THE
WOLF
PRINCE

THE WOLF PRINCE

KAREN KELLEY

BRAVA

KENSINGTON PUBLISHING CORP.
www.kensingtonbooks.com

BRAVA BOOKS are published by

Kensington Publishing Corp.
119 West 40th Street
New York, NY 10018

ISBN-13: 978-0-7582-3840-5
ISBN-10: 0-7582-3840-1

First Kensington Trade Paperback Printing: November 2010
10 9 8 7 6 5 4 3 2 1

Printed in the United States of America

CHAPTER I

"I need a man," Darcy Spencer said, moving her cell phone to her other ear.

The trail she was on ran through the park on her parents' country estate so she didn't have to worry about interruptions. Besides, it was too early for anyone else to be out and about. The sun was just coming up, painting an orange-red glow across the Texas sky with a wide stroke. The lush green grass was damp from the heavy dew and a slight chill hung in the air. Being outside this early felt good—fresh and clean.

"Do you realize what time it is?" Jennifer asked, her words thick from sleep.

"I don't know." She squinted toward the horizon. "Around six, I suppose. What does that have to do with anything?"

"It has to do with the fact I was still asleep, and besides, if you'd gone with me to the club last night, you could have found a man easy enough."

Darcy didn't sleep much, and often forgot her friends did. "A man from the club won't work," she told Jennifer. "And I'm sorry about waking you. I forgot you like to sleep late."

"Nine is not . . . never mind. Why wouldn't a man from the club work?"

"I don't want that kind of relationship. I need someone long term."

Jennifer's deep sigh came clearly across the phone. "What about Peter or Dick? Peter thinks the sun rises and sets with you."

"Peter was a mistake. Never date a man who's always been more like a brother to you." Darcy stopped walking and frowned. "Have you ever thought about my ex-boyfriend's names? I mean, in reference to the male anatomy."

"Merely a coincidence."

"I'm beginning to wonder." She continued walking along the edge of the dense stand of trees, but keeping in the open. "There was Willie—remember him? He loved garlic and onions, and always smelled faintly of . . . well . . . onions and garlic. Then there was Tom Johnson. And Woody."

"Wait, I don't remember a Woody."

"Woody Harrelson."

"You didn't date him."

"No, but I had a crush on him at one time. The guy has a seriously funny sense of humor."

"A crush doesn't count. Maybe you should date a guy with *boyfriend approved* stamped on his ass. Like FDA approved meat. Except this would be boyfriend approved meat." Jennifer chuckled at her own joke.

"I'm not sure the FDA approval stamp carries as much weight as it once did."

"I still don't know why you're looking for a man."

Darcy turned and started back toward the house. "I sort of told my mother I'd met someone."

"In other words, you lied through your teeth."

She nibbled her bottom lip. "That's one way to put it. I told Mom that she could meet him when she and Dad join me next month."

"Why do you do these things?"

Darcy shrugged. "It seemed like a good idea at the time." And it had. Now that she thought about it, maybe not so much. But no other plan had seemed plausible.

"You're twenty-five," Jennifer said. "You shouldn't have to lie to your parents. Just tell your mother you're not ready to settle down."

"Except then she would try her hand at matchmaking again. Remember Albert?"

Jennifer chuckled. "He did sweat a lot."

Shivers of revulsion ran up and down Darcy's spine just thinking about the guy. "He was flatulent. I am not going to get stuck with another one of my mother's attempts to fix me up with a man, and that's exactly what she'd do. She would drag him down here for the whole summer. Some trust-fund baby who's doing nothing but living off his parents' wealth."

"Uh, I hate to break it to you, Darcy, but you just described us."

Darcy flinched, knowing her friend spoke the truth and feeling again as though she were caught between her guilty conscience and her overbearing mother. Enough already! This was the summer she'd convince her mother to untie the apron strings. If her mom dragged another Albert along with her, it would never happen.

"So, just what are you planning?" Jennifer asked, breaking into her thoughts.

"I'm not sure, but I have a month to figure it out."

"The great procrastinator. Hey, keep me up to date with what you're going to do so I'll know which lie to tell if anyone asks. And don't stay gone too long. I get so bored without you in the city, but I loathe the country. Too much fresh air. I'll take smog and pollution any day."

They talked a little more, then said their good-byes, and Darcy closed the phone, slipping it back in her pants pocket.

She kicked at a rock, sending it flying into the woods. Jennifer was right. Darcy had to get more control of her life. She was twenty-five, and had a freakin' private investigator license, and a degree in business, except her mother cried every time Darcy even mentioned getting a job that might be remotely dangerous.

But Darcy was good at finding things. It was almost as if she had a sixth sense. She'd make a great investigator. She loved the thought of intrigue, stealth and danger. Actually, there probably wouldn't be that much intrigue, stealth or danger. It would be a lot of research on the Internet, or spying on wives or husbands suspected of infidelity. She didn't really think she would enjoy spying on cheating spouses. But finding things that might be lost intrigued her, making her pulse beat just a little faster.

Her shoulders slumped. That is, if she ever got the chance to work. She didn't have an ounce of courage when it came to standing up to her mother.

Darcy loved her mom, but the woman really had to loosen up. The rooms, no matter how opulent, were closing in on Darcy. Trouble was, she understood why her mother was so suffocating, which made everything worse. Mary Spencer had had four miscarriages before adopting Darcy. She'd been smothering her only child ever since.

A large dog jumped from between the trees and into her path. Darcy froze. The dog turned and glared at her. It wasn't unusual that people dumped unwanted pets in the country, but this dog was really big. Maybe not even a dog. She would swear it was a wolf.

Her palms grew sweaty. She glanced around, careful not to make any sudden moves. There was a large branch within reach. She cautiously leaned down and picked it up. Damn, it was heavier than she'd expected, but heavy was probably good.

"Go away or I'll clobber you." She spoke calmly, but fear coursed through her veins.

The wolf didn't make a move to leave.

A thick fog began to roll in. Should she run? What if the wolf attacked and ripped her to shreds?

She hesitated too long. The fog was so thick now, she couldn't see her hand in front of her face. There was a rustle in the brush. Darcy stiffened. Then she heard someone groan, and more movement in the brush.

Was someone else there? Had the wolf attacked somebody earlier? Maybe she'd interrupted the wolf eating its prey. Her stomach turned at the thought of finding body parts. Even worse the wolf might still be hungry and decide to eat her. She gripped the branch a little tighter.

The fog began to dissipate almost as fast as it had rolled in. She hugged the branch to her chest, ready for anything.

"Ow!" A deep male voice grumbled. "By the gods, is this place filled with thorns?"

"Who's there?" she croaked, then quickly cleared her throat.

He stepped out from behind a tree as the fog completely cleared.

Her gaze swept over him, then jerked back to his face. "You're naked," she said, her voice trembling. Oh, God, there was a naked man in the woods, along with a man-eating wolf. She was going to die!

The man stepped toward her, holding out his hand.

She screamed and brought the heavy branch down on his head with all the strength she could muster. There was a distinct thud. His eyes widened as he stumbled forward a couple of steps. She quickly stepped back. The naked stranger's eyes closed as he slowly collapsed to the ground in front of her.

Her legs were shaking so badly she had to lean against the side of a tree for support. Oh, God, she'd just knocked out a streaker. She closed her eyes and tried to slow her racing pulse. She could barely take a breath. Adrenaline surged through her veins.

Calm down. You're still alive.

She opened her eyes and curled her lip as she stared at the naked man. "Ha! That will teach you to walk around naked and accost women." Not that he'd accosted her. But he *was* naked.

Her eyes narrowed. And he wasn't moving.

Another kind of fear swept over her.

She stepped closer and nudged him with the toe of her tennis shoe, then jumped back. He still didn't move. Oh, crap, had she killed him? Dammit, he'd scared the hell out of her. What was she supposed to do?

If she said it was self-defense, would they send her to prison? What would she tell a jury, though? That he'd held his hand out to her and she'd killed him. Oh, yeah, that would go over good.

She could lie. That might work. Her mother still didn't know who'd broken the window in the living room when Darcy was twelve. But her mother would buy anything Darcy said. She might not be as lucky in front of a jury of her peers.

His chest suddenly rose and fell. Relief washed over her. Thank God, she wasn't going to prison. A good thing because orange was so not her color, nor did she like stripes or bars, for that matter.

She stepped closer, still hugging the branch. Who the hell was he? His raven-black hair was shoulder length, and his eyes had been a warm whiskey-brown with gold flecks. Maybe early thirties? His shoulders were broad. Nice biceps, too. Her gaze lowered. Among other things. She swallowed hard. Very sexy. Cover model sexy. Male stripper sexy. Freebie lap dance sexy.

Who the hell was he and why was he strolling through the woods stark naked?

Was he a vagrant?

A homeless man had risked his life to save her from a wolf, and he got hit over the head for his trouble. Not that he looked homeless. Only unconscious. Possibly dying. Cripes, she needed to get help.

She removed her jacket and laid it across his lower half. Thank goodness she had her cell phone. She pulled it out of her pocket and quickly punched in the number of the house, and then waited while it rang.

"Spencer residence," Ms. Abernathy said.

"It's Darcy."

"Are you okay?" the housekeeper asked, worry lacing her words.

"I'm fine, but I nearly killed a man."

"I'm sorry? Did you say you nearly killed a man?"

"There was a wolf, then this man stepped out from behind a tree, and I had a branch so I sort of clobbered him. He's still unconscious. Have Ralph bring the little trailer so we can get him back to the house. Oh, and call Dr. Wilson. He'll need to examine him."

Ms. Abernathy said she would be right on it. Darcy snapped her phone closed and exhaled a sigh of relief.

Ralph wouldn't waste any time getting here. He took care of the grounds, making sure everything always looked well manicured. He was practically like a father to her. He would help her without reprimanding her for hitting first and asking questions later. She hoped.

Even though she knew Ralph would hurry, time seemed to come to a standstill. She picked up the branch again, just in case the wolf came back or the guy regained consciousness. Though she had a feeling the stranger had scared the wolf away.

She glanced at the rising sun and looked up the path. She couldn't see the house, but it was just over the hill. Ralph would come from that direction. She glanced nervously at the stranger and silently prayed he wouldn't wake up before help arrived. What if he attacked her?

Darcy snorted. Had she really been thinking only a few moments ago how great it would be to have danger and excitement in her life? And how had she handled it? By knocking some guy over the head whose only crime was to run around the woods naked.

In her defense, he had startled her. First the wolf, then the naked stranger. She'd acted on instinct when she'd hit him. She had really good instincts. Most of the time.

She breathed a sigh of relief when the golf cart came chugging over the hill, the trailer bouncing behind it.

She tossed the branch and wildly waved her arms. It wasn't that hard to spot her since she was out in the open, but waving her arms gave her something to do. Ralph pulled up beside her and turned off the key.

"I'm afraid I hit him pretty hard," she said. "But he stepped from behind a tree and scared the hell out of me. He's still unconscious."

Ralph walked over to him. He nudged the stranger with the toe of his work boot. "Yep, you got him a good one." He raised her jacket, then let it quickly drop. "He hasn't got a stitch of clothes on. What kind of man runs around the woods naked? You did good knocking him over the head."

"Well, he did scare off the wolf." She had no idea why she would take up for the stranger. Remorse? That had to be it.

Ralph had brought one of his grounds workers with him and they started to pick up the stranger, but Ralph hesitated at the last moment. "Might want to turn your head, Miss Darcy."

Heat flooded her face when she caught the meaning of his words. Ralph had worked for the family before she was even adopted and he really was like a second father. She quickly turned around. There was a grunt, probably from Ralph, and then a thud as the stranger was placed on the trailer.

"Okay, he's as decent as he'll ever be. What do you want us to do with him?"

"Take him to the guest house," she said.

Ralph's brows drew together. "Are you sure about that?"

She nodded. "He saved my life." The wolf *was* gone.

"Then I guess you owe him something. At least until we know who he is." She jumped in beside Ralph, while his helper got in the trailer with the stranger.

Ralph started the golf cart up again and they made their way to the guest house. The estate sat on ten acres deep in the Texas hill country. The house had six bedrooms, besides the guest house. They had room for one naked stranger.

The trailer bounced over a bump. The stranger groaned. She bit her bottom lip and looked over her shoulder. What if she had given him brain damage or something? She would never forgive herself, even if it turned out he was a bad guy. Well, if he was really bad, maybe she wouldn't feel quite as guilty.

He hadn't looked like a bad guy. Oh, Lord, what if he was a neighbor who liked running around naked? The Bishops were on vacation, but they had their place up for sale. They would be gone all summer, unless it sold. What if this guy had purchased the property? It might not go so well for her at trial if she'd brain-damaged her new neighbor.

Ralph pulled in front of the guest house as Ms. Abernathy came hurrying out of the main house to meet them.

"Is he dead?" she asked, walking briskly toward them. Loose tendrils of gray hair had escaped the usually tight bun that sat on top of her head like a hummingbird's nest. "We could bury the corpse and not tell anyone a thing." She eyed Ralph's young helper as if he would be the one who'd snitch. The poor guy lowered his head and shuffled his feet.

Ms. Abernathy was very loyal. She was also thin, almost to the point of anorexia, which was ridiculous since she could out eat any man, and she was the best cook for miles around. She told everyone she was blessed with a fast metabolism.

"He's not dead." Ralph climbed out of the golf cart.

"You're not planning to put him in the guest house, are you?" Ms. Abernathy's eyebrows shot up. "Mrs. Spencer will fire us all."

"He saved my life," Darcy told her.

"Then why'd you whack him?" she asked.

"He scared me. Is the doctor on his way?" Darcy asked. Irritation laced her words. She just wanted everyone to stop asking so many questions.

"He'll be here soon enough." Ms. Abernathy reluctantly opened the French doors to the guest house, and stepped back. The men lifted the stranger out of the trailer. "Lord-a-mercy, he hasn't got a stitch of clothes on. What's a young man like him doing running around the countryside in his birthday suit? Your momma is going to skin all of us alive for letting a naked stranger stay in her pretty guest house."

"Then we won't tell her he was naked." Darcy wore the expression her mother always said was her daughter's stubborn look.

"But—"

Darcy held up her hand. "Not a word."

"Okay, but you know she's going to find out. That woman always knows everything that goes on around here."

"But *we* won't tell her. Right?"

Ms. Abernathy pursed her lips. "She won't be hearing it from me."

"Good." Darcy hurried to the bedroom and pulled back the bedcovers. Ralph and his helper placed the stranger on the bed.

Ms. Abernathy quickly pulled the covers up. When the stranger groaned, she jumped back. "Ralph, go get the gun."

"He's injured. I doubt he could overpower all of us," Darcy told her.

"They say the crazier they are, the more strength they have," Ms. Abernathy said.

"Well, there's four of us, and only one of him," Darcy reminded her.

"Hello!" Dr. Wilson called from the other room.

"In here, Doc," Ralph said.

Dr. Wilson came striding inside the room carrying a small black bag. The doctor was past retirement, but still saw a few patients, and he'd always been the Spencers' doctor.

The doctor glanced around, his gaze landing on the man in the bed. "Who is he?"

"We don't know," Darcy said. "He was in the woods. He startled me when he stepped from behind a tree so I sort of hit him over the head with a stick." Heat rose up her face. "A really big stick."

Dr. Wilson walked closer. After putting on exam gloves, he ran his hands over the stranger's head. "You bopped him a good one. He's got a big goose egg."

"Will he be okay?" Darcy nervously twined her fingers together.

"Don't know until we get X-rays."

The stranger groaned again, his eyes fluttering open. His head slowly turned, and he looked right at Darcy. His expression told her that he'd like to hit *her* over the head with a really big stick. This wasn't good.

The doctor reached toward the stranger. The man turned to

him, curling back his lips, baring his teeth. Dr. Wilson only paused for a moment. "I'm Dr. Wilson. You want me to see to your wound or not?"

Slowly, the man's facial expression relaxed, replaced by a look of confusion.

"That's better." Dr. Wilson removed his gloves, then took the stranger's pulse and blood pressure. "Everything checks out." He folded his stethoscope and put it back in his satchel.

"Then he'll be okay?" Darcy asked.

"X-rays, then we'll see. One of the guys is bringing the portable out." He glanced at his watch. "Should be here in a bit."

She nodded. This was just awful. She looked at the man again. He seemed almost animal-like the way he looked at everyone.

"What's your name?" Dr. Wilson asked.

His forehead wrinkled, and then he said, "Surlock."

"Last name or first?"

"I don't remember."

"Do you know what day it is? Where you come from?"

Surlock shook his head.

The doctor shined a light in Surlock's eyes. "Probably a mild concussion with temporary loss of memory. I've seen it a lot in cases like this. If he's not better in a few days, I'll order more tests."

Why hadn't she just taken off running? She was pretty fast. She could have thrown the heavy branch at him, and gotten a decent head start. She had a great pair of lungs and could have screamed loud enough that someone would've heard her.

Suddenly, Surlock's gaze swung her way. "You hit me over the head."

She cringed away from the condemnation in his eyes.

"See, he's starting to remember already." Dr. Wilson beamed.

Yeah, well, maybe that wasn't such a good thing. Was he the kind of man who would seek revenge?

"Where am I?" he asked.

"In the guest house. I didn't know where else to take you."

Oh, hell, he had amnesia because of her. Could someone die from that? She took a deep breath. "You can stay here until your memory returns."

Ms. Abernathy cleared her throat and cast a disapproving glance in Darcy's direction.

Darcy squared her shoulders and met Ms. Abernathy's gaze head-on. The housekeeper pursed her lips, but didn't dispute Darcy's orders.

Darcy breathed a sigh of relief. A good thing, too. She'd been the one to clobber him over the head. He was her mess, and she would clean it up. But when her glance fell on Surlock, she thought it might not be too difficult. He was the sexiest mess she'd ever made.

CHAPTER 2

Surlock eyed the people in the room. They made him uneasy, looking at him as if they expected him to pounce any second. Especially the young woman. The one called Darcy. Her gaze would fall on him, then skitter away. He frowned. Probably because she'd attacked him. That, he remembered. What he didn't remember was why he was in the woods.

He ran a shaky hand through his hair and felt the lump. He grimaced. It was tender. His gaze fell on her again, and once more a guilty flush stained her cheeks. She wasn't very big, but she'd wielded the branch like a warrior. She was also very beautiful. Pleasant to look upon.

He took a deep breath, then exhaled. Not that it mattered what she looked like. He needed to focus. There was something he was supposed to do. But what? His memory had been wiped clean. When he struggled to remember, the humming noise inside his head only got worse and his temples began to pound from the effort. Finally, he closed his eyes to block out everything—the people, the sounds—everything around him.

"Darcy, you stay, but the rest give us some room," Dr. Wilson ordered.

Good idea, Surlock thought to himself. When he didn't hear movement, he opened his eyes. No one had left. The skinny older woman hesitated until Dr. Wilson raised his eyebrows. Then she turned and marched toward the door. Surlock could tell she didn't want to go. The two men followed.

The doctor sat in one of the chairs, taking a small notebook from his jacket. He began to scribble something on it.

Darcy still refused to meet his gaze.

Who were these people?

Who was he?

Surlock only had sketchy recollections. He knew he had to keep his identity a secret, and he was looking for someone who might be in danger. Someone he needed to protect. But who? And why?

He remembered a wolf, too. They were friends. At least, he thought they might be. He knew he was called Surlock, but when he tried to remember more, his head felt as though it would explode. It wasn't worth the effort to concentrate.

He watched the young woman as she moved to a dresser and straightened one of the figurines. Not that it needed straightening. Yes, she was definitely beautiful.

Her blond hair was pulled away from her face, showing delicate features, and skin that looked as soft as a baby's. Deep blue eyes were fringed with dark lashes. Ah, but it was her mouth that drew his attention. It tempted him to pull her down to lie beside him and kiss away her anxiety.

What was she doing going around hitting innocent people over the head anyway? Did she often get violent?

There was a knock on the door. The doctor told the person to enter. When the door opened, a man came inside pushing a cumbersome machine on wheels. Surlock warily eyed this new person. What did he plan to do?

"No need to be concerned," Dr. Wilson said. "He's only here to x-ray your head. I don't want you moving any more than necessary until we make sure your skull isn't cracked."

"Do you think it might be? I'm pretty sure I didn't hit him that hard," Darcy said as she twined her fingers together again.

The doctor came to his feet, slipping the notebook back inside his pocket. "No, but better safe than sorry." He walked over and told the man with the machine what he wanted. Then the doctor and Darcy stepped from the room.

Surlock eyed the machine. It was big and unfamiliar. When the man carried over a large metal plate, Surlock growled. The man stopped, taking a step back, and hugging the plate to his chest.

"I'm . . . uh . . . Harold and I just need to get this X-ray to make sure you don't have a fractured skull or anything. I swear it won't hurt."

The man was of small stature. Surlock slowly relaxed, then nodded. It would not be hard to fight this one if he posed a problem. Surlock would take their tests. If the man had lied, and there was more to this X-ray, he would attack.

Harold hurried to finish, going back to his machine and pushing buttons that made clicking noises. He replaced the metal plate with another one, and repeated everything. Then he took his machine and rushed from the room. The doctor and Darcy returned.

"Your vitals are good. Even so, I'll have one of my nurses come out to keep an eye on you for the next twenty-four hours." Dr. Wilson turned to Darcy. "Either that, or I can admit him to the hospital for observation."

"Hospital?" Surlock didn't like the sound of being admitted into a hospital. He didn't even know what a hospital was.

"Will he be just as well off here in the guest house with a nurse?" Darcy asked.

"Better probably. Twila is an excellent nurse and will keep a close eye on him."

"Then send her out."

"I can't remember anything." Surlock's frustration spilled out of him. The man seemed to be a healer of sorts. He remembered healers helped make people better when they were sick. Maybe Dr. Wilson could give him back his memory. He didn't like feeling vulnerable. It put him at a disadvantage. And what of this person he believed he'd been sent to protect? How could he protect anyone if he didn't know who he was?

"Nothing to worry about, I'm sure," the doctor told him. "Sometimes when you take a blow to the head it can cause temporary amnesia. You'll probably start remembering as the day goes on." He turned to Darcy. "Someone will need to stay with him until the nurse gets here."

"I can do that." Darcy walked the doctor out, then returned.

Surlock watched as she fidgeted with her clothes, then smoothed a loose tendril of hair behind her ear. He noticed her hands trembled. She looked at him, then quickly glanced away.

"I'm sorry I hit you over the head." She sat in the chair closest to the bed. "It isn't every day a wolf steps into the open like that. Then there was this fog. Once it cleared, you stepped from behind a tree"—her cheeks turned red—"and, well, you were naked. You frightened me."

"Naked?"

She nodded.

He remembered the wolf, but it was an odd feeling. Then she had stepped forward. He was going to tell her something.

A sharp stabbing pain suddenly struck his head. He reached a hand up, closing his eyes. The light in the room made the pain worse, and the humming grew louder.

"What?" she frantically asked. "Do I need to call the doctor back?"

He shook his head, the pain easing. "No, it was something you said. I had a flash of memory."

"What kind of memory?"

"I don't know. It happened so fast I didn't have a chance to grasp it."

"But it's a good sign that you remembered something, even if you can't remember it now."

Nothing would be good until he remembered everything. How could it be? His whole life had been swept away. He was nothing, a nobody, without his memory.

He carefully eased open his eyes and looked at her. She wore an expression of hope. For a moment, he thought about telling her exactly how he felt, but one look into her anxious eyes, and the words wouldn't come.

"Yes, I would say that's a good sign." He had no idea if it was or wasn't, but he was glad he'd lied when he saw the relief on her face. He didn't want her to be concerned about him, even though she deserved to worry.

She smiled. His breath caught in his throat. It was as though she'd given him the gift of sunshine on a cloudy day. He had a feeling it would be difficult to concentrate when she was around, but he had to force himself to do just that.

"Why was I in the woods without clothes?" he suddenly asked.

Her cheeks turned red. "I don't know." Her gaze dropped to her hands.

Apparently, she had a problem with nudity. Apparently, he didn't have the same problem since he was running around the woods without clothes.

He closed his eyes and sighed deeply. Tiredness washed over him as if he'd been traveling for a long time from far, far away.

"You can't go to sleep!" she screamed.

He grimaced as the screeching noise shot through him. His eyes jerked open. "Why can't I?"

"The doctor doesn't want you going to sleep."

"Ever?"

She frowned. "Probably just for the next few hours."

It all seemed overly dramatic. He was tired, though, and the bed felt good. It wouldn't be that hard to fall asleep. He had a feeling it would throw her into a frenzy if he did, and then she would call the doctor back. "If I can't go to sleep, then you'll have to talk to me."

She hesitated. "You really don't remember a thing?"

He shook his head, then winced when pain shot through it. "No, nothing."

"Not even the wolf?"

He opened his mouth, then closed it. "I remember a wolf."

"I was afraid it would attack me. That's why I picked up the heavy branch, except you stepped from behind the tree after the fog lifted, and the wolf was gone." She shrugged apologetically. "You got hit instead. It was a knee-jerk reaction. I'm sorry."

"The wolf wouldn't have attacked."

"How do you know?"

He thought about it for a moment. Everything was a blank. "I don't. Something tells me I was close to the wolf."

"Close? You mean like a pet?"

"Maybe. Yes, I think so." The humming grew angry inside his head. She asked a lot of questions. He didn't have the answers. He closed his eyes. "I'm not going to sleep. Only resting my eyes."

"Of course. I'll just sit here and talk." Her voice was soft and comforting. She spoke about the countryside, and some friend called Jennifer who hated the country.

She'd looked small and defenseless sitting there. His brothers would laugh their fool heads off if they knew he'd been brought down by a slip of a female.

Brothers?

Yes, he had brothers. And he was pretty sure sisters. Also lots of animals. He remembered walking with animals. The wolf might very well be a pet. Maybe his memory would return, and then he would know why everything seemed so strange, as if he didn't belong in this place.

"The nurse is here." Darcy rose from her chair.

The two women spoke for a few minutes, then Darcy hurried away. The nurse said her name was Twila. She was short and plump with very dark skin. After checking his pulse and blood pressure, she wrote the numbers on a pad of paper.

"I'll be in the other room if you should need me, but I'll be checking on you from time to time. I'm a registered nurse. Have been for twenty years, so I'll know if something is not right."

"I'm tired," he said.

"I think it will be okay to sleep for a bit. You've had a rough day." Her gentle smile was comforting. He remembered someone else whose smile also made him feel like this, but he couldn't focus on a face. He finally stopped trying. Twila left the room.

Finally, silence.

He eased his feet over the side of the bed. The room tilted, then settled. By the gods, his head was killing him.

There was another door in the room. He stood, holding on to the nightstand until he felt a little steadier. When he thought he could trust himself not to fall, he made his way to the door and opened it. He knew this room, and quickly made use of the facility, then washed his hands.

The face that stared back at him in the mirror was unfamiliar. His hair was dark, shoulder length. His eyes were brown with gold flecks. His chin strong, skin tanned. It was as if he looked at a stranger, and the feeling made him uncomfortable. He didn't like not knowing who he was.

He left the room and went back to the bed, pulling the covers to his waist. At least, his headache had eased, but he was incredibly tired. His eyes were so heavy he didn't think he could keep them open even if he tried. It was a good thing Darcy had left or he would be forced to remain awake.

As quickly as that thought crossed his mind, he knew the words weren't true. He wasn't glad she had left. There was something about her. Something that made him want to know her better. Odd. Especially since she had been the one who had caused him to lose his memory.

He felt as though he'd always known her. Yet, he was certain they had never met until today. He was sure she didn't recognize him, either.

His body grew weary. It was too much to unravel right now. He yawned, then turned on his side as sleep claimed him. His last thought was that maybe when he woke, he might remember who he was.

Chapter 3

Something was different. Darcy didn't know exactly what, but as she snuggled her pillow closer, and the last bit of sleep drifted away, she knew something in her life had changed.

Then it hit her.

It wasn't a good different. She had almost killed a man yesterday morning. Oh, hell, what if he'd died during the night while she'd been dreaming. . . . Her mind was a blank. What had she been dreaming about?

Her face suddenly flooded with heat when she remembered. She'd been dreaming of a sexy, very naked, male god, worshipping at his feet like a horny woman who hadn't been laid in over a year. That wasn't true. She'd actually had sex eleven and a half months ago.

Except the man she'd drooled about in her dreams might very well be a corpse right now. Her heart began to pound.

Had Ms. Abernathy buried the body? Did the housekeeper know that would make her an accessory? Darcy grimaced when she thought about sharing a cell with her. Not that she disliked the housekeeper. She'd been almost as much of a mother to Darcy as her adoptive mother. Hmm, and bossy, now that she thought about it. But still, she didn't want Ms. Abernathy to go to prison because she was being overprotective.

Darcy flung the cover aside and jumped out of bed, glancing

at the clock. It was barely six. She rushed toward the closet, but stopped at the French doors that led to her balcony. Her room was directly across from the guest house. If something had happened to Surlock during the night, she would be able to tell from her room—maybe.

She opened the double doors and rushed out onto the balcony, then stumbled to a stop. The swimming pool was between her room and the guest house. Surlock stood on the diving board, his arms raised. The sun peeked over the horizon, casting everything in a hazy early morning light. There was enough light that she could see him, though.

She swallowed past the lump in her throat. The man was truly magnificent, and very naked. Right now, she didn't really mind that he disliked clothes. Boy, did she not mind!

His muscles weren't so big that he looked deformed. No, they were just right. His chest was broad with just a sprinkling of dark hair. Her gaze dropped lower. Nice. Very nice.

A burning need grew inside her. For just a moment, she wondered what it would feel like to lie naked in his arms, to have his body pressed against hers. The ache inside her grew until she trembled with need. Her last few dates had been losers. She had a feeling Surlock would be good in bed. He would know how to please a woman.

Her hands curled into fists, nails biting into her palms as she stifled the groan that threatened to explode from her. She needed good sex. Maybe Surlock was a gift from the sex gods and she was meant to have him. It could happen. Before she could get too far into her fantasy, he dove into the water, causing barely a ripple.

She leaned over the balcony. Nice ass. Firm. Hmm, with a tattoo on the upper right cheek. Or a birthmark. Odd, she had a birthmark in the same place. She squinted her eyes, but he was too far away for her to tell exactly what it was. What were the odds it would be the same as her birthmark? She quickly dismissed the thought as she lost herself watching him swim the length of the pool.

The muscles in his back tightened and relaxed as he reached forward in the water. He swam to the end of the pool, then turned and swam back. His movements were those of a professional.

Maybe that was what he was—a swimmer.

Yeah, right, he'd been running around naked in the woods looking for a pool. With a wolf at his side.

What if he'd been raised by wolves? He'd growled at Dr. Wilson. Surlock did come across as a little wild, untamed. A fantasy formed in her mind. Surlock was Tarzan of the wolves, and he was looking for a woman he could steal away and take back to his den.

She shook her head. Ridiculous. Besides, since she had hit him over the head, Darcy kind of doubted she would be in the running as someone he would whisk away. The thought of spending time lying in his arms was nice, though.

Surlock popped out of the water, levering himself to the side of the pool, slinging his wet hair out of his face. He sat there for a moment, catching his breath, before getting to his feet. Rather than go immediately back to the guest house, he looked up, their gazes locking, as though he'd known she watched him the whole time. He seemed quite unconcerned he was naked.

He didn't smile or wave. Not even a nod. He only stared at her for a long moment, his gaze slipping down her body, caressing her with his eyes, causing goose bumps to pop up on her arms. For a brief moment, something passed between them. He wanted her just as much as she wanted him.

He abruptly turned and walked to the guest house, stealing her breath as he did. The guy had a seriously sexy ass. Why had he looked at her so strangely? As if she was the one who was naked.

She glanced down and had her answer. She was wearing her thin white gown. The silky material clearly outlined her tight nipples, and was so low cut that it left little to the imagination. Great, now who was the exhibitionist? She turned and sauntered back into her room, a slight smile lifting the corners of her mouth. She had a feeling her life had just gotten a whole lot more interesting.

Just as quickly, her smile slipped. Where the hell was Surlock's nurse? A cold chill washed over her. What if he'd killed Twila during the night? She paused, hand on the doorknob. Darcy might very well be harboring a serial killer.

She shook her head, then went inside the bathroom. Of course, he hadn't killed Twila. If he had, he wouldn't be taking a swim in the pool. He'd have been long gone. Twila was probably still asleep. It wasn't like the nurse was that young. She was what? Getting close to sixty?

Darcy hurried through her shower, then dressed in shorts and a button-down blue top before she rushed downstairs. Two young maids were giggling in the dining room as they set the plates on the buffet for breakfast, but stopped when she walked past.

"Breakfast will be ready in a few minutes," Ms. Abernathy told Darcy as she walked from the kitchen.

"I'll let Surlock know," Darcy told her as if she hadn't planned to hurry over to the guest house anyway.

The two maids giggled and earned one of Ms. Abernathy's famous glares. They quickly stifled their laughter and hurried back into the kitchen.

Ms. Abernathy turned her gaze on Darcy. Whatever the housekeeper was about to say, Darcy didn't think it would bode well for her.

Shades of when she was fourteen came back to haunt her. She'd gotten caught cutting the coconut cake Ms. Abernathy had made for their neighbor, Ms. Bishop, who had just come home from the hospital. Darcy hadn't known it was for Ms. Bishop, though, but had still suffered a scolding. Darcy now felt as if she were about to relive that moment.

"I took Surlock clothes that belonged to your father," Ms. Abernathy began. "I was going to have them taken to Goodwill anyway. I also included a pair of swimming trunks. Since you insisted he stay in the guest house, please inform him I cannot have my staff in a state of agitation because he chooses not to wear clothes." She turned on her heel and went back to the kitchen without another word.

Not as bad as Darcy had feared, but still, she had been soundly chastised. Surlock went skinny-dipping, but she caught the flack. Not that she could blame the maids for having their heads turned. Apparently, he'd caused more than one heart to flutter.

She hurried out to the guest house, and tapped on the door. As she went inside, Twila was just coming out of the bedroom.

"His vitals are all good this morning," Twila told her. "I checked them on and off through the night and there was no change."

"Does he remember anything?"

She shook her head. "No more than he did yesterday. It might be a week or so before he's completely back to normal. Maybe longer."

Darcy didn't like the sound of that. What if he never regained his memory? Would he live in the guest house forever?

Surlock stepped from the other room wearing her father's old clothes. They were about the same height, but Surlock was broader in the chest so the white shirt didn't button, and showed a delicious expanse of bare skin. He'd rolled the sleeves past his wrists, giving him a casual beach look.

How could he look even sexier than when he was naked? Maybe he *could* live in the guest house for a few years. She didn't think she would ever get tired of staring.

"The shoes didn't fit." He glanced down at his feet.

"No problem, we'll get you some new ones." She met his gaze. "How do you feel?"

"I still can't remember anything."

"Give it time," Twila told him. She glanced at her watch. "There's nothing more that I can do. Dr. Wilson will probably call this morning."

"Yes, of course," Darcy said. "Thanks so much for coming out."

Twila gathered her things and left.

The room suddenly began to shrink. "Are you hungry?"

He nodded.

Surlock didn't talk a lot. Her theory that he was raised by wolves was beginning to sound more plausible. He followed as she went across to the house. She glanced at the pool.

"You should wear clothes next time you swim."

"Why?"

Why? She couldn't think of one good reason. It would be nice to wake up to Surlock swimming naked in the pool every morning. It might cause her mother to have a heart attack though.

"Because Ms. Abernathy will lecture me again if you don't," she finally told him. It was as good a reason as anything else she could come up with.

He nodded. She didn't ask if that meant he would or would not wear trunks the next time.

They went into the dining room. Breakfast was always buffet-style in silver warming trays on a side table. It had been this way as long as she could remember. No matter how many times Darcy told Ms. Abernathy a bowl of cereal or just some fruit would be fine, Ms. Abernathy still fixed her spread. She always said it wouldn't go to waste since there were plenty of mouths to feed at the estate.

When Darcy glanced at Surlock, he only looked confused. "Scrambled eggs, bacon and sausage, pancakes and fruit," she said, pointing to the different dishes.

He nodded. She watched in amazement as he loaded his plate with some of everything. She got him another plate for his pancakes, buttered them, and added syrup. After she carried it to the table, she fixed her plate—two strips of bacon and some strawberries.

She took a seat at the table, picked up a slice of crispy bacon and took a bite. Honey-cured bacon was a weakness. Surlock watched her until she began to feel uncomfortable.

"Go ahead and eat." She picked up her glass of orange juice.

He began wolfing down the food as if he hadn't eaten in days.

She choked on her orange juice when he picked up a handful of eggs and shoved them in his mouth.

He looked up, egg on the corner of his mouth. "What?"

She picked up her fork and waved it. "Use your fork for the eggs. You don't eat food with your hands."

"You did."

"No, I didn't."

"Yes, you did. I watched. You picked up meat and took a bite."

"But that was bacon." He still didn't look as if he understood. "Bacon is okay if it's crisp because cutting it would only make it crumble. The eggs are soft so you eat them with a fork."

Maybe he *had* been raised by wolves. He'd even told her that he remembered a wolf. Coincidence? Why else would he be running around naked? Wolf Boy?

He hadn't looked like a boy on the diving board.

Wolf Man?

Darcy could almost see him running through the woods, the leader of a pack of wolves. A shiver ran down her spine. He'd be completely naked, growling and snarling, ready to do battle. Or have sex.

"This is good," he said.

You better believe it was.

Darcy mentally shook her head and quickly brought her thoughts back to the present. She watched as he took a drink of orange juice. At least he knew how to hold a glass. He picked up the fork and looked at it, then plunged it down into the pancakes, bringing one entire pancake up and toward his mouth.

"No!"

He frowned. "I eat it with my hands?"

She shook her head. "No, you cut it first. Like this." She hurried over to him, took his fork and knife and cut the pancakes. "Now you take normal bites."

She turned to look at him. Their faces were close. She felt as if she could drown in his whiskey-brown eyes. He suddenly leaned forward and brushed his lips across hers. He tasted of orange juice. He deepened the kiss, pulling her head closer. Her heart pounded inside her chest, and her palms grew moist when his tongue stroked hers.

Someone cleared her throat.

Oh, go away.

This was nice. Visions of him carrying her up the stairs to her bedroom filled her head.

A throat was cleared again.

Damn! She moved back, guilty warmth flooding her cheeks. One of the maids held the cordless phone. "Dr. Wilson is on the line, Miss Darcy." The maid ducked her head, but a knowing smile played around the corners of her mouth.

"Of course." Darcy smoothed her hands over her hair, then took the phone from the maid. The girl hurried out.

Darcy cleared her throat. "Yes, Dr. Wilson." They spoke a few minutes, with Darcy agreeing to bring Surlock in later that morning. After saying good-bye, she set the phone on the table, and took her seat.

"Don't kiss me again, please." She primly laid her napkin across her lap, smoothing out the linen, but her hands trembled.

"Why?"

Why? Why did he always ask why? And why couldn't she ever come up with a plausible explanation as to why he shouldn't do something? The kiss had been nice. Better than nice. It had had made her feel warm all over. Hell, it made her want to straddle his lap and press her body against his and forget about everything except how he would make her feel.

She took a steadying breath and looked at him. Her insides turned to mush. He was way too tempting. "It's just not done."

"You don't kiss?"

"Of course, I kiss."

"But not me. You didn't enjoy it?"

"Of course, I enjoyed it. Very much, in fact." He was confusing her. "We don't really know each other. Maybe kissing wouldn't be a good idea right now."

He forked some of the pancake, but stopped halfway to his

mouth. "I enjoyed kissing you, too." He took the pancake and slowly chewed, but his heated gaze never wavered from her. His words pleased her more than she wanted to admit.

Good Lord, the guy was a stranger. His words shouldn't make her feel all giddy. She still wasn't sure he hadn't been raised by wolves. Maybe he just camped out a lot with the guys. Even if he had amnesia, he wouldn't forget how to eat, though. Would he?

She *had* used her hands when picking up her bacon. Maybe he just didn't recognize the food. He could be from a foreign country. She could believe that more than Surlock's being raised by wolves.

She studied him while finishing her breakfast. He held the fork correctly, so he was apparently familiar with utensils.

"You still don't remember anything?" she asked.

He looked up. "I remember you hitting me over the head with a big stick."

She cringed. He *would* have to remember that. She took a drink of orange juice, then studied him some more. His hair was neatly trimmed. She also noticed his fingernails looked as if they were manicured—no ragged edges. That kind of blew her raised-by-wolves theory.

Laborer was probably out of the question, too. Although it wouldn't be hard to imagine him stripped to the waist, frayed jeans riding low on his hips, his muscles straining as he held a jackhammer in place to break through concrete.

He finished his food and laid his fork across his plate, forcing her to abandon her newest fantasy.

"Would you like more?" she asked.

"No, that was sufficient."

Now what to do? She drummed her fingers on the table. He needed clothes that fit, but all the stores in town would still be closed. They couldn't just sit here staring at each other—no matter how tempting the thought.

"Would you like to see the rest of the house?" That would give them something to do before they went to town.

"Yes, I'd like to see how you live." He stood, but then grabbed the back of the chair.

She jumped to her feet, rushing over to him. "Are you okay?"

"Yes. I think I stood too quickly. The room spun for a moment. I'm fine now."

"If you would rather sit, we can."

"No, I'd like to see more of the house."

"Okay, but if you get tired, let me know, and we'll stop." When he nodded, she pointed toward the door the maid had come through. "That goes to the kitchen, but Ms. Abernathy doesn't like anyone in there who's not authorized."

"Ms. Abernathy was the one who brought me clothes this morning. I can see that she would be ruler of her domain. She has a commanding presence."

Darcy chuckled. "She does rule with an iron fist, but she takes good care of us." Darcy opened a set of double doors. "This is what my mother calls the music room. Not that any of us can play."

There were two sofas in an ice-blue floral print that were more pretty than comfortable. The four arm chairs weren't quite as bad. Long, ice-blue silk curtains framed the floor-to-ceiling windows. An antique, faded yellow rug with blue accents warmed the room.

Her mother called it her Victorian room and had done a lot of the decorating herself, spending an enormous amount of money on priceless vases and antiques. Darcy's father had said that if it made his wife happy, then what was the harm? He spoiled them both shamelessly, but they loved him anyway.

Surlock ambled over to the baby grand piano, running his fingers over the keys. "Nice."

"Do you play?"

"I don't know." He pulled out the bench and sat down, testing the keys again.

Suddenly, he began to play a melody she had never heard before. It was absolutely exquisite. She closed her eyes and let the haunting music wash over her. It was powerful and sensuous at the same time. He conjured a whole new fantasy in her mind.

Heat rushed through her. She closed her eyes and let the melody fill her. He stood naked before her, and when she glanced down, she was naked, too. He stroked his hands over her bare breasts. She moaned, arching her back.

The music called to her, exploding inside her. Throbbing vibrations caressed raw, exposed nerve endings. His body pressed against hers. He lowered his mouth, his kiss hot and fiery as he claimed her body as his own. She let him have his way, relishing the feel of his hands stroking her body, bringing her closer to his need.

The music rose to a deafening crescendo. It was all she could do to take a breath. Her chest rose and fell as her body strained for more. She bit her bottom lip; her body quivered with release.

The sounds grew softer as she brought her ragged breathing under control. Calm settled over her. Darcy opened her eyes, and looked around, surprised to find she still stood close to the piano, just behind Surlock, and that she was completely dressed.

Clapping sounded behind them. She turned to look. Ms. Abernathy stood in the doorway, wiping her damp cheeks with her apron. "That was so beautiful. I've never heard anything like it in my life. Such a sweet sound."

Sweet? Had they heard the same music?

A flood of heat rushed through Darcy. She hoped what she had felt didn't show on her face.

Surlock came to his feet. "Thank you," he said humbly.

"Was there something you needed?" Darcy asked.

"No, I heard the music and knew it wasn't you playing. I just thought I'd peek in to see who was making such a wonderful sound."

She couldn't fault Ms. Abernathy for thinking Darcy wasn't the one playing. The help had worn earplugs every time the music teacher came to the estate. Even the teacher had worn them. Finally, Miss Crump had had enough and explained to Darcy's mother that Darcy was tone deaf. After that, her mother had stopped the lessons.

"I'll just go back to my work." Ms. Abernathy left the room.

Yes, please go away. When Ms. Abernathy was gone, Darcy stole a look at Surlock. He studied her as though he knew exactly what she'd experienced, which was completely ridiculous, of course. He couldn't, could he?

She cleared her throat and kept her expression bland. "You play like a professional." He was thoughtful for a moment and she wondered if he might have felt something, too.

"Which doesn't tell me much," he finally said.

She sensed his frustration. "I'm so sorry I hit you over the head."

"As you said, I scared you. Even so, I can't continue to accept your generosity. What if it's a very long time before my memories return? I doubt you would want me to reside in your guest house indefinitely."

The way he talked baffled Darcy. He didn't talk like most people. His speech was more refined, besides the fact he could play like a genius. He was exactly the kind of man her mother would love to see her dating.

Oh, that was a thought. She studied him for a moment. "How would you like a job?"

"A job?"

"You could live in the guest house and work for me, but the arrangement would have to be between the two of us. No one else could know."

"What exactly would I do?"

"Be my boyfriend."

"Boyfriend?"

"You know, like we were dating."

His forehead wrinkled. It was odd how some things he knew, and other things went right over his head, as if he didn't quite understand the English language. She was leaning more toward the idea he might be from another country. She was pretty sure Surlock wasn't an American name—first or last.

"Pretending we were in love," she said.

His eyes widened. "That would be a good job. Yes, I would enjoy that kind of work." His gaze roamed over her in a way that only a blind person wouldn't guess what he was thinking.

"No fringe benefits. It would only be pretend." She wanted to get that straight right up front.

"I don't understand 'fringe benefits,' " he said.

"Then I'll make sure I explain them very well."

And then she thought about what she was saying. Had she lost her freakin' mind? No fringe benefits? *She* wanted the fringe benefits, dammit!

Of course, he didn't know what no fringe benefits meant. She didn't have to tell him it had anything to do with sex. She could lie and say it meant something else.

Her gaze slowly traveled over him.

She wasn't stupid. The guy was seriously sexy. If he could give her an orgasm while playing the piano, just think how good it would be if they actually had sex.

Her body tingled at the thought of the two of them in bed together. Naked bodies pressing close. No, she didn't think she would explain what "no fringe benefits" meant.

CHAPTER 4

Surlock glared at the man who measured him for clothes—Mr. Barnes he was called. He didn't like him. He kept licking his lips as if he wanted to do more than take measurements.

"I just need to get the width of your chest," the tailor simpered. "My, you do have a broad chest, don't you? I'd bet you're a bit of a wild one." His voice went husky when he said *wild*. "I love a man who can wear his hair long and still look ruggedly handsome. There's no doubt that person is a real man."

Surlock fisted his hands. Darcy had said he would need the clothes, and since he worked for her now, he knew he had to act accordingly and not pound this man into the ground. It didn't feel right, though. Not the way the tailor let his hands linger a little too long in all the wrong places.

"Now, if you would please be so kind as to step up on the bench, I'll get your inseam." He licked his lips. "I have to tell you that you have a very nice inseam."

Surlock narrowed his eyes, but the tailor was more interested in keeping his gaze below the waist as Surlock stepped up on the bench.

Darcy shouldn't have left him alone with the tailor. He had beady eyes. When the tailor neared his crotch, Surlock growled from deep in his throat just as Darcy pushed the curtain open and walked inside the small fitting room. She stopped in her tracks, then cast a warning look in his direction. *Now* she decided to return. Surlock wondered how much trouble he was in.

The tailor's hands fluttered close to his face, and his eyes grew wide. "Oh, my." The little man's hands began to tremble.

"Is there a problem?" One of Darcy's eyebrows shot upward as her hard gaze was redirected at the tailor. At least she'd changed the direction of her displeasure. Maybe he was in the clear.

"No, no problem. I'll just take these last measurements and be done," Mr. Barnes stuttered. He took out his pad and pencil and jotted down numbers. There was a snap, and the pencil broke, one end flying across the room. "Oh, I pressed too hard," the tailor said. "I'll . . . I'll just get another pencil so we can finish up." He pulled a white cloth out of his pocket and mopped his forehead before hurrying through the curtains.

"You have to stop glaring at poor Mr. Barnes," Darcy whispered. "And for heaven's sake, stop growling at people. You're scaring them."

"I don't like the way he touches me," Surlock snarled. "I think he enjoys it too much."

"He probably did in the beginning, but I think he's had a change of heart."

Mr. Barnes hurried back in, took one look at Surlock and visibly swallowed, his face turning pale. "I just need a couple more measurements. I promise."

Darcy willed Surlock to meet her look of warning. He sighed. "Then continue," Surlock said, keeping his gaze on Darcy, rather than looking at the tailor.

A memory flashed of another time, another person taking his measurements, but it had been a female with dark green eyes and a saucy smile.

The memory was gone as quickly as it had flashed across his thoughts. Frustration filled him. Why did his memories stay blocked? He fisted his hands and growled.

"I'm finished," Mr. Barnes squeaked as he quickly straightened, then stepped a good distance back. "I think we have a few things he can take with him until we get his other clothes ready," he told Darcy. When she nodded, he scurried from the room.

"You scared him again," she accused.

"I apologize." He hadn't meant to frighten the little tailor again, even if the man deserved to be frightened. It was the flash of memory that had caught him unaware.

When would he remember everything? He felt as if there was a huge hole in his life, and he desperately wanted it filled. Who was he supposed to keep from danger? Why did his identity have to remain a secret?

"It must be difficult not remembering who you are," Darcy said softly.

There was something in her voice that soothed the beast inside him. He felt his tension ease. "Difficult? I feel as though I've been turned loose in a place where I don't know the people or their customs. I'm like a child learning to walk, but stumbling with every step." He glanced her way, and saw the sympathy in her eyes. He wasn't sure he wanted her compassion.

"I'm sorry." She looked down at her hands, twining her fingers.

He hadn't meant to make her feel guilty again. She was so beautiful, so perfect. And now she felt bad she'd caused him to lose his memory.

From somewhere deep inside, a door unlocked. He remembered someone telling him women enjoyed compliments. "You look nice," he said. He told the truth. She did look nice. Before they had left for town, she had changed into a loose skirt and a sleeveless top. There were sandals on her feet and her toenails were painted dark red to match her fingernails.

He remembered how she was dressed this morning when she stood on the balcony with only a thin bit of material clinging to her naked body. He had clearly seen the outline of her breasts, the exposed curves. He'd felt an almost overwhelming urge to climb up to her balcony and take her into his arms. She'd looked at him then, just as she did now, her need palpable. Desire rose inside him.

"I want to mate with you," he said, his words husky with need.

Her mouth dropped open. "You want to . . . what?"

He stepped off the stool and sauntered to where she stood. Before she could offer a protest, he took her into his arms and pulled her against him.

He stared into her eyes. "I want to mate with you. I want to feel your naked body pressed against mine. I want to plunge inside the heat of your body, stroking you," he whispered close to her ear. Then he was kissing her, tasting her, tongues sparring, his dominating, catching her moan, feeling her press tight against him.

Someone cleared his throat. Surlock was hearing that a lot and wondered if there was something in the air. Darcy pushed out of his arms.

"I'll leave you to change," she said as she hurried from the room.

Surlock watched her leave, then turned to the tailor.

"Here are the things you can wear now," Mr. Barnes said hurriedly, then shoved the clothes toward him.

Too many interruptions. He wanted Darcy. She stirred something inside him and he found it harder and harder to restrain himself.

But rather than cause the little man in front of him to keel over dead from fear, Surlock took the clothes. Mr. Barnes fled the room as if demons from the night were after him.

The clothing was much the same as what Ms. Abernathy had brought, and looked as restraining as what he now wore. He examined each piece to see where he thought it might be worn, then dressed. He didn't like the shoes. He preferred bare feet.

He closed his eyes and could see green fields; he was running through the grass, his feet pounding the ground, breathing labored. Not him, but yet it was. He grabbed the back of the chair as the vision abruptly ended. The humming inside his head grew louder.

Who the hell was he? Where did he come from?

"Are you okay in there?" Darcy's voice floated to him.

The humming quieted. Her voice had a calming effect on him. A musical sound, much like a finely tuned instrument. It relaxed him.

He walked to the curtains and parted them, standing before her. "Will this do?"

For a moment, she didn't say anything, then he caught the slight flare of her nostrils, her quickened breathing. She cleared her throat. "Yes, you look fine. The clothes fit . . . um . . . nicely."

"I'll send the other ready-made clothes out to the estate," Mr. Barnes said. "There will be one last fitting." He cleared his throat. "It shouldn't take long, though."

"Just call when they're ready," she said. She briskly made her way to the door, head held high, shoulders squared.

She wanted him. It wasn't hard to see, but yet, she would deny them both. He wondered why. Maybe he would ask her about it when they returned to the estate.

They arrived at the doctor's office a short time later. Darcy breezed up to the glass-fronted wall. There was a nameplate that read RECEPTIONIST.

Darcy strode to the window. The receptionist glanced up. "Dr. Wilson is expecting us. Darcy Spencer."

Surlock gauged the woman's reaction. She quickly rose to her feet. "Yes, Miss Spencer. He's expecting you both." She hurried to the door that led to the back and opened it. "Come this way." She took them to a small office. "Just have a seat and he'll be with you shortly."

"You're staring at me," she said after they were both seated.

"Am I?"

She frowned and he realized how tempting she looked. He wanted to lean across and kiss away her displeasure.

"Yes, you're staring." Her frown only deepened.

Odd woman, very complex. He discovered something different each time he was around her. "You're very highly regarded by people. They give you deferential treatment wherever you go. The tailor did, as did the doctor yesterday, and now this young woman. Are you special in some way?"

Her cheeks turned rosy red. "My parents do a lot for the community," she finally told him. Then she sighed. "That, and they have money."

"Money is important."

"Money will buy you anything you want."

"It won't buy my memory. Nor the true worth of a man, I think. It can't buy a sunset, or a sunrise. It can't buy laughter, nor dry tears." He thought about it for a moment. "Maybe this money only means something to a small group of people." She looked at him as if he'd lost his mind.

"It will be interesting to discover where you're from and exactly what you do for a living," she said.

Their conversation ended when the doctor entered the room. "Well, you look better than you did yesterday," he said as he went behind his desk and sat in the chair. "Your color is back. Twila said you had a good night, too. Vitals stable. Have you remembered anything?"

"Only flashes," he said. "Nothing of importance."

"And he can play the piano like a professional," Darcy spoke up.

"Good." The doctor beamed. "That's a start. I'm sure it won't be long before you remember everything."

"How long?" Surlock asked.

The doctor leaned forward, resting his elbows on his desk. "Let's not push it. It will come naturally." He shuffled some papers on his desk. "There is one thing. The X-rays came back with some abnormalities."

Darcy drew in a sharp breath, the color draining from her face. "What?"

Surlock gripped the arms of the chair.

"Oh, no, nothing like what you're imagining," the doctor quickly reassured them. "It was just an odd bone structure. Almost as if there were animal bones mixed with human." He laughed. "Of course, that can't be right. I think someone must have x-rayed a family pet and not changed the film. I called the tech and told him to recalibrate his machine and check his plates. Of course, we'll shoot some more."

"No, I don't want more pictures of my bones," Surlock told Dr. Wilson. Something warned him away from more tests. Why couldn't he remember? His stomach churned as he tried to draw forth a memory . . . anything. Nothing came.

"Relax." The doctor's softly spoken words reached out to him.

The doctor was right. It would happen when it happened. Trying to force his memory only made his head hurt.

"I want to draw some blood, and do a quick evaluation. It will only take a moment. Then you'll be free to go."

Surlock looked at Darcy. She nodded, then came to her feet. "I'll meet you in the waiting area."

He didn't want her to leave, but there wasn't a lot he could do about it, except watch as she left the room, quietly closing the door behind her. He didn't like the idea of the doctor taking his blood, but he wanted to be done here. The walls were closing in on him. Letting the man draw his blood seemed the quickest way to escape.

"Have you been experiencing anything out of the ordinary?" the doctor asked as he stood.

"I don't know what the ordinary is."

Dr. Wilson chuckled. "Good point. Okay, have you had any dizziness?" He checked the bump on top of Surlock's head. "Much better."

"If I stand too quickly or if I have a flash of memory, everything turns upside down."

Dr. Wilson nodded. "Perfectly normal." He took an instrument off his desk and bumped it against his palm. A light immediately came on. He shined it in Surlock's eyes. "What a strange shade," he murmured. He changed tips and looked into first one ear, then the other. "Any ringing?"

"Humming."

The doctor straightened. "What kind of humming?"

"Like a voice, but I can't understand the words."

"We'll check your blood count. That might tell us something. Do you swim a lot?"

"I swam this morning."

"You may have swimmer's ear." He went to the other side of the desk again and picked up the phone. "Yes, Marcia, see if I have some samples of eardrops for ringing in the ears. When you come to my office, bring the things to draw some blood. I'll need a complete workup."

He walked back to Surlock. "She'll be here in a moment. After she draws your blood, you're free to go, but I'll want to see you next week. You are planning on sticking around?"

"I have nowhere to go." He realized how true his words were. He felt completely hollow on the inside.

"Don't worry, son. Your memory will all come back. Give it time. When you get to my age you learn to enjoy life and not worry so much about tomorrow."

The nurse came in a few moments later. Before the doctor left, he told Marcia to make an appointment for the following week. The woman took one look at Surlock and visibly swallowed.

Surlock wasn't too sure what she was about to do. She put a band around his arm, then came toward him with a needle. But when she inserted it, she did so expertly, causing only a small prick of pain.

"Sorry if I hurt you," she said. Her gaze flitted to his face, then quickly dropped. "Are you a relative of Miss Spencer?" She loosened the band and put a white ball on his wound, taping it down.

"No." He remembered the job he was supposed to do. "We're dating." She looked crushed by the information. He wondered why. He had met some very strange people this day. "Are we done?" he asked.

"Yes," she sighed.

Darcy was in the waiting area. She looked up when he walked into the room. A smile spread across her face.

"Are you finished?" she asked.

"We're supposed to return next week."

"Here's your appointment card." The receptionist handed it to them from her place behind a desk. "Take care." She grinned at Surlock.

He noticed Darcy didn't seem pleased by the attention he was getting from the female staff. That might work in his favor.

On the drive back to the estate, she was unusually quiet. "I told the nurse we were dating," he announced.

Her head whipped toward him. "Why would you do that?"

Again, she confused him. "I thought that was what you wanted."

Comprehension showed on her face. "Oh, yes, I forgot. That was fine."

"If I'm going to pretend to be your boyfriend, then I should know more about you." Yes, he had an ulterior motive. But he did want to know more about her. She was interesting, and he was lonely. He felt empty not having memories. She helped to fill the void inside him.

"You're right, you do need more information. My mother will definitely grill you." She was thoughtful for a moment. "I'm twenty-five."

"What do you do all day?"

"You mean my job?"

"Yes."

"I don't have one."

"But to earn money to buy all the things one would want, a person needs a job. Is this not correct?"

"My parents have a lot of money, so I don't have to work." She shifted in her seat.

"So, you do nothing all day."

"No! I do lots of things. I go to charity functions and . . . and . . ." Her shoulders dropped.

Again, he felt sorry he'd caused her to feel bad. "There is something you want to do, though," he guessed.

She glanced across the seat. Her gaze returned to the road. "I want work as a P.I.," she said as if telling him a big secret. "I have all the training. I took some college courses, but then I took classes outside of college so I could get licensed."

"What's a P.I.?"

"A private investigator. I want to find things or people who are lost. I'm good at hunting."

He closed his eyes against the blinding pain that shot through his head. He could see himself hunting, going after game in the night. Hunting, watching, attacking. But it felt more as if he were in another body. The humming grew more intense. He grabbed his head, groaning.

"Surlock, what's wrong?" The car slowed, crunched across gravel, then stopped.

The pain was easing, but he kept his eyes closed, his hands holding his head. "I saw something. Hunting. But not me. I was someone else. Then the humming in my head. It's confusing."

She pulled his head against her chest. "I'm so sorry."

"Not your fault," he managed to tell her.

"Shh, don't talk. Just keep your eyes closed and try to relax."

He took a deep breath, and caught the exotic aroma of the scent she wore. The pain stopped, but was replaced with a different kind of hurt. She absently kissed the top of his head, smoothed her fingers across his forehead. He tilted his head until he could see her face. She hesitated, then lowered her lips to his in a gentle kiss.

At least, he was pretty sure she meant it to be gentle, but as soon as her tongue stroked his, she awakened something inside him. Something he couldn't control. Or maybe he just didn't want to control it. He cupped the back of her head, bringing her closer. The humming quieted.

He slid his hand under her top, under her bra, and grazed his thumb over her nipple. She moaned, surrendering to his touch, pressing closer.

The blast from a car horn broke them apart. Someone called out for them to "get a room," which was ridiculous. He was quite happy where he was.

"I'm sorry," she stuttered as she straightened her clothes.

"Why?" Surlock groaned in frustration.

Her face was infused with a rosy tint. "Because I didn't mean for my comforting to go quite that far."

"I liked it." He reached toward her, but she quickly pulled away so he let his hand drop to the seat.

"That's the problem. So did I, and I know nothing about you." She started the car, then backed out into the road. She continued toward her family's estate.

"Sometimes you can know everything there is to know about a person and not know them at all," he told her.

She pulled up to the iron gates and pushed a button inside the car. The gates swung open and she drove to the house.

"I still don't know anything about you. How can I pretend to be your boyfriend?"

"I'll make a list."

"I don't want a list. That won't work. We'll need to spend time together if we are to convince anyone. And we'll have to convince the staff first."

She cast a wary look in his direction before returning her gaze to the road. "You're right."

"And I want to know more about this P.I. business. My mind is lost. Maybe you can help me find it."

And maybe she could explain the incredible pull he felt toward her. It was almost as though there was some kind of connection between them. He had a feeling Darcy might be part of the reason why he was here.

CHAPTER 5

Adrenaline rushed through Darcy as she stepped outside. She needed to figure out what her first step would be to discover who Surlock was, and why he'd been running around the woods naked.

Deep in thought, she wandered aimlessly down the path that wound through the garden at the side of the house. Still, she couldn't stop the flutter of excitement that swept through her. Her skills would be put to the test. Someone had offered her a job.

She chewed her bottom lip. Of course, she had been the one who caused Surlock's amnesia, so it was only right that she should be the one who helped restore it. And she would. She would discover Surlock's identity, solve the mystery and soothe her guilty conscience.

Darcy truly did love her mother, but having a real job was like a dream come true. Maybe this was fate. She was achieving her goal, grabbing the brass ring as it went by. She hugged her middle, barely able to keep a shout of joy from escaping past her lips. She could do this. She only had to piece everything together. Like one big puzzle.

Doubt suddenly reared its ugly head, and her excitement plummeted. But what if she couldn't do this? All this time she'd told herself she wanted to be a P.I., but what if finding out who Surlock was or where he came from proved to be too difficult? What if she was only fooling herself, using her mother as an excuse so that Darcy wouldn't have to face the fact she might be a failure.

"You look deep in thought," Surlock said as he came up beside her. He glanced around. "It's nice out here." He leaned forward and brought one of the delicate pink flowers to his nose. "It smells nice. What is it?"

"I'm not sure about that particular flower. Ralph takes care of the garden, so you would have to ask him. I know some of the names, but mostly I just enjoy their smell and how pretty they are." She tilted her head and looked up at him. "Most men would never admit they liked flowers."

"Why?" he asked.

Again with the whys. She shrugged. "Too feminine, I guess."

"But you enjoy this place." He waved his arm in front of him.

"I find solace out here." She strolled farther down the pea gravel path. He walked beside her. "Dad had the fountain put in because Mother loves the water. They have a beach house on the coast, too." She was rambling, but she couldn't seem to stop herself. How could she tell Surlock that she might not discover anything about him?

"Your father must earn a lot of money."

Startled, she looked at him, but didn't see the usual calculating gleam. That was another thing about her boyfriends: Most of them liked the idea that her parents were wealthy. Did Surlock fit into that category?

She continued to study him for a moment, then dismissed that idea. Surlock had stated it more as a fact, rather than anything else. She breathed a sigh of relief, then wondered why she should care. Okay, so maybe she was attracted to him just a little—or a lot.

"Dad has his own business," she told him. "That, and my

parents inherited from their parents. They've also made wise investments over the years."

"But you're not happy?"

She stopped at a bench and sat on the flowered cushion. Surlock chose a chair angled slightly toward the bench. Wisteria grew thick over the arbor, creating a shady canopy. In the spring, large, grapelike clusters of flowers would hang from the branches.

"I have everything I could ever want," she finally told him. And she did. Her parents had always given her anything she desired.

"That's not what I asked. Sometimes material possessions can only give short-term gratification."

She studied him. "Maybe you're a monk."

"A monk?"

"Yes, a priest. They don't put much stock in worldly goods, but rather in life." She brushed strands of loose hair behind her ear and shifted to a more comfortable position on the cushions.

He nodded. "Then maybe that is who I am."

"They're also celibate." When he didn't seem to recognize the word, she explained, "They have taken a vow of chastity. No sex."

Good Lord, could she have knocked a monk out cold? Maybe he'd been on a pilgrimage, giving up all worldly possessions, including his clothes. She was pretty sure lusting after a priest would get her a ticket to hell.

Surlock's eyes widened. "Why would they do something so crazy as to give up mating?"

"Because of their religious beliefs," she explained. Okay, he probably wasn't a monk. Thank God.

"I'm not a monk." He squared his shoulders and sat straighter.

"No, I didn't really think you were." Not the way he kissed. But who was he? "Let me see your hands."

He stuck them out and she took one. It was warm. His heat

quickly transferred to her body. He had strong hands. Darcy could almost feel them caressing her, stroking.

She cleared her throat and her thoughts. She was here to help him, not pounce on his body. It was a sexy body, though.

She ran her hands over his, trying to act like a professional. They were a little rough in places, but the nails were manicured, smooth. His other hand was the same.

"You weren't raised by wolves," she murmured.

"Why would you think that?"

When she looked up, she forgot what he had asked. For a moment, she lost herself in his warm whiskey eyes. The gold flecks sparkled in the sunlight. Very unusual. She mentally shook her head.

What had he asked? Oh, yes, why she would think he was raised by wolves. "Because you were with a wolf. At least, there was one in the area when you stepped out from behind the tree. You also look sort of rugged." In a very sexy way. "You didn't have any clothes on, either, and you ate with your hands, and you growl at people."

His eyebrows drew together. "Because you were eating with your hands." His frown darkened. "I don't growl at people."

"The doctor? The tailor?"

"I don't like being probed, nor did I like the way the tailor measured. Maybe I did growl a few times," he conceded.

She chuckled. "You can see how I might come to that conclusion," she said. "All the facts pointed in that direction."

"What changed your mind?"

"You play the piano beautifully. If you had been raised by wolves, you wouldn't have learned how to play. Besides, your nails are manicured, and it looks like a professional did them." She let go of his hands and leaned back against the bench.

"But I still don't have a clue to who I am."

"You remember nothing?" When he hesitated, she knew he wasn't telling her something. She leaned forward, willing him to meet her gaze, and he did, eventually. "How can I discover who

you are or where you come from, if you don't tell me everything?"

"It's not that I have anything solid. It's more like a feeling."

"What?" Still, he didn't say anything. "It won't go any further
than me."

He clasped his hands. "I think there's someone I'm supposed
to protect."

"And?"

"I'm supposed to keep my identity a secret. But I can't continue from day to day not knowing who I am."

She sat forward again. "Wow, that sounds very James Bond."

His eyes widened. "You have already discovered my identity?
Is that who I am? This James Bond?"

"I'm sorry," she quickly told him. "James Bond is a fictional
spy, but there are people like him—secret agents. Maybe that's
what you are."

She studied him for a moment. It actually did make sense. He
had the build, the muscles. That was probably why he remembered that he would need to keep his identity a secret. She was
pretty sure secret agents had that drilled into them. And, he'd
said he needed to protect someone. Definitely secret-agent stuff.

A thrill of excitement swept through her. Her very own sexy
secret agent living in the guest house. She wondered if he had all
of James Bond's bedroom moves.

"What are you thinking?" he asked.

Heat flooded her face. She really had to stop fantasizing. But
it was such a good fantasy. She regretfully brought her attention
back to the present. "I think we might have just discovered what
you do for a living."

"But I still don't know what a secret agent is."

She jumped up and grabbed his hand. "Come on, I'll show
you. My dad is a big Bond fan. He has a media room full of his
movies. If that's what you are, maybe it'll jog your memory."

Her father's addiction to Bond had probably sparked Darcy's
dream of becoming a private investigator. She'd watched every

Bond movie at least twice with her father. They'd bonded over Bond.

She was really losing it.

They went into the house and upstairs. When they walked inside the media room, she realized she still held his hand. She quickly dropped it, and went to the DVD player. Holding his hand had felt nice, though. Too nice. The relationship had to stay platonic, professional. Her gaze landed on him and lingered for a moment. At least platonic until she knew his background.

The media room could seat up to twenty people in chocolate-suede covered, oversized recliners. The screen filled one entire wall. There was even a popcorn machine at the back and a small bar where you could get a soda or alcoholic beverage. Not that she had been allowed alcohol until she turned twenty-one, and by then she discovered she preferred soda.

But her favorite part of the media room was the lights. When they were dimmed, the ceiling automatically began to twinkle with thousands of fiber optic lights. The atmosphere created a feeling of being outside under the stars.

She motioned Surlock toward one of the chairs and went to the library cabinets. Her organized father had every movie alphabetized and arranged by genre. She quickly found the Bond movie she wanted and grabbed the remote. Her father had hundreds of movies. Collecting them had gone way beyond the hobby stage and become an obsession.

Darcy inserted the DVD, then took the chair next to Surlock's. With just the push of a few buttons, the lights dimmed, and the movie started.

Out of the corner of her eye, she watched as Surlock really got into the movie. Halfway through, she realized one thing: All guys were alike. It wasn't hard to tell that he enjoyed action flicks.

But she'd forgotten about the sexual tension, the love scenes. She shifted in her seat as James Bond became Surlock and she became the female lead. It was Surlock touching her, flirting with his eyes, seducing her.

Darcy was glad when the movie finally ended. She jumped to her feet and turned the lights on, rather than using the remote. She needed to put some distance between them.

"What did you think?" she managed to ask with only a small catch in her voice.

He shifted in his seat until he met her gaze. "Yes, I think I might be a secret agent."

"You've remembered something?"

He shook his head. "Nothing. But being a secret agent feels right."

Which didn't really tell her a lot since most guys would like to play the part of James Bond in real life. She was no closer than she had been before they watched the movie. The only thing it had created was more sexual frustration, and confusion about who Surlock might be.

So, how to find out for sure? She thought about it for a moment before coming up with an idea. "We can fingerprint you."

"What will that do?"

"If you work for the government, your prints might be on file. You could work in intelligence of some kind and not necessarily be a secret agent. There are a lot of possibilities."

A slow sexy grin curved his lips upward. Her toes curled in response. Damn, the man was devilishly handsome.

"I don't know, I kind of like the idea of women falling all over themselves to mate with me."

Her mouth went dry and swallowing was suddenly not an option. The way he looked at her, she had a feeling he wanted to mate with her right here, right now.

What he'd just said finally sank in. "That's not the first time you've referred to sex as mating. I've never heard anyone call it mating. That might be a clue to where you're from."

"Mating is not correct?"

"It is, but most people refer to it as sex or making love. Mating is usually associated with animals. That's why I think you're probably not from around here."

He still looked at her as if he was more interested in making love than finding out who he was. She understood the feeling perfectly. There was a strange current that seemed to pass between them. It was hard to explain. It was almost as if she'd known him all her life, but that wasn't possible.

"You're very beautiful," he said, reaching over and brushing some loose strands of hair behind her ear.

His fingertips grazed her cheek. A shiver of anticipation rippled through her. She knew he was going to kiss her. One kiss wouldn't hurt.

Darcy leaned forward, welcoming his touch, needing his touch. Instead of pulling her closer, his hand slipped to her arm. He ran his fingers lightly up and down in an absentminded caress. It was all she could do to stop herself from jumping his bones.

"You feel it, too," he said.

"Feel what?"

"The attraction."

Her cheeks grew warm. "You're a nice-looking man—of course I feel attracted to you." That was an understatement if she'd ever heard one.

"No, more than that. I've never felt anything such as this. I want you so much, my need has become a deep ache inside me. Do you feel this?"

As if an electrical current passed between them. Yes, but she'd been afraid to say anything to him. She finally nodded, unable to speak.

"I think if I can't touch you, I will explode." He moved his hand to the shoulder ties on her shirt. He didn't hurry as he untied first one, then the other.

Darcy knew that he was giving her time to protest, to stop him, but she couldn't. Instead, she reached for the remote and dimmed the lights. She refused to remind herself she'd only been going to let him kiss her, nothing more. She'd think about the consequences later.

She started the movie playing again to drown out the noise she knew they would make. When she faced him again, she reached for the hem of her shirt and pulled it over her head, tossing it to the floor.

Her hands trembled when she unbuttoned the first button on his shirt. He didn't try to stop her, either. Not that she had really thought he might. It was a good thing, too, because she wanted to touch him.

When his shirt was open, she pushed the sides off his shoulders, relishing sliding her hands over his sinewy muscles. Her body quivered with anticipation as he stood, letting the shirt fall to the floor with a shrug of his shoulders.

She stood as well, kicking off her sandals. He toed off his shoes, then removed his socks before reaching for her again.

Her mouth went dry when he unfastened her shorts, tugging the zipper down. His palms caressed her at the same time as he pushed her shorts over her hips. She stood in front of him wearing only a lacy pink bra and a matching thong.

"You're so beautiful."

"So are you."

"I'm a man, a hunter, not beautiful."

She stilled. "A hunter?"

He frowned, then grabbed his head. He groaned, then closed his eyes tight, his expression pained.

"What?" Worry shot through her. She touched his arm, guiding him back down in the chair. "Surlock, what's happening?"

"Noise," he gasped. "In my head." He fumbled in his pocket, but he wasn't having much luck retrieving whatever he was trying to get.

"What? How can I help?"

"The doctor gave me eardrops."

She brushed his hand out of the way and reached inside his pocket, bringing out the small bottle. "Got it. Move your hands and I'll put some drops in." He moved one hand. She put in several drops and hoped it wasn't too many, then repeated in the other ear.

As soon as she finished, he put his hands over his ears and dropped his head between his legs. She could see he struggled to keep from crying out. Once again, guilt flooded her.

"Maybe I should take you to the hospital."

"No, it's easing. It only happens when I remember something. It's not so much painful as it is loud. Like someone screaming in my ear."

A few moments passed until he straightened. She breathed a sigh of relief. He slowly lowered his hands as if he was afraid the noise would return.

"Better?" she asked, nibbling her bottom lip.

"Better."

She stood, reaching for her clothes. "Maybe this wasn't such a good idea. It's probably too soon after your injury." Could she feel any more guilty? Or embarrassed?

When she straightened, he was beside her, taking her into his arms, lowering his mouth to hers. She let the clothes fall to the floor, forgotten as she lost herself in the man. She wrapped her arms around his neck, pulling him closer still. He undid the clasp of her bra, then his hands slipped under to cup her breasts. He teased her nipples. They tightened and became more sensitive.

When the kiss ended, she was breathing hard. She rested her head against his chest, and heard the pounding of his heart. He slid his hands down her back, cupped her butt and pulled her close. She wiggled against him, and smiled when he groaned.

He stepped away from her. Her body tingled as she watched him undo his pants, then slide the zipper down. Her pulse raced when he shoved them downward, his briefs going with them. The man was truly magnificent. He was thick, swollen with need. She imagined what it would feel like to have him buried deep inside her. Hot, scorching, stroking . . . unprotected.

Damn!

"I'll be right back." Before she gave him the chance to say anything, she was at the door, cautiously opening it. All clear. The maids always cleaned the upstairs first. She prayed they were gone now as she ran naked down the hall—a thong didn't really count as clothes. Her bedroom was only two doors down, thank goodness.

Once inside, she hurried to her dresser and yanked open the top drawer. In the far back corner she found the condoms. She rifled through them until she found an extra large. Her fingers trembled as she hurried back to the door. She cracked it open. All clear. Her pulse raced as she darted back to the media room and slipped inside.

"Protection," she said, completely out of breath as she waved the condom in the air, then realized what the hell she was doing. God, how embarrassing. She was acting as if she had never had sex before. She'd just never had really, really good sex, but she had a feeling this time would be different.

"Protection?" His forehead wrinkled.

"You know, sexually transmitted diseases?"

"You are diseased?"

She frowned. "Well, no, but it's better not to take any chances." She thrust the condom toward him. She had a feeling he had no idea what to do with it. "I'll show you." Right before she died of embarrassment.

She tore open the foil packet and removed the condom. "It, uh, sheaths your, uh, erection." She was so glad she'd dimmed the lights. He jerked when she brushed across the head of his penis. She had an insane desire to wrap her hands around him and slide his foreskin down. But she didn't. Instead, she slowly rolled the condom onto him. It was a snug fit.

She swallowed past the lump in her throat. Was he too big? She hadn't had sex in almost a year.

"I want you," he said, his voice husky.

Screw it. She couldn't stand not feeling him buried inside her. She jerked her thong down and kicked it away. He pulled her close, sliding his hand down, slipping between her legs. She drew in a sharp breath when he scraped his fingers through her curls.

"Yes," she breathed, moving closer. "More."

He slipped a finger inside. Her body quivered from the small eruption he caused. She bit her bottom lip, moving against his finger. "More," she cried.

But rather than give her what she asked, he slipped his finger out and moved to a recliner, tugging her hand so that she went with him. At this point, she would've done anything he asked, followed him anywhere, just as long as he promised to give her more of what he already had.

He sat first, then pulled her onto his lap so that she straddled him. She rubbed against his erection. He groaned. She raised herself enough so he could move inside her, then slowly brought herself down on him. Each inch of him was an explosion of delight. She waited until her body adjusted to his size. It didn't take long.

He watched her, also waiting, and seemed to know when she was ready. He raised his hips. She moaned with pleasure, raising and lowering her body.

"Feels so good," he gasped.

"Yes," she cried out.

In the background James Bond raced across the screen. Shots rang out, a car crashed and burst into flames. A woman screamed. More shots, running feet.

Darcy ran her hands through her hair. He massaged her breasts, tugging on the nipples. Heat filled her. The blood pounded through her veins. She moved her body against his. Faster, harder.

She heard an old familiar humming in her ears, growing louder. She blocked the sound, only wanting to feel what he was doing to her body. Blocked it as she had when she was younger. The humming stopped as suddenly as it had begun. She only wanted to feel what was happening to her body, the incredible sensations that were exploding inside her.

"Look at me," he said, his voice hoarse with need.

She opened her eyes, made the connection. Something passed between them. More than just making love. It was almost as if they were becoming one. Words were no longer necessary between them. She knew what he wanted, needed, without his saying a word.

The fire built inside her. Rising to a crescendo.

Release shook her body. She stilled. Muscles clenched. Heard him cry out and was glad the sound was turned up on the movie. His body suddenly tightened, then slowly relaxed.

She melted against his chest, a film of sweat covering her body as she tried to bring her breathing under control. She'd never, ever had an orgasm like the one she'd just experienced. She was afraid Surlock had ruined her for other men. Right now, she really didn't care.

She rose slightly, looking into his face. "That was good," she said, then laughed.

"Yes, it was." He smiled, but then his face contorted into a grimace of pain. He grabbed his head.

"What? What is it?"

"The screaming," he gasped. "It won't stop."

She quickly slipped off him. "What can I do? The eardrops. I'll get them." She rushed over to his slacks and grabbed the bottle out of his pocket, then hurried back.

But when she looked at him, for a moment, she could've sworn she looked at the eyes of the wolf. She rubbed her eyes. The wolf eyes were gone and she saw Surlock's eyes again.

"Ahh . . . I can't stand it."

She ran to him. "I have the drops." She moved his hand away and hoped she got some inside. It was so dim in the room she could barely see.

She moved to the other ear. He growled from low in his throat. She jumped, but didn't pause. He was only in pain. She put drops in the other ear. He began to quiet, and when she leaned down and looked into his face, she saw his eyes, not the eyes of an animal. It had only been a trick of the light. That's all it could have been.

"Better?" she asked.

He nodded, letting out his breath. "I felt as though something tried to pull me away."

"What do you mean?"

He shook his head. "It doesn't matter."

"No, it does matter. There could be something seriously wrong. I should take you to the doctor again. This isn't normal. You could have swelling of the brain or something."

He shook his head. "I'm feeling better now. No more screaming in my head. And I don't want to see the doctor."

"I still think I should call him." She worried her bottom lip.

He squeezed her arm. "And tell him what? That we mated, then the humming in my head got louder?"

She cocked an eyebrow. "I'd leave out the part about us making love. I'd tell him you overexerted yourself."

He gave her a wobbly grin. "You think I did?"

"Well, no, I mean—"

"I enjoyed mating—making love with you."

She smiled. "I enjoyed it, too." And she was now naked in front of him and she was more than a little self-conscious. "There's a bathroom on the other side of that door. I'll slip to my room and freshen up. I'll meet you back in here. And I will call Dr. Wilson just to see what he thinks."

He nodded. "If it will make you feel better."

"It will." She scooped up her clothes and hurried from the room. As she slipped inside her bedroom, she wondered exactly what she thought she saw happening to Surlock. She might have tried to dismiss it as the light, but something strange had happened.

And why had the humming in her ears suddenly started up again? She'd actually forgotten about it until now. She dropped her clothes in the hamper, then turned the water on in the shower.

Strange things were starting to happen. She'd never felt this connection with someone when she had sex. Hell, she'd never felt any connection.

Darcy shook her head and stepped in the shower. Nothing strange had happened. The humming had started because she'd been—excited. Nothing more. And it was just as she'd thought, Surlock knew how to please a woman. She'd only had the best orgasm ever and was still in shock.

Right?

CHAPTER 6

Surlock stared into the bathroom mirror. What had happened in there? For a moment, he'd been someone else. No, something else, and that something else had tried to take over his body. A deep shudder washed over him.

The humming grew louder in his ears. Not as loud as before, but enough that he knew it was there. Maybe he was crazy. Maybe the blow to his head had affected him more than he'd thought. Maybe . . . He scraped his fingers through his hair.

Who the hell was he?

He turned on the water, splashing some on his face. He didn't belong here. He could feel it all the way to his bones. Could he be this secret agent man like the James Bond character? He'd remembered he was a hunter, but not much else.

Was he one of the good guys? There had been killers in the movie as well. Darcy had said they were the bad guys. If he could be one of the good guys, couldn't he be a bad one just as well?

He jumped when someone tapped on the door of the bathroom. "Yes?"

"Are you okay?" Darcy asked.

He patted his face dry on the hand towel, tossing it on the counter. When he opened the door, he was in control again. "Yes, all better." He smiled.

"You look worried," she said. She took his hand and squeezed.

Worried? Surlock had thought he could hide what he felt from Darcy. Apparently not. She had easily picked up on his emotions. Again he wondered at the bond between them.

"I'll find out who you are, don't worry. The doctor said your memory would come back naturally. He said the humming you're hearing might be from trying too hard to remember."

"He's probably right. There's no pain now."

His gaze swept over her. Darcy was fresh from the shower. She smelled sweet. He'd loved mating with her. She'd given as much as he had. By the gods, he didn't want to hurt her if it turned out he was a criminal.

He caressed her cheek with the back of his hand. Her skin was smooth, soft. She smiled and his pulse quickened. "Am I one of the good guys?" His voice sounded raspy.

"Of course, you're one of the good guys," she said softly.

"But how can you be sure?"

She stepped closer, and his arms automatically went around her, settling on her hips.

"You're one of the good guys because I'd know if you weren't. I have fantastic instincts. Besides, remember what you said? You're here to protect someone, not hurt them. What kind of bad guy would protect someone?"

He sighed, knowing she was probably right. "I don't feel like one of those killers in the movie."

She leaned back and looked him in the eye. "Exactly."

Her lips were too soft and inviting. He lowered his mouth to hers, then pulled her closer as he deepened the kiss. She was sweet and hot all mixed together, and he wanted her again. But he wasn't sure he could go through another episode where it felt as though something was trying to possess him. He ended the kiss.

She took a deep breath, stepping out of his arms. "Wow, you're a good kisser."

He smiled.

She shrugged one shoulder. "Well, you are. I have a tendency to speak what's on my mind. Unfortunately."

"I like that about you." He studied her for a moment. She was beautiful, sexy and very tempting. "Why did you need me to pretend to care about you? Men should be falling all over themselves to be your boyfriend."

She abruptly turned and went to the machine that had played the movie, removing the disk. "Most of the men I've dated seem only interested in my money. The ones who haven't been, well, they didn't work out." She put the round disk into the case and snapped it closed. "My parents will be joining me here in one month. I told my mother I had a boyfriend."

"And this is important to your mother?"

She walked back over to where he stood. He liked the way she walked—smoothly, gracefully.

"Oh, yeah, it's real important. My mother wants me married. She wants me to be a social butterfly."

"You don't want this?"

She shook her head. "I want to get my hands dirty. Do you know what I'm saying?"

He didn't, but her expression said she hoped he would agree. "Yes," he lied.

She exhaled a deep breath. "I'll find out your identity, too. It'll be the first real job I've ever had." She glanced at her watch. "Ms. Abernathy should have lunch fixed. Let's eat, then we'll run down to the sheriff's office."

"You enjoy running?"

She smiled. "An expression. I'll drive us in my car."

He followed her out of the room. "What is at the sheriff's office?"

"Jillian's brother works there. She's one of the maids. She called her brother and he said we could drop by this afternoon. He's going to run your prints. If you're in the system, we'll know who you are."

He gripped the railing on the staircase. "I need to keep my identity a secret."

She glanced over her shoulder. "Don't worry, Eddie will be discreet."

His world felt as though it was unraveling around him. He wasn't sure discreet would matter.

If he was supposed to keep his identity a secret, he was doing a great job. Even he didn't know who he was. He had a feeling he needed to fill in the blanks as quickly as possible. Maybe Darcy could make it happen.

Darcy glanced at Surlock from the corner of her eye. He was hesitant when he got out of the car. Right now he looked at the sheriff's building as if he was about to go to jail. She only hoped that she was right, and that Surlock was one of the good guys.

"It'll be okay," she told him. "I've known Jillian and Eddie a long time. Her brother will be careful when he runs your prints." Of course, all bets were off if Surlock was wanted by the law. Eddie would have Surlock picked up and behind bars before she had a chance to get him out of the country.

She missed a step and stumbled. Surlock grabbed her elbow to steady her. Crap, would it come to that? Would she end up just as much a criminal?

No, that wouldn't happen. She refused to even think about it as a possibility.

"It'll be okay," she said, more to reassure herself.

He nodded, but he still didn't look too sure about any of this. Her instincts were usually spot on, which was why she wanted to open her own agency. There was no way Surlock could be the bad guy.

But who was he?

If he was supposed to protect someone, then who? Could he have been trying to do his job and maybe been captured? Robbed of everything he had, including his clothes? Had he somehow escaped? Great, then when he'd stepped out of the woods, she'd whacked him over the head, and added to his problems.

She only hoped the person Surlock was supposed to protect

was okay, maybe in hiding. She'd hate to think she'd caused someone to be in more danger, or worse, killed. Ack, she didn't even want to go there.

They stepped inside the dim interior of the building. It was a typical small-town sheriff's office. The dispatcher's cubicle was behind glass panels. There was a short hallway, the doors on both sides closed. On the other side were locked double doors that led to the jail and fingerprinting area.

Darcy knew the doors were locked because she'd been here before. If her mother ever found out, there would be hell to pay. *Ohmygosh, her daughter had been near bad guys who were locked away because of the crimes they'd committed.*

Usually the only crimes committed around here were minor. This wasn't the big city. Summerville was only fifty thousand in population. It did have a nice country club and a few really good restaurants. But hardened criminals? Pftt . . . no.

"It's like the receptionist at the doctor's office," Surlock said as he looked around the department.

"Similar, but with much different jobs."

The glass window slid open. "I'm here to see Eddie," she told the dispatcher.

"I'll buzz him," she said, then slid the glass closed again.

"What do they do here?" Surlock asked.

"They maintain order. Make sure the town is safe and secure."

He nodded. "My brother Kristor does that."

They looked at each other. "You remembered something." She grinned. "That's great. If your brother maintains order, then I bet he's in law enforcement, and I really doubt you're one of the bad guys." She noticed he looked relieved by her observation. So was she.

There was a loud *click* and the heavy double doors opened. Eddie smiled at her. He was a nice-looking man. Tall, with bright orange hair, but the color seemed to suit him.

"Hey, Darcy, I haven't seen you in a while. How's it going in the P.I. business?"

She grimaced. "It isn't." Just as quickly, she brightened. "Until now. Surlock is my first case. I'm trying to help him find out who he is."

Eddie nodded. "Oh, this is the guy you walloped."

She inwardly cringed.

"I scared her," Surlock spoke up. "She had a reason to knock me out. Next time, I'll make sure I don't step out suddenly in front of someone."

Eddie laughed. "I don't know, there are a lot of guys around here who wouldn't mind if Darcy hit them over the head, especially if she nursed them back to health."

"Are you one of them?" Surlock asked conversationally, but there was a rigid set to his jaw.

And the testosterone flowed. Sheesh.

"Nope, my wife would kill me if I looked twice at another woman. Not that I would. She's the best thing that ever happened to me."

Surlock looked at Darcy with a question in his eyes. She realized he didn't know the term *wife*. "A wife is like a . . . a mate. They're bound together by love."

Surlock relaxed and they went to the back. The light was dim, and apparently the prisoners had been cleaning because there was a distinct smell of disinfectant in the air.

Eddie stopped at a desk. "I've got everything ready. I'll get the prints, then call you when the results come in. Now, if we were in the city, this wouldn't take long at all, but our equipment is a little dated. Still, it shouldn't be more than twenty-four hours."

Eddie took Surlock's hand and inked a finger, then pressed it on the paper. When he finished printing all his fingers, he handed Surlock a tissue. "That's it." He closed the inkpad and casually asked, "You going to be around for a while?"

"Yes, I have nowhere to go."

"Good." His gaze met Surlock's. For a moment they just stared at each other.

Darcy looked between the two and knew they were taking

each other's measure. Eddie suddenly smiled, relaxing. Apparently, Surlock had passed his test.

"As soon as the results come in, I'll call Darcy," Eddie repeated, then walked back to the heavy doors and opened them. "Take care, Darcy. Surlock, it was nice meeting you. We'll do everything we can to help."

They left the sheriff's office and walked back to her car. Surlock was quiet.

"That wasn't so bad, was it?"

He stopped at the passenger door. "No, it wasn't bad at all. I liked your friend."

She grinned. "His wife is very nice, too."

"What?"

"You were jealous."

He frowned.

"Do you know the word?"

"Yes." He opened the door and got in. When she was inside, he glanced across the seat. "I was jealous until I knew he had a mate."

She hadn't expected him to admit it. It was kind of nice knowing that he cared. "Want to get something to drink?"

"Yes."

A man of few words. She eyed him as she backed out of the parking space. But sexy as hell.

There was a Sonic a couple blocks over. She drove to it, then pulled into a parking spot, and rolled the windows down before turning off the key. "What would you like?"

"I don't know."

She pointed to the menu. "This is what they have."

He moved closer to her, close enough that she could feel the heat coming off his body. Their gazes met and held for a moment. She saw his mouth move, but her brain was in a fog and she didn't hear what he'd said.

"What?" she asked.

His grin was slow and lazy.

Ass.

"I asked what was good," he repeated.

She drew in a deep breath, but caught his earthy scent. She quickly turned to the menu. "I like the lemon-cherry slush."

"Then that's what I'll have."

She cleared her throat. "I just need to give them our order." She quickly leaned out the window and pushed the button.

"Welcome to Sonic, I'll take your order whenever you're ready," a pleasant voice announced over the speaker.

Darcy gave the girl their order. Surlock had already moved to his side of the car. A shame. She didn't mind a bit that he'd been in close proximity. It had been very nice.

Damn it, she just had to discover Surlock's identity. She sent up a silent prayer that he would turn out to be one of the good guys. But wouldn't she know if he was bad? She hoped her instincts were that good.

Their drinks came and she paid for them, then handed one to Surlock. After the carhop left, she showed Surlock how to insert the straw. "Now you suck on it," she said, then demonstrated.

He tried and managed to get a drink. "This is good," he said, taking another big swallow.

"I like them," she said.

Suddenly, he set his drink down and grabbed his head.

"The humming? Did you bring the eardrops?"

"No, no, it's something new. My head feels as if it'll explode. The pain is almost unbearable."

"No! This isn't good. I'll get you to the hospital and . . ."

He lowered his hands. "It stopped." He looked surprised. "It wasn't like before. There was no loud humming." He reached for his drink.

She chuckled when she realized what had happened.

"What?" he asked.

"I think you've just experienced your first brain freeze." When he still looked puzzled, she explained, "You drank your slush too fast. The cold rushed to your head, which created a brain freeze."

"My brain froze?'

"Technically no. It feels like it, though. Drink the slush a little slower."

"I like the taste."

"So do I, but I hate brain freeze."

He picked up his drink again and took a slower drink this time. His expression turned solemn. "Do you think when Eddie checks my prints, he'll find something?"

"I don't know."

He nodded. When he looked at her again, he was smiling. "But I do remember I have a brother named Kristor."

"Yes, you do." She could see the worry behind the smile. She worried, too, but for more than one reason. There was a muted humming in her ears. Why, after so many years, had it returned?

CHAPTER 7

He was running. Surlock felt the wind on his face, but it was another's face, another's eyes he saw through. He felt free and alive.

"Hear me, Surlock, you know me. I am Chinktah. Let me past the barriers you have erected. Hear me!"

Surlock sat straight up in bed, drenched in sweat, gasping for air. What had just happened? He looked around. The room was dark. He was in bed. A bad dream? It must have been. By the gods, it had seemed real. Too real for comfort.

He shoved the cover off and stood, his movements jerky. Rather than turning on a light, he went to the other room, to the French doors. He opened them wide, breathing deeply of the night air. The stars were out, the moon was almost full. He stepped to the patio and raised his arms, drawing strength from the orb in the sky.

What had he dreamt? It was fading away, but he needed to remember. He'd felt the wind on his face, but he was in someone else's body. A voice had spoken, not his thoughts. Confusion warred within him. What if he was losing his mind?

The humming was back. He put his hands over his ears, trying to block out the noise, but it grew louder. "Stop," he cried out. "I don't know who or what you are, but leave me in peace!"

The noise didn't abate. Surlock walked to the edge of the pool and dove in. Beneath the water, the noise lessened. Here was peace at last.

He began to relax as he swam beneath the water. Long strokes carried him to the other end of the pool and back. Blue and red lights shimmered around him, making it all seem surreal. He didn't care—the noise in his head had stopped now, and that was all that mattered.

He surfaced, flinging his hair out of his face, and when he did, he saw Darcy at the pool's edge, wearing a silky nightgown that left little to the imagination.

Did he still dream? If so, he didn't want to waken. He needed her now more than he ever had. He needed the connection with another human being. He needed her to tell him he wasn't going crazy.

As if she heard his thoughts, she grasped the hem of her gown and pulled it over her head, tossing it behind her, then laid a small package on the edge. When she straightened, she stood there for a moment, then slowly brought her arms up. He could only stare at the ethereal beauty before him. Her lips curved slightly upward, and then she pushed off the side, diving over his head. He turned, watching as she swam to the other side. She turned beneath the water and swam toward him, emerging in front of him. She pressed her naked body against his, and looked into his face.

"I dreamt you were running, but it wasn't you. I came awake, sitting up in bed, and knew you needed me." She stroked the side of his face. "What does it mean? Did it even happen? Are we . . . connected in some way?"

He shook his head, pulling her tighter against him. "It happened, but I don't know what it means. I was dreaming, too. A voice spoke to me. Has a voice ever spoken to you?"

"No." Her eyes were sad.

He hadn't thought so. "I think I'm going crazy. I should leave. What if I'm putting you in some kind of danger?"

She placed her hands on either side of his face. "Look at me— you're not going crazy. If you are, then so am I. Why else would

I share your dream?" She wrapped her arms around him. "There's some kind of connection between us. I felt drawn to you in the guest house that first day."

"And it gets stronger each day," he added.

"Yes," she whispered close to his ear. "There's more."

"What?"

"I heard a humming sound in my ears when I was younger. My mother took me to so many specialists. None of them could discover the cause. She became so agitated that I finally woke one morning and lied to her. I told my mother the humming had stopped. Eventually, it did. Since you've shown up, it has started again."

"I'm sorry."

She leaned back and looked at him. "For what?"

"I've caused the noise to return."

"I don't think so, but I have a feeling once we discover who you are, and where you're from, we'll also know why we have the noises in our heads."

"Are you scared?"

She hesitated, then said, "Not as long as I'm with you."

He could see the fear in her eyes, but maybe she hadn't lied because he felt better able to cope as long as she was with him.

"Make love to me," she said, running her hands over his back.

How could he not when he ached so much to do just that? He kissed her, his tongue stroking hers, feeling the heat, the need that rippled through her at his first touch. Knowing that he could make her tremble was a heady feeling. He wanted to make her do more than tremble. He wanted her to cry his name. He wanted her to need him as much as he needed her.

He cupped her breast, teasing the nipple, taking it into his mouth. She gasped, pulling his head closer. He picked her up and carried her to waist-deep water, then lifted her to the edge.

"I want to see all of you, taste all of you." He parted her legs. She covered herself. He nipped at her hands, and she jumped. "Lie back. Please."

She cast a wary gaze upon him. "I'm not sure I can," she said. "Please," he repeated.

She hesitated, then lay back, but her hands still covered what he most coveted. He began to place tiny kisses on the insides of her thighs while his fingers lightly stroked her hands. He knew the minute she relaxed. He eased her hands away.

The light from the pool cast her body in a warm glow. By the gods, she was magnificent. He lightly brushed his hands through her curls, then ran his thumb over the fleshy part of her sex. He scooped up a handful of water and let it drizzle over her. She gasped.

He wanted her to feel more, and she did when his mouth covered her, stroking with his tongue instead of his finger. Loving her, tasting her musky scent, sucking her inside his mouth.

She cried his name, her breathing becoming labored. When her body trembled, he opened the small package she had brought and sheathed himself, then took her hands, bringing her into the water with him. He nuzzled her neck as he slid inside her. She wrapped her arms around him.

"Yes, I need you now," she cried out.

"You're beautiful," he said close to her ear as he thrust inside her. He braced himself against the side of the pool when she wrapped her legs around him. He sank deeper inside the heat of her body.

In and out he plunged. Her body was hot, caressing him with her moist heat. He growled from low in his throat as the fire began to burn hotter inside him.

She cried out, clinging to him. Water splashed around them. He stiffened as spasms shook his body to the very core of his being.

When he could catch a breath, he leaned back and looked at her face. Tears ran down her cheeks. "Did I hurt you?' he asked, fear filling him. Had he been too rough?

She shook her head. "No, I've just never felt like this with anyone else."

Before his grin could form, his gut clenched. "Ahhh," he cried out, grabbing his head. The humming was even worse than the last time they had mated. It grew stronger within him and it was all he could do to fight it.

"*I am a part of you!*" the voice screamed. "*Do not fight against me! Accept who you are!*"

"No, leave me be!" Surlock cried out.

He sank beneath the water. The noise inside his head eased, but he knew he would have to surface soon. He'd hoped the voice had only been part of his dream. But he wasn't dreaming now.

The next thing he knew, Darcy was in front of him, stroking his hair. Somehow he knew everything would be all right. They came up for air, then went under again. They held each other, lightly caressing, letting the other know they would get through this.

And when the humming eased, they went to the guest house and curled up on the bed. They had gone through something together and survived.

The sun streamed into the room the next morning, waking Surlock. He stretched and yawned as the last vestiges of sleep drifted away, and remembrance of the night before came flooding back. He'd had a dream that he was running, but it hadn't felt so much a dream as a memory. The humming in his head had gotten louder, becoming a voice.

He sat up in the bed, glancing around the room. He and Darcy had made love in the pool, and once again, he'd felt as though something had tried to possess him.

Darcy had stayed with him. If not for her, he didn't know what would have happened. But now she was gone. Did she regret agreeing to help him?

Nothing would drive him closer to the edge of losing his mind than if Darcy decided he wasn't worth the effort. He scraped his fingers through his hair. He had to remember. He closed his eyes and concentrated on the moment before Darcy had hit him over the head.

There'd been a wolf. Darcy had said so. He remembered a wolf—vaguely. The humming grew more intense. Rather than fight it, he let it come. Colors and sounds swirled inside his head. He felt as if he was suffocating.

"Surlock."

He stilled. Someone had spoken to him. This wasn't the voice in his thoughts.

"Surlock, are you awake?"

His eyes jerked open. Had he only heard Darcy's voice? Or had he heard another's?

"I'm awake," he called out.

The door opened. She grinned. "I told Ms. Abernathy we were going to have a breakfast picnic. You should have seen her scowl of disapproval."

"Picnic?"

"I have everything set up on the private patio." Her gaze lazily drifted over him. "Join me." She opened a drawer in the dresser, tossing him a pair of lightweight pants. "Just in case we get interrupted, you might want to wear some pajama bottoms." She left the room.

He could get used to waking up to her smile every morning. She made him feel whole. He grabbed the bottoms and slipped them on before making use of the bathroom. There was another set of French doors that led to a private patio. He walked out to it. She had breakfast laid out on the table.

"Better hurry, I'm getting hungry."

"As am I." But he barely glanced at the food. He would much rather look at her. When she raised an eyebrow, he assumed she had more than mating on her mind.

"We have a lot to do today," she said.

"What would that be?"

"We're going to re-create the scene where I hit you." Excitement practically bubbled out of her.

He wasn't too sure about getting hit over the head again. In fact, he was certain he didn't want a repeat performance.

"Don't worry. You won't get hurt this time. I promise."

He breathed a sigh of relief.

Her eyebrows rose. "Did you really think I would hurt you again?"

"No, of course not." He picked up a piece of the food she called bacon and bit into it. It had a smoky flavor that he found pleasing. Darcy had shown him a lot in just a few days time. Yet, it all seemed unfamiliar.

He watched as she filled their plates. She smiled and laughed, her eyes twinkling with mirth as she flirted with him. Did she know what she was doing? He thought maybe she did a little. He liked that she found him worth seducing.

He thought he could probably be content to live the rest of his life here with her and never remember who he was. It didn't matter that he might have family. He didn't miss what he couldn't remember.

Darcy said she'd had the humming in her ears when she was young but suppressed it until it finally went away. Maybe he could do the same. He was starting to feel that the only thing that mattered was being with her.

CHAPTER 8

Darcy had a hard time keeping her gaze on the trail in front of her. Surlock was way too tempting. Every time she remembered the night before when they had been in the swimming pool making love, goose bumps popped up on her arms. It was all she could do to concentrate on the matter at hand.

What was it about him that made her want to draw closer? There was a definite connection between them. He'd felt it, and so did she.

"Tell me about the humming in your ears," he said.

She stooped and picked up a stick off the ground, swinging it in front of her until she caught his worried glance. What? Did he really think she might whack him over the head again? She doubted the branch would do much harm if she did. It wasn't nearly the size of the other one. Still, she tossed the branch away, noticing how much he relaxed when she did.

Okay, he wanted to know about the humming in her ears. Gosh, it seemed so long ago, she had all but forgotten about it. "I was adopted when I was a little girl. I was three. I didn't have the humming then."

"Adopted?"

"My parents left me on the doorstep of an orphanage."

"What is an orphanage?"

"A place where people leave their kids if they can't take care of them." She swallowed past the lump in her throat. "Or if they don't want them anymore."

"So you know nothing about your true parents." He pulled her close and hugged her tight.

Darcy knew that Surlock might not understand all the words, but he knew the emotions behind them. He felt her pain and she understood his need to make her feel better. She felt the same about him, and didn't want him to hurt, either.

"But then someone came along who did want you," he said as they continued down the path. He kept his arm across her shoulders. She was glad he did.

"You're right." She smiled to let him know everything was okay. "Steve and Mary Spencer couldn't have children of their own so they went to the orphanage and brought me home to raise as their child."

He nodded. "That was good of them."

She smiled. "I love them very much." She kicked at a clod of dirt. "Except my mother worries about me a lot. I want to work as a private investigator, but she's afraid I'll put myself in danger. I've spoken with Dad and he thinks it's a good idea." She grinned. "We're going to double-team her when they get here."

"And that will work?"

"I think so.

"But you need a boyfriend, too."

"Definitely. If she thinks I'm unattached, she'll try her hand at matchmaking, and so far, her choices for me have been nothing short of scary."

"Then it's a good thing I came along when I did."

"Yes, it was." She frowned. Except that she'd hit him. His timing could've been a little better.

"When did the humming in your ears start?"

She'd forgotten what he'd asked. "Sorry, I have a tendency to veer off course." She thought back. "When I was seven—no, eight, I think. I remember it was after the birthday party with the pony. My dad had a clown, who brought a pony. I remember it because the pony wanted to follow me around all day. Everyone thought it was funny, but it kind of made me nervous."

"You don't like animals?"

"It's not that I don't like them. They seem to want to get close, and that makes me a little uncomfortable."

"Close?"

"They have always been friendlier with me. You know, invading my space. The humming started that night. My mother was certain I had a brain tumor and that I wouldn't live to see another birthday."

"What was the noise like?"

"Loud. Much like what you experience." She glanced at him. "Do you think we might be connected in some way?"

"As in?"

"You don't think we might be related, do you. If we are, I don't think I want to know."

"Why would you think that?"

"We have the same birthmark in the exact same place. A rose." She nibbled her bottom lip. "I saw it very clearly last night after we, well, when we were in the pool."

His eyebrows drew together. "Show me."

She turned her back to him and pulled her shorts down just enough for it to show. He lightly ran his finger over the raised surface. Goose bumps popped up all over her body. This was not the time nor the place to have sexual thoughts. Sheesh. This was serious.

"And now we share the humming in our ears," she told him.

"I have a mark just like yours?"

He didn't sound convinced. "Exactly like mine." She readjusted her shorts and they continued. "What do you think it means?"

"I'm not sure."

"Here we are." She wasn't sure she wanted him to dwell on their birthmarks too long. She'd absolutely croak if she discovered they were closely related. No, life could not be that cruel.

"Okay, step into the woods. Try to visualize the moment before I hit you over the head."

"Do you think it will work?"

She shrugged. "What have we got to lose except a little time?"

He nodded, then disappeared behind the trees. She waited. Nothing stirred. She was beginning to worry that something might have happened to him when he stepped from behind the trees.

His eyes were glazed over as he stood staring at her as if seeing her for the very first time. Oh, God, something *was* happening. She felt in her pocket to make sure she had her cell phone, breathing a sigh of relief when she felt the hard surface.

"What's happening?" she asked.

"No, we're not related," he said, almost as if he were speaking to himself.

"How can you be sure?"

"Because our entire race has the birthmark."

Their race? Cold chills ran up and down her arms and it was suddenly hard to breathe. "Why are you here?" She spoke softly, hoping she wouldn't break what he was seeing.

"To protect you. Your life is in danger." His eyes immediately cleared. He hurried the rest of the way to her and grabbed her shoulders. "I remembered something!"

He hugged her close, then swung her around as if she weighed nothing at all. He was thrilled, but he'd scared the hell out of her. He only grew serious when he set her back on her feet and saw her expression.

"Why aren't you happy?"

"Oh, I think it's great you remembered something. Even better that we're not related. I just don't know why the hell I'm in danger. You're here to protect me, but we don't know where you're from. And what exactly did you mean when you said we were from a race that bears the same rose birthmark? I've never heard of any race that has an identifying birthmark." Her voice rose with each word. "Not every single person."

He grabbed her shoulders and looked her in the eyes. "It will be okay. I was sent here to take care of you, and I will."

"Sent here from where?" She took his hands in hers. This was crazy. None of it made sense. She didn't have any enemies. "I'm not sure it's an accurate memory. We did watch the James Bond movie. That might have influenced you in some way. I can almost say for certain that my life is not in danger."

At least, she hoped it wasn't. No, it couldn't be. The only people who might be pissed off at her were a few old boyfriends. No, she really doubted she was in danger from them.

"I think it was a true memory," he broke into her thoughts. "I'm here to protect you."

"But I'm not in danger," she repeated.

"We don't know that for sure."

She frowned. "I know for sure." She was learning one thing about Surlock—he was stubborn. "And I'm damned tired of people trying to protect me. I refuse to let anyone else wrap me in cotton."

"Fair enough."

If it wasn't for the twinkle in his eyes, she would think she had won. "You're laughing at me," she accused.

He pulled her close. She felt the rumble in his chest. "You are as fierce as any warrior. Anyone who tried to harm you would put himself in danger."

"You better believe it," she muttered.

The humming in her ears was just a bit louder than the day before. She only hoped they discovered what caused it. She'd never heard of a race having the same birthmark or humming noises. Maybe the humming signaled impending death? That could be why she'd never heard of the race. There were only a few of them because everyone else had died.

Was that what had happened to her parents? Maybe they had started hearing the humming, and it got loud enough that they knew they were going to die. She sniffed. Maybe they *had* loved her. Deep inside, Darcy had always wondered. Now it was more important than ever to discover Surlock's identity.

"Maybe Eddie has information," she said. The mystery could be over sooner than she thought.

But she noticed as they walked back, Surlock seemed to be on guard, his gaze darting past the trees and up the trail. He also put himself between the wooded area and herself. He was wrong about her being in danger.

Great, she had her very own cover-model-sexy bodyguard by her side. Okay, that might not be so hard to adjust to—as long as he didn't smother her.

"Don't worry so," he said. "You'll discover my identity, and we'll learn why I'm here."

As they rounded the corner past a row of bushes and walked up the steps that led to the swimming pool, she leaned closer to Surlock, slipping her arm around his waist. It felt right when he draped his arm across her shoulders.

"You two seem awfully cozy," a male voice put in a little petulantly.

Startled, her head jerked up. "Peter, what are you doing here?"

Surlock gripped her arm, but showed no other outward sign that he'd slipped back into protective mode. Good grief, Peter offered no threat. She'd known him all her life. When they'd reached their teens, they'd even briefly dated, but it hadn't lasted. He was more like a slightly older brother to her. Best buds. But why was he here now?

"Is that any way to greet an ex-boyfriend?" His gaze strayed to Surlock, a smile playing about his lips.

Did Surlock growl? It was a barely perceptible noise, but she was almost certain it was a growl. She squeezed his hand to reassure him she was in no danger.

She hurried to Peter and let him embrace her in a hug. "I'll murder you later," she whispered, then quickly stepped away. She certainly didn't want Surlock going into attack mode. Not that she really thought he would. Just in case, she hurried back to Surlock, who looked quite grim.

"Peter is an old friend. I've known him all my life," she quickly assured Surlock. "Peter, this is Surlock, a new friend."

Peter stepped forward, reaching out with his hand. "Ouch. You make me feel quite ancient, Dar." He followed his words with laughter.

Peter was nice looking, very GQ, with light blond hair. He was always impeccably dressed. Today he wore a beige pullover top and deep green slacks.

"It's nice to meet a friend of Darcy's," he said.

Surlock looked at Peter's hand, but didn't take it. Peter's eyebrow rose.

"He's not from around here," she quickly intervened, turning to Surlock. "It's customary to shake someone's hand." She took Peter's hand and shook it, then aimed Surlock's hand toward Peter's. Surlock was not being very cooperative, but he did take Peter's hand finally and they shook.

"That's some grip you have there. Almost like you actually work for a living," Peter said. "Where exactly are you from?"

"Sweden," Darcy said quickly. "How long are you down for, Peter?"

"A few weeks." His cell rang. "Excuse me. It would seem I can never get away from business and since I am the vice-president of my father's paper company . . . Well, I'm sure you understand." He took his cell out of his pocket and walked a short distance away.

"I don't like him," Surlock said, continuing to glare at Peter's back. "Maybe he's the danger."

Oh, good Lord! "I've known Peter all my life. His parents' estate is next to ours. We dated a few months, but he's always seemed more like a brother to me so I broke it off. Believe me, he's no threat. You can relax."

"Why did you tell him I'm from Sweden?" He turned his attention back to her. "What is Sweden?"

"Sweden is a country." She blushed. "I didn't want him to think you were a freeloader or anything."

"What's a freeloader?"

"Someone who . . ." She shook her head. "It doesn't matter. You're not. I just don't want anyone to know you have amnesia. Remember, you're supposed to be my boyfriend. It might be kind of tricky convincing someone that we're dating if neither one of us knows who you are."

He studied her face, then nodded. She breathed a sigh of relief.

Peter snapped his phone closed. His shoulders were stiff as he shoved it in his pocket before turning to face them again. She would have thought he was angry, except for the smile on his face.

"Sorry about that." Peter rejoined them. "What did you say you do for a living?"

"I didn't," Surlock said just as easily.

Peter laughed. "No, you didn't, and I'm being crass. It's just that I've known Dar for some time now and I'd hate for her to get mixed up with the wrong kind of person. There are a lot of people who would only be interested in her money."

"Peter!"

"Not that you would be, of course," Peter said. "I never meant to imply you would. No offense."

"Of course not," Surlock said.

Darcy looked between the two men again. Great, a pissing contest. That was all she needed.

"There's a band at the club tonight," Peter said. "I stopped by to see if you'd like to go. The invitation is open to you both, of course. I'll bring a date."

Darcy looked between the two men again. "I don't think that would be a good idea."

"Yes, I would like that," Surlock said.

Now what was he up to?

"Good." Peter beamed. "I'll drop by at eight to pick you both up."

Darcy had a feeling nothing good would come of this. As

Peter walked away, she turned on Surlock. "What was that all about?" she whispered, not wanting Peter to overhear.

"I like to keep my enemies close." Surlock's gaze was fixed on Peter's back.

"Peter is not an enemy. I told you that."

"I think he is."

Stubborn, stubborn, stubborn. She was not looking forward to tonight. Not one little bit.

CHAPTER 9

Surlock didn't like Peter. He liked him even less sitting in the back of what Peter had called a limo. The man acted as though he were superior to everyone else, and he looked at Darcy like she was a stack of pancakes with syrup drizzling over the sides and he was starving. Peter was careful not to let Darcy see. He didn't seem to care that Surlock did.

"Have you ever ridden in a limo?" Peter asked, casually draping his arm around the woman who sat beside him. He'd called her Annette. She seemed unsure of herself, as if she had no idea what she was supposed to be doing. Surlock could relate to the feeling.

"No." He had no memory of riding in a vehicle like this. He had no memory of any vehicles, but Darcy didn't want him to tell anyone.

"Remember the first time we rode in a limo," Peter asked, turning his attention to Darcy.

Darcy chuckled, then tried to cover it with a cough. Peter laughed.

"You know I have to tell them the story." He smiled at Surlock, but his eyes revealed something entirely different. They were calculating. "It was much like this one. It was back in the city and our fathers wanted us to go to the prom in style. They forgot to ask that the alcohol be removed. We were only going to have a taste."

Darcy shifted in her seat. "I don't think they want to hear this." She glanced warily at Surlock.

Surlock reached over and took her hand, squeezing it lightly, before bringing it to his lips and lightly kissing her knuckles. "But I do. I want to know everything about you."

She returned his smile, but when he grazed his thumb across the palm of her hand, she drew in a sharp breath and automatically leaned toward him.

"See," Peter said, interrupting what was going on between Surlock and Darcy. "I told you they would want to hear the story." He cleared his throat. "By the time we got to the dance we were both tipsy."

Darcy leaned her head against Surlock's shoulder. He put his arm across hers, and she leaned more into him. Surlock watched Peter from the corner of his eye and saw the flare of his nostrils, the anger he barely held in check.

"We were very young back then," Darcy said, but she looked into Surlock's eyes as if Peter and Annette weren't even in the car.

"Dar and I go way back. We were practically raised together from the cradle. We probably know each other better than anyone. And how long have you known her?"

Darcy stiffened beside him.

Surlock was not intimidated. "Not long, but I'm sure we'll make our own memories. In fact, we already have."

"What's that supposed to mean?" Peter fisted his hands.

Darcy laughed. "Peter, you're acting like an overprotective big brother."

Peter visibly forced himself to relax. "You're right, of course."

"Annette, tell us about yourself," Darcy said, changing the subject.

Annette preened. "I own a hair salon. I'm up to three chairs and a manicurist. If the place keeps growing, I'll have to rent a bigger shop."

Her voice was sharp and high-pitched. For a moment, Surlock thought the horrible humming was back, but then she cleared her throat and continued in a softer voice.

"I'm doing very well," she went on, fidgeting with her hands, smoothing the material of her slacks.

"It sounds like it," Darcy said.

"Oh, I am. I couldn't afford to catch the eye of one of the sexiest bachelors in the county if I wasn't. I spent one hundred and fifty dollars on this pantsuit."

"It's very glittery," Darcy said.

"A girl has to have her bling-bling." She looked at the others, then slunk down a little farther in the seat.

"We're here," Peter called out, looking vastly relieved that Annette would have to stop chattering.

The driver pulled to the curb. Annette started to reach for the door handle, but Peter stopped her.

"Oh, yeah, I forgot," she said. "I'm not very sophisticated."

Peter's face changed colors almost as fast as the tiny lights on the interior roof of the limo.

Surlock wondered why Peter had brought the young woman. They didn't seem to suit each other very well. Peter acted embarrassed by her.

The driver opened the door and they slid across the seat. Surlock preferred Darcy's car. It was much easier to get out of. He was grateful to stand on the walkway and stretch his legs.

"Welcome to the Lavender Club," a man in a dark uniform said, then opened the door.

Peter led the way inside.

"Oh, wow, talk about fancy-shmancy!" Annette breathed.

"Could you please lower your voice," Peter said between gritted teeth. "And try not to let it show you're a country bumpkin."

"I'm sorry." Annette looked at Surlock, then Darcy, biting her bottom lip. Her hands began to tremble and tears filled her eyes.

Peter sighed deeply. "No, I'm sorry. I'm a little on edge. Problems at the office."

Darcy glared at Peter, then took Annette's arm in hers. "It is pretty fancy-shmancy, isn't it?" Darcy said, staring at the lavender carpet, then the chandeliers. "You know, Annette, I need to make an appointment to get a trim. You're the expert, what do you think?"

Annette brightened. "Maybe just a little off the ends. You must have a great hairdresser, though. The style suits you."

"But I don't have one in Summerville. Well, until now, if you can squeeze in another client."

"Certainly. It would be an honor."

"Great, I'll call this week and make an appointment."

"If you two are through *chatting*, our table is ready," Peter told them.

"Don't get your briefs in a wad, Peter," Darcy said in a soft, silky voice before she breezed past him.

Surlock was grinning when he caught up to her. "You handled that very well."

"I loathe Peter when he gets like this." She made a face.

"Why did you ever date him?"

She shrugged. "He isn't always a snob. I think he's only angry that you're a part of my life. He's always been very protective of me."

Surlock picked up on one phrase. "Am I a part of your life?" He pulled her chair out and she sat. "Am I?" he asked again when she didn't answer.

"Well, yes." She fiddled with her lavender napkin, refusing to meet his eyes.

"Good," he said. "Because I think you're a part of mine, too."

"What are you two whispering about?" Peter asked as he pulled Annette's chair out for her. After she was seated, Peter went to his, gripping the back until his knuckles turned white, then pulling it out very easily, as if nothing brewed inside him.

"Now, Peter, a girl isn't supposed to tell all her secrets," Darcy told him.

"So what do you do?" Annette asked Darcy.

"I'm a private investigator," she said, sitting a little taller.

Peter snorted, then brought his napkin up to his mouth. "Sorry, darling," he told Darcy, then turned to Annette. "She has the title, but she's never walked the walk."

"Actually, I've hired her to discover some vital information that I need. I've been quite pleased with the job she's done so far," Surlock informed him.

Peter's eyebrows rose. "Does your mother know?"

Darcy frowned. "I don't need my mother's permission. I'm over eighteen."

"Then she doesn't."

"No, and you're not going to tell her. I'll do that myself, thank you very much."

"Now don't get in a tizzy. Of course, I wouldn't dare bring it up to Mary." He smirked. "Do you think I'm crazy? Why, she'd have my head for not stopping you."

"I'd love it if I didn't have to work," Annette said with a sigh.

"No, you wouldn't," Darcy said. "It makes me feel incomplete."

"There's always charity work, Dar," Peter told her. "No need to get your hands dirty—unless it's when you're counting all your daddy's money."

Surlock watched and saw the anger beginning to rise inside Darcy. If a man hadn't come by and asked if they would like something to drink, he had a feeling Darcy might have leapt across the table and strangled Peter. That would make the evening a lot more interesting.

"And for you, sir?" the waiter asked him.

He had no idea what to order. Or maybe he did. "Orange juice."

Peter snorted again. "What, are you in training?"

"I order what I like. Isn't that what you did?"

Peter frowned, but didn't say anything.

By the time their meal arrived, Darcy was ready to call it a night. Peter was being particularly obnoxious, and Surlock was making sure Peter knew which man she belonged to. She felt as though she was being pulled in both directions.

And then there was poor Annette, who was way out of her league, even though Darcy was trying to make her feel more comfortable. The only thing good about their evening was the food.

The band was assembling just as they finished their meal. Darcy used to refer to their offerings as elevator music. Her parents often brought her to this club when they were staying at their country estate. Her mother called the music soothing. Darcy supposed it was, but sometimes she longed for more.

Jennifer, her best friend, knew how to party. She went to all the in clubs. Darcy had been a few times, but she'd always had it drilled into her head how she was supposed to conduct herself. And so she had.

All that was about to change. As soon as she got up the nerve to tell her mother that she was going to get a real job. This time she would do it, too. No matter how many tears her mother shed. She cringed at the thought of her mother getting upset again and all because Darcy wanted to go to work. They would both have to be strong.

"Darcy, would you like to?" Peter asked, breaking into her thoughts.

She blinked, forgetting for a moment where she was. "Would I like to what?"

He stood and came around to her chair. "Dance with me. I'm sure Surlock wouldn't mind." He smiled and held out his hand.

Darcy didn't have much of a choice. It would be impolite not to accept his invitation. She and Peter had been friends for a long time. So maybe he was acting a bit of an ass tonight, but he had always been very protective of her. He'd also saved her butt a few times, if she remembered correctly. He'd never told her mother that Darcy was the one who broke that window when she was twelve, and he was fourteen. Peter could have said something, but he hadn't.

So she stood and took his hand. She couldn't help comparing it to Surlock's. His grip was strong and firm. Peter's was, well, a little on the soft side.

Once they were on the dance floor, he pulled her tight against him. She wiggled away until there was some distance between them. He laughed.

"What? Do you think Surlock will get jealous?"

"Why are you trying to start a fight with him?" She leaned back until she could look into his face.

He sighed deeply. "I care about you. I always have."

"I can take care of myself."

"Okay, so tell me about this guy." He nodded his head toward Surlock. "How much do you know about him?"

"Enough," she hedged.

"That's what I thought. You barely know the guy."

"That's not true. Can we talk about something else?"

"Fair enough. How about this? I love you and I always have. I've wanted you to be my wife since the night of the prom, but you always wanted to do something else with your life. I've been waiting patiently for you to see what's been right in front of your face. Now it seems I need to rock the boat before you run off with this Surlock guy."

"Oh, Peter." She felt awful. "I never guessed." But she should have. All those years of the laughing and playing together. He'd been her first kiss. Nothing more than that, but he had been the first guy she'd ever petted with. She had to admit that he was a pretty good kisser.

"Then say yes. Tell me that you'll marry me and make me the happiest man on earth. We have everything in common. The same backgrounds. And your parents would be thrilled if we married." He raised her chin with one finger. "You've always wanted to make your parents proud. This would do it."

The music stopped and he pulled her toward the table before she had a chance to say anything. He was beaming when they stopped beside it.

"Champagne!" He snapped his fingers toward the waiter. "We have reason to celebrate. I've just asked the love of my life if she will marry me."

"Peter!"

He hugged her close. "It's okay, sweetheart. They're both thrilled for us."

She met Surlock's fiery eyes. *Thrilled* was not the word she would have used to describe him. And poor Annette looked as if her heart were breaking in two.

How the hell did she get herself in these predicaments?

Chapter 10

Darcy looked at Surlock, hoping he didn't think she had said yes. His expression told her nothing, though. He slowly got to his feet. Oh, God, please no fight.

"You left out one small detail, Peter," Darcy said.

"What's that, Dar?" Peter turned away from Surlock's steady gaze. His words didn't sound as strong and confident as they had a moment ago.

"I didn't say yes."

"I just assumed you would." His expression was genuinely puzzled. "It's what our families would want."

"But it's not what I want. And I really doubt it's what you want." She tried to be as gentle as she could. She might do a lot for her parents, but marrying a man she didn't love was not one of them. She really didn't think they would ask that of her.

"Darcyyy," Peter whined.

How embarrassing. And Surlock was glowering. At least she didn't have to wonder what he was thinking anymore.

She looked at Annette, who was starting to look more than a little pissed off. Not that Darcy blamed her. Annette's date had just asked another woman to marry him.

"I have an early day tomorrow. Since this date is a bust, I'm ready to leave." Annette rose to her feet, dropping her napkin on the table.

"Good idea." Darcy followed suit. "I think in light of the circumstances, Surlock and I will take a taxi home."

"Darcyyy." Peter was starting to look like a whipped pup. Old times reared up in front of her. He *had* always been like a brother to her. She could feel her resolve weakening.

"You have a problem with that, Peter?" Surlock stepped closer to Darcy, slipping his arm around her shoulders. "If I were you, I wouldn't push my luck. Darcy's with me, not you."

Darcy glanced up and watched as a feral gleam entered Surlock's eyes. His lip curled slightly. Her mouth dropped open as she stared. Then his expression changed, softening, almost as quickly as it had hardened. For a moment, Darcy could've sworn she had been looking into the eyes of the wolf.

Yeah, right. She mentally shook her head and glanced up at the twinkly crystals on the chandelier. A reflection from them must have gleamed in his eyes. Nothing more.

Well, duh, of course, that's all it had been. What, did she imagine Surlock was part wolf? Now that was ludicrous. She stifled a laugh. Maybe he was a werewolf.

They weaved their way through the crowd, stepping outside into the warm night air. Thousands of stars were scattered across the sky.

"We need a taxi," she told the doorman just as Annette and Peter stepped from the restaurant.

"No, Darcy. I promise I'll be good. Just ride back with us. I apologize to you all for what I did. I've ruined your evening and it wasn't my intention."

Darcy looked at Surlock. He finally sighed, then nodded.

"We've changed our minds," Darcy told the doorman. "We'll go back in the limo."

"As you wish," he said with a slight bow as the limo pulled to the curb.

They got in, no one saying a word as they drove away. They stopped first at Annette's modest little house.

Annette pulled a business card from her purse and handed it

to Darcy. "Call anytime for your appointment. That is, if you're still interested."

She took the card, lightly squeezing Annette's hand. "I am, and I will."

"Well, it's been—interesting." She glared at Peter. "Keep your seat. I can make it to my own front door," she told him, but smiled at everyone else, then turned and walked to her door. They waited for her to unlock it and go inside before they drove away.

"You don't have to keep staring at me like that," Peter told Surlock, finally breaking the silence when they were nearly home. "It's not like she said yes."

Darcy squeezed Surlock's hand. He broke his demonic glare at Peter and smiled down at her. She breathed a sigh of relief when they pulled up to the gate. It slowly swung open and the limo drove inside the compound.

A few moments later, the car came to a stop and the driver opened the back door. She slid out of the car, glad the evening was finally over.

"I'll join you in a few minutes," Surlock said and shut the door.

There was a distinctive click as the door locked. Then a high-pitched scream came from Peter. Oh, no, this wasn't good. She tapped on the window.

"Surlock?"

Nothing.

She hit the glass with her fist.

"Surlock!"

"Should I call 9-1-1?" The driver asked.

He was starting to look as worried as she felt. Before she could tell him that that might not be a bad idea, the door opened, and Surlock stepped out, straightening his jacket and tie.

"Is Peter okay? You didn't kill him, did you?"

She glanced in the backseat. Peter was curled into a ball, tears running down his face, and he whimpered.

She slammed the door closed and glared at Surlock. "What the hell did you do to him?"

"I merely told him that you were already taken and that he shouldn't bother you again."

Her eyes narrowed. "That wasn't all you did." She watched as the limo pulled away.

"No, but I didn't touch him if that's what you're afraid of. I only spoke to him."

She shook her head. "I saw him. Peter was terrified. He'll probably need therapy."

"He'll be fine in a day or two."

"Are you sure?"

"Yes, well, almost certain." He reached for her, but she side-stepped him.

"I think there's been a little too much testosterone flowing tonight. I'm tired of being pulled in different directions by men who want to take care of me. If you don't mind, I think I'll just go up to my room."

She started past him, but he pulled her into his arms and lowered his mouth to hers. His kiss stole her breath away and sent heat spiraling to every part of her body. Before she could wrap her arms around his neck and pull him closer, he stepped away, running the back of his fingers over her cheek.

"I hope your dreams are pleasant." He walked around the side of the house and disappeared.

Darcy wanted to call him back. Her body was on fire, the ache to have him make love to her almost unbearable.

No! She needed to make him pay for treating her as if she couldn't take care of herself. She would not be spending the night with him tonight. That would teach him a lesson.

"Yeah, right," she mumbled before flouncing into the house.

Running through the woods, breathing hard. Overhead branches. Something near.

Chasing.

No, just running together.
A wolf. More than one.
Fear, trembling.
No, there was no fear. This was right. As it should be.
"Who am I?" Darcy asked.
"One of us. Symtarian."

Darcy sat up with a start. There was humming in her ears, and sweat drenched her nightgown. What had happened? She held her head as tears streamed down her face, her body trembling. She was losing her mind.

The French doors opened. She gasped, head jerking around. Surlock stood in the doorway. The light from the moon bathed his naked body.

"I had a nightmare," she whispered.

He hurried to her, enfolding her in his arms. She laid her head against his chest and listened to the comforting beat of his heart.

"It was only a dream," he whispered close to her ear.

"I was running through the woods."

"I was there."

"What's a Symtarian?"

She felt him shake his head.

"I don't know," he finally told her. "I don't know. I think it might be who we are."

"Animals? Wolves?" She swallowed past the lump in her throat. "Could we be werewolves?" Oh, God, she didn't want to be some kind of monster that went around scaring little children.

"I don't know what you speak of," he said.

"Werewolves are creatures that rip off the heads of humans."

"No, I don't think we're monsters."

"Just Symtarians."

"We may be."

"I've never heard of a place called Symtaria."

"Maybe it was just a dream."

She leaned back and looked at him. "Do you really think so?" She studied his face. He hesitated. "The truth."

"I don't think we're like everyone else. Why would we share the same dreams?"

She leaned back against his chest. "You're right. I've never heard of that until now. Maybe we're both crazy and we're in denial."

"I'm glad that we're in this together."

"Me, too."

He laid her back against the pillow. A breeze drifted in through the doors he'd left open. She was glad he didn't leave, but scooted in next to her.

"How did you get into my room?" she asked.

"Climbed."

"That's dangerous. Please don't do it again. I'd hate to wake some morning and find your battered corpse lying on the ground below my balcony."

His chest rumbled again. "Sleep," he told her. "I'll stay and chase the bad dreams away."

"Promise?"

"Yes, I will always be here for you."

Darcy had a feeling he told the truth. It didn't seem to matter that he'd gone into protective mode again. Just as long as he didn't go overboard. She yawned and snuggled against his bare skin.

Darcy yawned and stretched as she came awake. The night came rushing back. Her gaze flew to the French doors leading out to the balcony. They were closed. Had she dreamed Surlock's coming to her last night? That he had somehow shared her dream?

She flung away the cover and swung her feet off the bed, padding barefoot to the doors. She hesitated before opening them, then stepped onto the stone balcony. She breathed easier when she didn't see Surlock's lifeless body lying all bruised and bloody on the ground.

Had any of it really happened? She shook her head and went back inside. When she went downstairs, Surlock was laughing with Ms. Abernathy as they stood in the hallway.

Laughing?

"Good morning," she said.

Ms. Abernathy smiled. "Good morning, child. Did you sleep well?"

"Yes," Darcy hesitantly told her.

"Good, good. I've got a fine breakfast. Hurry in before it gets cold. French toast this morning. Your favorite."

"Thanks." Darcy looked at Surlock and wondered what exactly he'd been up to.

"No trouble at all," Ms. Abernathy said as she hurried back to the kitchen.

"You've been busy this morning," Darcy said. "What exactly has been going on?" She led the way to the dining room, needing a lot of coffee.

"Nothing."

She glanced over her shoulder. "Nothing. Hmm, why do I doubt that nothing has been going on while I was asleep?"

"Nothing much," he expanded.

"And what has put the housekeeper in such a good mood?" She took a plate off the stack and began to get her food. "She was practically glowing."

He shrugged. "I played her a song."

"A song?"

"She hummed it and I picked up the tune. It made her happy."

She took her food and coffee to the table and sat down. He joined her. Surlock acted as if nothing had happened last night. Maybe it hadn't. It could all have been a dream. She picked up her cup and took a drink.

"So, you have no idea who or what a Symtarian might be?" he suddenly asked out of the blue.

She jumped, then carefully set her cup back on the saucer. "I thought I'd dreamed last night. It happened then? I mean, both of us having the same dream? That we were wolves running in a pack. That I heard one of the wolves thoughts telling me I was Symtarian?"

He picked up a slice of bacon and bit into it, slowly chewing. "Yes, it all happened."

She moved the food around on her plate with her fork, but didn't eat any of it. "You still don't think we might both be crazy? I mean really—wolves?"

He shook his head, then smiled. A soft, gentle smile that wrapped around her and held her close. "No, I don't think we're both crazy, but I certainly think we're different."

Different? That was an understatement. She had no idea what her background was. Maybe her parents had been certifiable and she was following in their footsteps. None of it made sense. Surlock hadn't been sent here to protect her. Unless it was to protect her from losing her mind, and she wasn't so sure anyone could help her with that.

"Eat, we have a lot to do today." He shoved part of the French toast into his mouth, then closed his eyes as if he'd died and gone to heaven.

There was a little bit of syrup at the corner of his mouth. She raised her hand, but his tongue came out of his mouth and licked it away. God, how could he make the act of licking away a little drop of syrup look so damn sensual?

She swallowed hard, then cut into her French toast. "What exactly are we going to be doing?"

He opened his eyes and looked at her as if she should already know the answer. "We have to find Symtaria. If we can find this place, we'll have our answers."

She should've figured that one out. She was the P.I., after all. And she would've, too. He'd just beat her to the punch. She would be the one who actually found it, though. How hard could it be to locate a place called Symtaria?

Chapter 11

Finding Symtaria was proving harder than Darcy could have imagined. "I've Googled it and there is no Symtaria." She spun her computer chair until she faced Surlock. "Nothing, nada, zip. This proves it. We're both crazy."

"No, we're not crazy," Surlock told her.

"Okay, then neither one of us exists."

He reached over and pinched her.

She frowned and rubbed her arm. "Ow, why did you do that? It hurt."

"So you did feel it," he said.

Okay, Surlock won hands down. He was crazier than she. "Of course I felt it."

"Then you exist." He suddenly grinned.

For a moment, she forgot that he'd pinched her and just lost herself in his smile, the way the gold flecks twinkled in his eyes—the way his mouth turned up on one side. It was all she could do to draw her attention away from him and back to the screen.

"So maybe we do exist, but Symtaria doesn't. I can't fathom a whole race of people who bear the same birthmark, either, if you want to know the truth."

"Why not? There are people on earth who share the same characteristics."

He was right again. It still didn't change the fact that this place she was searching for was nowhere to be found. Life was getting too complicated. She longed for simpler times when she only *thought* she'd make a good P.I. A time when the dream was still alive within her. Now she wondered if she had been totally off the mark. She hadn't found anything of significance so far.

"Maybe we only thought we heard the name Symtaria," he said. "It was a dream. If we're off on the spelling, wouldn't that make a difference?"

She brightened. "You're right. It would." Just as quickly as her heart began to pound with excitement, it slowed to a slog. Again, Surlock had found the problem, not her. He made a better P.I. Her confidence slipped another notch.

Her cell phone rang. She slipped it from her pocket and looked at the caller. Eddie. Maybe now they would discover Surlock's identity.

"Hi, Eddie. What did you find out?"

"Hi, Darcy. Well, as far as I can tell, the guy has a clean record."

Adrenaline rushed through her. Great, she wasn't harboring a criminal. Not that she'd really thought Surlock was a serial killer or anything.

"Did you find out who he is?" she asked.

"Not exactly."

Her eyebrows drew together. "What do you mean, 'not exactly'?"

"It means he's clean. Although, his prints were kind of strange."

"Strange? As in?"

"Just what I said, they're different. Not intentionally so. Some criminals will burn the pads of their fingers so you can't run their prints." He chuckled. "That usually sends up a red flag. No, Surlock's are just . . . different. Like he was born that way. We still don't have him in the database. Sorry I couldn't be more help."

"Well, at least we know he's not a criminal."

"True. If you find out who he is, let me know. Now I'm curious. Has he remembered anything at all?"

"Little things. I don't suppose you've ever heard of a place called Symtaria."

"Is that in Africa?"

"I have no idea."

"If I can be any more help, just let me know."

"Will do."

She slipped her cell back inside her pocket and looked at Surlock. "At least you're not wanted by the law."

Her cell rang again. She brought it out and glanced at the caller I.D. Peter. Ugh! Knowing him, he would keep calling until she answered.

"It's Peter," she said.

Surlock didn't say anything. His expression was as bland as low-calorie ice cream.

So much drama. "I've known him all my life. Yes, he can be an ass, but sometimes he was the only friend I had."

He continued to stare.

"Why are men so damn stubborn?" She answered the persistent ringing. "Yes, Peter, what do you want?"

"I'm so sorry. I shouldn't have asked you to marry me. You're my best friend, Dar. I would never do anything to jeopardize that. Say you forgive me."

"I forgive you."

"And Surlock, will he forgive me, too?"

She glanced at Surlock. His face was still devoid of all expression. Well, except for the barely discernible twitch in his jaw. "That might take a little more time."

"I was afraid of that. He's quite taken with you."

"He'll come around." She was probably lying through her teeth.

"I hope so. I'm having a party at my house this weekend. Say you'll come. Please, please, please. It's a masked costume ball. It will be great fun, and you know I give the very best parties."

She hesitated.

"I couldn't bear it if you didn't."

He was whining again. "Okay, okay, we'll be there. Now, I really do have to go."

"'Bye, Dar."

"'Bye, Peter."

She slipped the phone inside her pocket, and went back to the computer without saying a word.

"Where will we be?" he asked.

"What do you mean?" she stalled.

"You said we'd be somewhere. Where?"

"Peter is having a party."

"We're not going."

She slowly turned in her chair. "I beg your pardon?" She crossed her arms in front of her.

"Peter is in love with you. He might be the person I need to protect you from."

"Peter? That's highly unlikely. Besides, your protecting me has to be connected to the James Bond movie we watched. Believe me, I don't need protecting. And, I *am* going to the party. You're invited if you want to come along, but it makes no difference to me."

He pulled her chair closer to his, and cupped the back of her neck. His lips brushed across hers, sending flames shooting down to her lower regions. She lost herself in the kiss, the way his tongue stroked hers, the way his fingers caressed her nape.

When the kiss ended, it took her a few seconds to regain her senses, and then a frown turned down the corners of her mouth.

"It won't work," she told him.

"What?" he asked, all innocent.

"Kissing me until I forget who I am."

"Did I do that?" His voice turned silky, seductive. "Do I make you forget who you are?"

She swallowed hard, then turned away. "You know damn well you do."

"Does this party mean that much to you?" he finally asked.

"No," she told him. "But it's Peter's way of saying he's sorry."

She hesitated, then continued. "Peter is Peter. He'll never really change. He's spoiled because his parents have given him everything he could ever need or want. The only thing they haven't given him is responsibility . . . and their trust. His place in the company is just a title. He has no real authority. The only major decision he's been allowed to make is where he wanted to place his furniture in an office he rarely uses." She wanted Surlock to understand that Peter wasn't a threat. That he was just Peter, her friend.

"Whenever I've needed him, Peter has always dropped everything to be there for me. It's not because he loves me or anything. He just doesn't have anyone else that he's close to. I understand who he is, and I accept him and all his flaws."

He studied her for a moment. "We'll go to his party."

Darcy grinned, liking the man even more. She got up out of her chair and went to his, parking herself on his lap. "You're a pretty great guy, did you know that?"

He seemed to think over her words. "Yes," he said, nodding. "I had started to suspect as much."

She rolled her eyes. "Lord, save me from men and their egos." But when he kissed her, she knew there was one thing she didn't want to be saved from.

Annette fastened the cape over Darcy. "Your shop is really cute," Darcy said. It was done in black with pink polka dots. The floor was black and white checks. There were wigs on white Styrofoam heads sitting on shelves.

Annette beamed with pride. "I was going for a sixties look."

"I think you did a fantastic job."

"Thanks." Annette ran a brush through her hair. "What do you want me to do today?"

"What do you think? Just a little off the ends?" Darcy wasn't too sure about having Annette cut and style her hair, but she'd made a promise, and she never went back on one.

"You don't have to do this if you don't want to," Annette told her.

"What do you mean not want to? Of course, I do."

Annette met her gaze in the mirror. "I know you're only doing this because you're a really nice person, but I'm a damn good hairdresser. I might not be very polished socially, but I come from good stock." Her smile was crooked. "At least that's what my daddy always tells me. He only has a sixth grade education, but he's one of the smartest men I know."

"Then let's throw in a shampoo, too."

"You've got it."

They talked about the weather being unusually nice, and agreed that fall was in the air. They talked about the new restaurant opening next week.

Darcy knew there was something else Annette wanted to know, but Darcy didn't pressure her, knowing she would ask when she felt comfortable. Besides, Darcy was almost positive it had to do with a certain man.

"How's Peter?" Annette blushed, finally getting to what she most wanted to ask about. "Not that I care about him or anything. It's just that I knew Surlock looked fit to be tied when Peter announced you two were getting married."

Annette had actually seen that in Surlock's expression? Amazing. He'd seemed carved out of stone to Darcy.

"Peter's having a party this Saturday so I'd say he's recovered from my rejection."

"A party?"

Darcy had a sudden lightbulb moment. "Why don't you come? I bet Peter would like that. He throws the best parties and this one is masked, so it should be a lot of fun."

Annette's eyes sparkled for a brief moment, but just as quickly, the glitter faded, and she shook her head. "It was different when it was just a double date. Besides, Peter only took me out to get to you. It's you he loves. He made that very clear the other night."

"No, he only thinks he's in love with me. I'm familiar. Like an old shoe. Now that Surlock is in the picture, Peter is like a puppy who doesn't want to give up his favorite toy."

Hope flared in her eyes. "You think so?"

"I know so." Darcy narrowed her eyes on Annette. "How did you two meet?"

She shrugged. "He came in here one day for a trim."

"Peter?"

Annette nodded.

"Wow."

"Wow what?"

"Peter is very particular about who cuts his hair. Hmm, that's very interesting. Let me get this straight. He came in here, and you cut his hair?"

"Yeah."

"Then he asked you out."

She nodded. "That's pretty much it. No biggie."

Darcy shook her head. "Nope, that's a very big deal."

"Do you think so?" Annette sighed, a dreamy look on her face. "I've seen him around town, you know, and every once in a while I'd feel him watching me. I think he's so handsome."

"I bet Peter is sweet on you, too, but he's not ready to admit it. Now you have to come to the party."

Annette paled. "Oh, I couldn't mix with all the upper crust. And I still don't believe Peter really likes me."

"Phooey. It doesn't matter where you come from or where any of us is positioned in life. We all have problems of our own. Including Peter."

"Yeah, but having money makes the solving a whole lot easier," Annette mumbled.

Darcy chuckled. "You're probably right about that. But look around. You have your own business. From the number of people I've seen walking through that front door just since I arrived, I'd say you're doing pretty darn well."

Annette ducked her head, but Darcy could see her proud smile.

"I'm not doing too badly. Business has been pretty good."

"Then come to the party. If for no other reason than it will be great for your business. You can network."

Annette seemed to be thinking it over. "That's not a bad idea." She nodded. "Okay, I'll come, but you have to show me what to wear. I know my taste tends to run a little on the discount side. Maybe you could give me some suggestions."

"I'll do even better than that. I have a closet full of costumes. We can see what I have that would look great on you." She eyed Annette's figure. "We're about the same size, so I bet I have something that will fit."

"Oh, I couldn't wear anything of yours. I'd be afraid I might spill something on it."

"It won't matter if you do. There's a good dry cleaner in town. But won't it be fun trying on costumes? You can help me decide what to wear. I want to look nice for Surlock."

"I don't think you have to worry about him. He's a man in love."

"You think so?"

"I've seen that look before. He's definitely taken with you."

The thought of Surlock's being in love with her made butterflies flutter in Darcy's stomach. Then it hit her. How did she feel about him?

He was her client, sort of. What did she really know about him? Absolutely nothing except he might come from some place called Symtaria that just happened to not be on any map whatsoever.

He could have an obnoxious family.

No, she really couldn't picture that. He was too nice.

Okay, what if he had a wife and half a dozen kids running around? Her spirits plummeted. She hadn't thought he might have a family somewhere. A wife who wondered where her super-sexy husband had gone.

A wife who believed in revenge and knew karate.

Annette lathered Darcy's hair. Usually, getting her hair washed was very relaxing, but right now her stomach was filled with knots. Maybe she had started to care for Surlock a little too much.

There was only one way to discover if he did have a wife

somewhere. Find out who he was and where he came from. Trouble was, she kept running into roadblocks. Did other P.I.'s have this much trouble?

Peter's party could be the break she was looking for. If she knew Peter, he would invite everyone he knew and they would probably bring along their friends. Most of his parties were so big, they spilled out into the yard. Maybe, just maybe, someone would recognize Surlock.

A few more days and the mystery could be solved. She should feel elated that she might have found the solution to their problem, but her gut rumbled uncomfortably, telling her to run away as fast as she could. Her gut was almost always right.

CHAPTER 12

Surlock closed his eyes and concentrated. The humming in his ears worsened. He refused to give in this time and gritted his teeth. Sweat dampened his skin. He didn't move, but continued to sit on the floor of his bedroom trying to break through the barriers that kept him from his memories.

Darcy had shown him how to work the computer and while she was getting her hair fixed, he'd done his own research. He read almost everything there was on memory loss. Meditation had helped in some instances.

With legs crossed, he attempted to empty his mind. Breathing in, then out, and concentrating on each breath and not the noise inside his head.

It wasn't working. The noise only grew louder.

Concentrate! Who am I? Where do I come from?

"Argh!" He grabbed his head, closing his eyes tight against the pain, and rolled to his side, willing the noise to go away. "Stop!" He gasped for air, drawing breath into his body as the sounds eventually subsided, and he could breathe a little easier. He lay there, curled on his side on the hard floor waiting to see if the noise would return. It didn't. Slowly, he eased his eyes open. The noise had escalated over the last few days, but it hadn't been quite so bad this time. Maybe he would eventually conquer it.

At that thought, the sounds inside his head returned with a

vengence. He put his hands over his ears again as he tried to block the noise. The intense screaming slowly subsided.

Surlock felt as though something lived inside him. A shudder wracked his body. He'd also read about demon possession. Maybe that's what was wrong. He was possessed by a devil who wanted to take over his body.

A knock on the door drew him out of his thoughts. He slowly came to his feet. Relief filled him when he opened the door and saw Darcy. Every bit of the tension inside him drained away. He knew she would help him find his path.

"You look like death warmed over," she said. "What have you been doing?"

"Meditating."

Her eyebrows rose. "Do you do that often?"

"No. I just started."

"And the reason being?"

"I read about it on your computer. I was trying to get in touch with my inner self."

"Did you find it?"

"What?"

"Your inner self."

He opened his mouth, but saw the twinkle in her eyes. She was teasing him. He scooped her up in his arms and twirled her around. She screamed, then laughed.

"I think you're making fun of me."

She grinned. "I think you're right."

He carried her over to the bed, then pretended he was going to drop her.

Her arms encircled his neck and held tight. "No!"

"You're right, the pool would be much better."

"You wouldn't!"

"I wouldn't?" He carried her toward the doorway.

"No, Surlock, you can't. I just had my hair done. Annette is dropping by later. Do you want to tell her you messed up my hair?"

"You don't think she would understand?"

"Surlock!"

He laughed and eased her down to the side of the bed. Once she was out of his arms, she stood and moved to the door, walking through to the other room. He supposed they wouldn't be having sex so he followed.

"I've had this brilliant thought," she told him.

He grinned, enjoying the way she paced around the room. He crossed his arms in front of him and leaned against the door jamb. "I think all your thoughts are brilliant."

She stopped and stared at him. "You do?"

"Exceedingly so."

"Now you're teasing me, but I don't mind because this one actually is brilliant. Peter's party."

His spirits plummeted. He had managed to go all day without thinking about Peter.

"You're not getting it, are you?" she asked.

"Apparently not. I can see nothing good about going to this party. No matter what you say, the guy is in love with you."

"Forget about Peter for a moment."

Not easily done since Peter was in love with Darcy. They had had a talk about her in the back of the limo, though. Surlock was pretty certain Peter wouldn't bother her again. At least, not while Surlock was around.

"I know Peter and his parties. He invites everyone. There will be a lot of people there."

He still didn't understand where she was going with her new idea to discover who he was.

"Someone might recognize you," she continued.

"You're a good P.I."

She beamed. "Yeah, I think I might be."

"But if there are a lot of people around, won't that put you in more danger?"

She rolled her eyes. "Believe me, I'm not in danger."

"You'll stay close to me."

She opened her mouth to argue, but then seemed to change her mind. "Yes, I'll stay close to you, but only because I don't want you wandering off alone."

She glanced at her wrist, where she wore some kind of device that told her what time it was. For some odd reason it seemed very antiquated.

"Annette will be here any time. You'll be okay on your own?"

"I think I can manage to stay out of trouble for a while."

She eyed him. "Yeah, well, just don't step out from behind any trees."

He deliberately widened his eyes. "Do you have a sister?"

She stuck her tongue out at him. "That was not funny."

He pulled her against him and kissed her long and hard. When he let go of her, she stumbled. He caught her.

"You might just be a secret agent because your kisses are lethal," she said.

"I see you've found your man." The sound of a feminine voice interrupted them.

They both turned, Darcy stepping from his arms. There were far too many interruptions around here. He looked at the woman. She was tall, with black hair that was cut short. If he had one word to describe her, he would say stunning.

"What, aren't you going to say hello?" the woman drawled.

"Jennifer!" Darcy screamed and ran to the other woman, throwing her arms around her. She hugged her tight, then stepped back. "What are you doing in the country?"

"Peter's party, of course. I'd never miss it. Didn't you get the message I left for you?"

"I've been at the beauty shop. I guess I didn't hear my phone."

Jennifer studied Darcy. "New hairdo." She smiled. "I love it."

He studied Darcy, but couldn't see anything different. She was beautiful and had been since the moment he saw her.

"Surlock, this is Jennifer, my very best friend who rarely comes to the country. Jennifer, this is Surlock."

Jennifer's eyes trailed over him before coming back to his face.

"I think I'm going to have to come to the country more often. Exactly how did you two meet?"

Darcy looked at him, then back at Jennifer, clearly trying to come up with something plausible.

"We met in the woods," he said. "I stepped from behind a tree and saw her. One look and I felt as though I'd been hit over the head with a heavy branch. After that, I couldn't think of anything except her." He remembered the gesture Darcy had shown him and walked forward, sticking out his hand. Jennifer took it. Her hands were soft, but her handshake was firm.

Darcy frowned, but quickly pasted a smile on her face when Jennifer looked her way. He hadn't lied about how they'd met; he'd just worded it differently.

"You always have the best luck," Jennifer told her.

"You know me." Darcy shrugged. "You'll be staying, right?"

Jennifer nodded. "For a few days."

"Good, then let's get you settled in. Surlock, we'll meet up later." She turned and tugged Jennifer along with her as she went back to the main house.

Surlock watched as Darcy hurried away. Damn, she was beautiful, and not a bad kisser herself. He was smiling when he went back inside, but just as quickly, the smile vanished.

But she was in danger. Yes, they had watched the James Bond movie, and maybe it had given him some ideas that might have mixed with his thoughts. Still, everything was telling him that he was right about this. He had been sent to protect her for some reason. Anger rose swiftly to the surface. If anyone dared harm her, he would strangle them with his bare hands.

It was time he did a little investigating of his own. There had to be a clue somewhere that would bring back his memories. He would start at the beginning. He and Darcy might have overlooked something when they'd reenacted their first meeting. Maybe he would be able to find something on his own that they had missed. He headed out the door.

As he walked down the well-worn path, he looked around.

Tall trees dotted the landscape. There was a small lake surrounded by lush plants and flowers. He could understand why Darcy loved to walk through the meadow. There was serenity here.

He slowed his steps when he came to the spot where he'd stepped out. There were footprints—his and Darcy's. He knelt down, noticing there was another set of prints, smaller, like Darcy's, but they left a different print. Who was the other person?

Was this the danger she faced? This unknown person? Frustration rose inside him. It could be anyone. One of the maids even. How could he protect her when he didn't know who he was?

No, Surlock wouldn't let this situation beat him. Maybe they hadn't looked far enough. He moved through the brambles. They scratched his arms, but he didn't stop.

Why had he been out here? The underbrush was thick and hard to fight his way past.

He stumbled into a clearing. For a moment, he stood there looking around. It felt familiar. He slowly turned in a circle, then closed his eyes.

Thoughts rushed toward him all at once. Jumbled, hard to decipher. He'd been in an aircraft of sorts.

He stilled, could feel the blood coursing through his veins. Had he crashed? No, he didn't think so. Or were all these memories because he'd watched the James Bond movie? He raked his fingers though his hair. He didn't know what might or might not be real anymore.

"Who am I?" he called out as he walked across the clearing.

Silence was his answer.

The pig watched him leave, then cautiously stepped into the open, sniffing and grunting. A thick fog rolled in and the pig shifted into a woman. She strolled across the clearing, uncaring that she was completely naked.

Laughter bubbled out of her. "Surlock, what have you done

that you no longer remember who you are?" This should prove very amusing. The great and mighty Surlock brought to his knees because he didn't know who or what he was . . . and with no way to guard his little impure.

Greed filled her. What worth would the king place on his youngest son if he was captured? She expected it would be a huge treasure, maybe his entire kingdom.

Surlock had once rejected her. Her lip curled in a sneer. She knew he'd slept with women of lower class, but he'd dismissed her advances. And now, he wanted to protect the impures, who were nothing at all. Maybe he had even slept with the one she knew he'd been sent to protect.

Revulsion washed over her. The impures were part Earthling and part Symtarian. She didn't care about them one way or the other, but she disliked the idea one might have been chosen above her.

Not that any of it really mattered now. The impure no longer seemed as important. She would be destroyed eventually. No, Surlock would be the bigger prize. Finally fortune smiled on Excoria.

Chapter 13

"So, who is he?" Jennifer asked as she looked out the bedroom window.

"I told you his name is Surlock." Darcy shrugged, smoothing her hand across the satin bedspread. Maybe she shouldn't have put Jennifer in the bedroom next to hers. It was a nicely decorated room with clean straight lines, done in yellow and soft white. Still, she'd have to warn Surlock about coming to her room late at night. What if Jennifer heard him? Darcy's relationship with Surlock was new and she wasn't sure if she was ready to share it yet.

Jennifer turned, capturing Darcy's gaze. "We've been best friends since college and we've always kept each other's secrets. Remember when I was thrown in jail for breaking and entering? You bailed me out and we didn't tell a soul." She visibly shivered. "My father would've had a stroke, right after he cut off my allowance, if he'd found out."

"But once you were inside Jack's apartment, you were able to destroy the naked pictures before you were caught, so it was worth it."

Jennifer laughed. "And almost burned down Jack's apartment in the process, which was why I was caught. He was such a jerk. If he hadn't gotten me drunk, I wouldn't have let him take the damned pictures." She took a deep breath and exhaled. "But the thing is, you bailed me out and you never said a word. We've always had each other's back. Except this time you're not talking."

Jennifer was right. They had shared a lot, and Jennifer always kept her word. "Okay, but you have to swear not to say anything, no matter how bizarre or strange any of this sounds."

"That good?"

Darcy planted her hands on her hips. "Swear."

"Cross my heart." Jennifer made a motion of crossing her finger over the center of her chest, then hurried to the bed, kicked off her heels and piled in the middle of it. "Tell me everything," she said, patting the other side of the mattress.

Darcy had to wonder if she was doing the right thing. But then, they had been friends for a long time, and she could always threaten to tell about the pictures if Jennifer breathed a word.

She climbed up in the middle of the bed and sat across from Jennifer. "Remember when I was talking to you the other morning?"

"You mean when you called at some ungodly hour and woke me up?"

"Yeah, whatever."

"I remember."

"I saw a wolf, so I picked up this big branch to protect myself."

"Ohmygod, a wolf?" Jennifer's gaze quickly scanned Darcy. "Did it hurt you?"

"No, now let me finish."

"Okay, just don't leave me in suspense."

"While I was standing there grasping the branch, this really dense fog rolled in and I couldn't see a thing. When it finally cleared, Surlock stepped out from behind a tree completely naked. He startled me, so I sort of hit him over the head. Now he has amnesia."

Jennifer pursed her lips. "If you didn't want to tell me, all you had to do was just say so." She started to scoot off the bed, but Darcy grabbed her arm and stopped her.

"No, that's really what happened. I swear."

She narrowed her eyes. "The truth?"

Darcy nodded. "Swear to God."

Jennifer's mouth dropped open, then snapped shut. "Darcy! He could be a vagrant, a serial killer. God, you are so damned gullible."

"I beg your pardon." She squared her shoulders.

"You are. I'm sorry to be the one to tell you, but you fall for everything."

"No, I don't."

"Yes, you do."

She shook her head. Now was not the time to get into a *did too, did not* argument. "There's more."

"More. Oh goody. I can't wait to hear the rest." She plumped a pillow behind her and lay back. "Please, go on."

"We have the same birthmark."

Jennifer's eyebrows shot up. "The rose?"

Darcy nodded. "He remembered enough to know that he's here to protect me." She frowned. "But I don't think that's right because I don't have any enemies."

"Have you had sex with him?"

Her face felt as though it were on fire.

"Oh, Darcy. Whatever will we do with you? This has to be some kind of prank. Maybe an ex-boyfriend is setting you up."

"But we have the same mark. Surlock said our whole race has the same mark."

Jennifer grabbed a throw pillow and pulled it over her face, making some kind of muffled noise that sounded a lot like a groan. She tossed the pillow away. It rolled end over end and fell off the bed, landing on the floor with a dull thud.

"Darcy, he could've had a rose tattooed on his ass. Did you really look at it?"

Darcy's forehead wrinkled. "Not up close. From what I saw, it looked the same." Was it all a setup? Okay, maybe she could have pissed off a couple of people, who just might set her up because they were really bored, and had more time on their hands than they knew what to do with.

"I wouldn't put anything past that bitch Amy. Remember how her boyfriend dumped her, then turned around, and asked you out in front of her. She definitely had sparks flying out her eyes."

That seemed to be happening to Darcy a lot lately—men asking her out in front of their current girlfriend. Jarrod, Amy's boyfriend, then Peter. She shook her head. "But there's more."

"Pray tell." Jennifer's words dripped sarcasm.

"We've shared dreams."

One of Jennifer's perfectly tweezed eyebrows shot upward. "Shared dreams," she repeated. "I have so got to hear this one."

"It's just what I said. We've shared dreams."

"Explain."

Darcy thought back. "The first time I knew what he'd dreamed. It was about a wolf."

Jennifer suddenly sat up, her eyes wide. "You're joking, right?"

Darcy shook her head, and goose bumps popped up on her arms. "No, why?"

"This is really weird. I had a dream about a wolf the other night."

That was too strange. What if it was all connected—wait, something was wrong. She stared at Jennifer, who was looking way too innocent. "No, you didn't. You're lying."

"But I did. I dreamed I was . . . running. And you?"

Could she have had the same dream? "It almost felt as if I was one with the wolf."

"That's exactly the way it was for me."

There was something about Jennifer that didn't quite ring true. Darcy didn't trust her. "And then there was this big mountain lion."

"It scared the hell out of me when it showed up out of nowhere," Jennifer said.

"Caught ya! There was no mountain lion."

Jennifer shrugged and lay back again. "See how easy it would be to make believe we had shared the same dream? Surlock probably did the same thing."

"I don't think so. There's more. He has a humming in his ears that turns to screaming. I had the same thing when I was young. My mother took me to all kinds of doctors until I finally told her it had stopped. Eventually it did."

"It all sounds a little too weird if you ask me. Besides, if this is a setup, and Surlock wanted to find out more about you, it wouldn't have been too hard to discover that your mom had taken you to a bunch of doctors when you were a kid because you heard humming noises."

"That's why I didn't want to tell you." Darcy slid off the bed and walked to the window. She saw Surlock going inside the guest house and wondered where he'd been.

It wasn't a setup, all of it a lie just so someone could get even. He did have amnesia. He did. She closed her eyes and thought back to when she'd first hit him over the head. Maybe he'd faked amnesia, too. The bump on his head had been real. He couldn't fake that. Great, now she was starting to question everything.

She turned back and glared at Jennifer. "It's real. I feel connected to him. It's hard to explain." That was it in a nutshell. She did feel connected to Surlock, as if they shared something that no one else shared. Jennifer always questioned everything. Why should Darcy think this time would be any different?

"Just be careful," Jennifer told her with a sigh. "I don't want to see you hurt."

Someone tapped on the door.

"Come in," Darcy called out.

The door eased open and Annette looked inside. "Ms. Abernathy told me to come up," she said, looking at Jennifer, then back to Darcy. "You have company. I'll come back some other time."

Darcy hurried over. "No, come in. I want you to meet Jennifer. Jennifer is my best friend, who never ever comes to the country, but she made an exception for Peter's party."

Annette seemed to hunker down inside herself. "I probably should go so you can visit with your friend."

"Nonsense." The girl was really feeling out of her element.

"Jennifer loves my new hairdo. Annette was the one who cut and styled it. She's wonderful with hair. In fact, she has her own shop in town."

"Really?" Jennifer ruffled her hair. "Do you think you would have time to do something with mine? I mean, before Peter's party. I'm going as a snake and would love something dramatic."

"That's it!" Darcy laughed. "We'll each go as an animal, or in your case, a reptile. It will be great fun."

"I can do makeup, too," Annette shyly put in. She studied Jennifer for a moment. "What if I put a bright red streak in it? One that will wash out, of course."

"I love it," Jennifer said. "It sounds so wicked. Wait until you see my costume. It's sexy as hell." She jumped off the bed and went to the suitcase that had been placed on a luggage rack. After she opened it, she pulled out a long black-and-gold leotard that had more cutouts than material.

"Wow, that's—" Annette looked at Darcy.

"Skimpy," Darcy finished.

"I call it my get-laid costume." Jennifer grinned.

Annette nodded. "Have you got another one in there that I can borrow?"

They laughed, but Darcy had a feeling Annette might have been serious.

"Follow me. I have a ton of costumes." Darcy led the way to her bedroom and swung open the door to her closet.

"Oh, my goodness," Annette breathed. "This is almost as big as my whole house." She wandered inside, her eyes trying to take in everything.

"Annette is interested in Peter, so we have to make sure he notices her," Darcy said.

"Our Peter?" Jennifer asked.

Darcy nodded. "He went into her salon and had her cut his hair."

"Our Peter?"

"The one and only."

"Do you think it means something?" Annette asked.

Jennifer grinned. "Oh, yes, it definitely means he's interested in you. We have got to find something really fantastic for you to wear."

"I like sequins. But on second thought, maybe not too sexy. I usually wear pantsuits."

Jennifer winked at Darcy. "Oh, yes, we'll make sure we stay conservative."

Annette breathed a sigh of relief. "Good." She wandered back to the row of costumes.

Jennifer and Darcy looked at each other, then smiled knowingly. Darcy had a feeling Jennifer's idea of conservative would not be quite what Annette had in mind. Not that Darcy would let Jennifer get too wild, but it was a masked ball and they were so much fun. They still had all week to convince Annette that if she wanted to grab Peter's attention, then she had to go for a totally different look.

The afternoon slipped by as they tried on different costumes. As much as Darcy enjoyed having Annette and Jennifer there, she missed Surlock. She had to admit, she was sort of glad when Annette said she needed to get back to her salon for an appointment.

"You're dying to go to him," Jennifer said as they waved good-bye to Annette.

"Who?"

"The gardener, who else?" Jennifer drolly replied.

"Very funny."

"I could say the same thing."

"I am trying to discover his identity. I actually have a job."

Jennifer shuddered. "I'll never understand your fixation with being a private investigator."

"Don't you get bored with all the parties? There's no substance in our lives."

"I'm actually going to start my own business, so there."

Darcy's eyes widened. "Really? You?"

Jennifer frowned. "You don't think I can?"

"It's not that. I'm just surprised you would go to that much trouble."

"I'm not, really. Daddy's hired people to do all the financial stuff. And don't go giving me that you-know-everything look. I've always wanted to be a party planner. At least something good will come from all the parties I've attended. Peter has been the only one who could actually throw a decent one."

"You're really starting your own business?" Darcy asked, with more than a little amazement.

She shrugged. "Celebrities start businesses all the time. Daddy has skads more money than most of them." She suddenly grinned. "It will be fun. We're going to start with one showroom that will display what I plan to do. You'll come to the launch party in a few months, of course." She gave Darcy a saucy wink. "You're not the only one who wants to put her stamp on life."

"I guess not. I'm proud of you." Not that she thought Jennifer would actually be doing any real work. She would have most of it done for her. Still, she was making an effort.

"I told Peter I would help him with the details of his party. It will be good practice. Want to go with me?"

"Well . . . I . . ."

Jennifer held up her hand. "Of course, you don't want to go with me. You've been away from Surlock all afternoon." She grimaced. "Just remember what I said. Don't trust him completely. He might just be after your money."

"I'll be careful."

Darcy watched as Jennifer left, then hurried through the house, and out the back door. She looked up when Surlock stepped out from the French doors.

"I missed you," he said.

All of her doubts immediately vanished. Maybe she had been a little gullible in the past, but not this time. He could have faked amnesia and the birthmark, but he couldn't fake the dreams that bound them together, or the humming in her ears, or the fact that she felt an incredible bond with him.

She ran the rest of the way and threw her arms around his neck. "I missed you, too." God, she wanted this man so badly, she ached deep inside her belly.

He kissed her, taking her to new heights. Her body tingled with the pleasure he created inside her. When the kiss ended, she laid her head against his chest and heard the erratic beat of his heart and knew he wasn't immune to what they'd just shared.

"What spell have you cast over me?" he asked.

"I could ask you the same thing." She laughed lightly.

"My mother and sisters cast spells. Once, my mother made sure my brother was celibate for days." He chuckled as he softly ran his fingers up and down her back. "He was careful not to anger her again."

Darcy tried to stay as quiet as she could, letting Surlock talk. She didn't think he realized that he was remembering.

His hand stilled. "I have a mother and sisters." He spoke barely above a whisper.

She leaned back and looked into his face, smiling. "It's just like the doctor said, your memory will return. You only have to give it a little time."

He stepped out of her arms, lost in thought, and walked back inside the guest house. She followed.

"I think I have three sisters." He turned back around and faced her. "I think they're very bossy, too."

She smiled back. "And they cast spells." Her smile dropped. "They cast spells?"

He nodded. "To the gods and goddesses."

"Gods and goddesses," she mumbled. Her eyes suddenly widened as she let it all sink in. "Where the hell are you from?"

"Symtaria, I think."

She began to walk back and forth across the room. "Except it doesn't exist. And your family prays to gods and goddesses. What are they? Gypsies? Modern-day witches? This is getting really strange, Surlock."

"Yes, I think I do pray to the gods and goddesses. You don't?"

"I pray to God. Just one." Oh, Lord, her parents weren't religious fanatics, but they'd always told her that they would like her to marry a nice Baptist boy.

"Darcy, are you okay?"

"I don't know."

He wrapped his arms around her. "Does it matter who we pray to as long as we are good people?"

It wasn't like they were going to marry, so Surlock's religion didn't really enter into the equation. Right? "No, it doesn't matter at all." Then why did she have a feeling it would matter a lot someday?

Hadn't she once wondered if he might have an obnoxious family or something? She'd rather face obnoxious than to explain to her parents that Surlock and his family were practicing witches or gypsies.

Drat, even if nothing came from this relationship, she wanted her parents to like Surlock as much as she did.

"What are you thinking?" he asked.

"That it might be a good thing to keep your religious beliefs to yourself for now. Not that I disapprove or anything, but it might just be easier all around. Most people wouldn't understand." And she hadn't thought she could feel any worse.

"If you think it's best."

"I do."

There was a tapping on the door. They moved out of each other's arms. Darcy went to the French doors and opened them. "Ms. Abernathy, did you need something?"

Ms. Abernathy looked between the two of them, then pursed her lips. "Your mother called. She said she hasn't heard from you in a few days. I told her I would have you call her right back."

Cripes, why hadn't she called her mom first? Darcy glanced at Surlock, then turned her attention back to the housekeeper. "You didn't mention . . . uh—"

Ms. Abernathy squared her shoulders and sniffed loudly. "No, I didn't, but I think you'd better. It's not right keeping things from your mother."

Sheesh, more drama. "I'll tell her."

"And you'll call her? I told her it wouldn't be more than a few minutes." She glanced at her watch. "You should call her soon."

"I will." She shooed the housekeeper from the room. "I'll call her from here."

"And you'll tell her about"—she lowered her voice—"him."

"Surlock. His name is Surlock. Yes, I'll tell her."

"I know his name," she whispered. "Just because he can play the piano like an angel, you should still be careful."

"Okay, okay." Darcy shut the door.

"I don't blame her for not completely trusting me," Surlock said after the housekeeper left.

"She needs to get over it." She went to the sofa and sat down, reaching for the phone. Still, Darcy hesitated. What exactly was she going to tell her mother? That she really felt drawn to this man whose whole family worshipped gods and goddesses?

"Prince," Surlock suddenly said.

"What?"

"I think that's part of my name. It's familiar."

Excitement fluttered through her. Another piece of the puzzle. "Surlock Prince," she tested the sound. It didn't really go together. "At least we have a last name. It should prove easier to find out exactly who you are and where you come from." And why his whole family worshipped gods and goddesses.

She called her mom and waited. The phone rang only once before her mother answered.

"Darcy, are you all right? You haven't called."

"I'm fine, Mom. I've just been busy."

"Busy? Doing what?"

"Well, Surlock is staying in the guest house."

"Surlock who?"

Darcy bit her bottom lip. She had a feeling this was going to be a long conversation. "Surlock Prince. You know, I mentioned him to you. The guy you're supposed to meet when you and daddy arrive. And Peter is home and planning a huge party. And

Jennifer is here, too." Thank goodness she'd filled the fake boyfriend slot.

"Jennifer is there, too?"

"Yes, Mom." Darcy heard her mother's sigh of relief.

"Tell me about this young man."

She really hated lying to her mom. "Surlock?" she hedged.

"Yes, dear, I already know all about Peter."

"Peter likes Surlock."

"Which tells me absolutely nothing. I know he covered for you when you broke that window. You were what? Twelve. I haven't completely trusted him since."

"You know about the window?" Wow, all this time and Darcy had thought she'd gotten away with breaking it.

"Yes, dear, I'm your mother. It's my job. Now tell me about this young man."

"He's wonderful, Mom. You should hear him play the piano. You'd think he was a professional. He brought tears to Ms. Abernathy's eyes."

"He's musical?"

Darcy breathed a sigh of relief. "Yes. Absolutely wonderful."

"Who are his parents?"

Almost home free. "They're from Sweden." She said a silent prayer for forgiveness. "Very upper crust."

"Are they Baptist?"

"I don't believe so."

"Well, no matter. Your father and I will meet your young man soon enough."

Darcy swallowed past the lump in her throat. "Meet him?"

"Yes, we're leaving the city early. Your father is quite exhausted and needs a vacation. We'll be there next week."

Darcy looked toward Surlock. He had his back to her as he stared out the window. "That's great. I can't wait to see you both."

"We'll have to plan a party. I just hate that we have to miss Peter's."

"His are so big, though," she quickly reminded her mother. "You know how you hate crowds."

"You're so right. We'll just have a small get-together. Not more than twenty or so of our closest friends. What do you think about prawns and those cheese puffs I so adore for appetizers?"

Darcy listened while her mother planned her party, only occasionally agreeing with her. Her mother was in her element when she had friends over. Darcy had to smile. Her mother was the queen bee of her social circle.

"Oh, you know Jennifer is starting her own party planning business. You should talk to her about it. I bet she'll have some great ideas."

"Jennifer? Our Jennifer?"

"Yes, our Jennifer."

"Well, it should at least keep her out of trouble. I have to say I worry about that child the way she likes to go out all the time. It's good she's found something to keep her occupied."

Darcy opened her mouth, but then closed it without saying anything. Now was not the time to get into an argument about why it was okay for Jennifer to have a job but not Darcy. She would tuck the information away, though. It might add a little leverage to her argument about having a real job.

Eventually, they said good-bye and Darcy replaced the phone in its holder.

"You love your mother very much, don't you?" Surlock asked.

Darcy stood. "Yes, very much. I know she didn't carry me for nine months, but I feel very close to her. As close to her as any daughter is to her mother."

"I wonder about my family. Who they are, and if they're worried about me."

She walked to him and wrapped her arms around his waist. "We'll find them. I have a gut feeling all our questions will be answered soon." She smiled up at him. "My gut is always right."

Her stomach chose that moment to growl and they laughed.

"And right now my stomach is telling me it's time for dinner. I'm starved."

As they walked hand in hand back to the main house, Darcy couldn't help wondering if her instinct was correct. Would she find out who Surlock was and where he came from? For some odd reason she felt a little queasy. That probably wasn't a good sign.

Chapter 14

Excoria paced the back room in the dusty, dingy warehouse they had chosen for their base of operations. If her suspicions were correct, then she would have good news to tell Nivla as soon as he arrived.

If he arrived.

He'd better arrive.

She was having second thoughts. Nivla frightened her. He was much older than her thirty years, at least sixty and his eyes were big and buggy. He also sweated a lot, and grunted when he moved. But he was still the second in command, now that Zerod was confined on New Symtaria, and she had to respect him, even if she didn't like it.

She sucked in a deep breath when she heard someone approaching. Her hand automatically rested on the weapon holstered at her hip. She didn't relax until the door opened, and Nivla walked inside. She immediately bowed her head, touching the back of her hand to her forehead in respect. "Oh, Great Leader."

"Excoria, this had better be good."

She looked up, then regretted meeting his gaze. His cold gray eyes bored into her. She quickly downed her head as fear trembled through her. What if she was wrong? If that were the case, Nivla would make her pay for her mistake.

"Well, are you going to tell me or make me guess?" He walked behind the desk and pulled out the chair, dusting it lightly before sitting.

"I have found Prince Surlock."

"And the impure. Have you destroyed her?"

"No, Great Leader."

He clamped his lips together, slapping his gloves on the desk, stirring a small cloud of dust. "Then your mission isn't complete. Please, tell me exactly why you called me here, and it had better be good."

"Prince Surlock doesn't know who he is," she blurted out.

Silence.

She shifted her weight from one foot to the other.

"Explain," he said, then mopped the sweat that dampened his face.

"He's staying with the impure. Today I followed him as he walked down a path to the woods. He made his way through the brush until he came to a clearing. I watched as he seemed to search for something. When he didn't find what he was looking for, he raised his face toward the sky and called out in a strained voice, 'Who am I?' I don't believe he has his memory."

"No memory?"

She shook her head. "No, Great Leader."

Nivla began to tap his fingers on the surface of the desk. Excoria dared to look up. Nivla didn't look angry. Maybe the news was worthy of his attention.

Nivla laughed. A deep rumbling sound that sent tingles of excitement down her arms. She knew then that she had gained his favor.

"This is exactly the break I've been hoping for," he said.

"We could ransom him for his father's great wealth," she eagerly suggested, then wished she'd kept her mouth shut when he turned his stony glare on her.

"It's more than wealth, you idiot. When we capture Surlock, we can trade him for Zerod's release. The true leader will rejoin our ranks."

Great. Excoria would rather have had jewels to drape over her beautiful body. It didn't look as though that would be happening anytime soon. While she had watched the impure, her envy had grown for the finer things that life had to offer.

That was one of the reasons she had joined the ranks of the rogues. The rogues wanted to wipe out all the impures—Symtarians who had mated with other species and created abominations of mixed blood. Not that she really cared one way or the other, but the rogues had promised her great wealth. Except she hadn't seen any of it yet. She was beginning to think joining their ranks had been a big mistake.

"You will watch them and report back to me. See if you can get closer and discover more."

"There will be a party in a few days' time. A masquerade ball."

He frowned. "What is the purpose of this masquerade ball?"

"People dress up in costumes. They can be anything they want."

He nodded. "You will go to this party."

"I'll need money for clothes to wear so I can blend in." If Nivla had a database he could easily produce a magnificent wardrobe, but only those of royal blood owned them. It was not fair everyone else had so much while she had so little. It would be a great pleasure taking down one so mighty as Surlock.

"You say you can be anything you want?"

"Yes, Great Leader."

His laugh held no mirth. "Then go as an alien." His gaze swept over her. "It's the perfect costume."

Anger swept through her. She'd brought him vital information and this was how he treated her—as if she was worthless.

"I see you're upset with me," he said in a silky voice.

She quickly hid her expression, becoming meek once again. "No, Great Leader, my reward is your pleasure."

"I'm glad you feel that way because I've journeyed far to be here." He grunted loudly as he came to his feet and unfastened his coat, tossing it on the desk. "I will mate with you. That will be your reward."

She cringed. No, she didn't want to mate with him. He sickened her.

"Well, hurry and remove your tunic. I have other pressing matters to attend."

Excoria was going to seriously rethink her role with the rogues. This was not what she'd been led to expect.

Nivla jerked her into his arms and planted his big wet lips on top of hers. Her stomach rumbled as he slid his humongous tongue inside her mouth.

She'd eaten what they called a burrito that she had bought at a small dingy store. It was all she'd had money to buy, and it hadn't smelled good. Now her stomach rumbled. She tried to push away from Nivla as fear raged through her. She couldn't shame herself.

"You taste good," he said as he pulled slightly away. "Being on Earth suits you." He grunted as he reached for the fastener on his pants.

She belched and the area around her filled with the sour smell of the burrito she'd eaten—that, and Nivla's strong body odor.

Her mouth opened and she belched again.

He grimaced. "You would make this noise when I offer my skills as a lover? Do you mock me?"

"Oh, Great Leader, I'm sorry. I haven't felt well all day," she lied. Her stomach rumbled and she belched again.

He waved his hand in front of his face, glaring at her. "As soon as your mission is over, I will see you punished for this!"

"Yes, Great Leader." She bowed her head, but smiled when he stomped out of the room, slamming the door behind him. There was nothing like loud belching to cool a man's amorous advances. It served him right.

As she straightened, she belched again. Her stomach churned and she had to run to the bathroom, where she got rid of the offending food.

She would definitely rethink staying with the rogues when she finished this mission. It wasn't quite the romantic experience she had imagined. Nor were there riches and jewels to be had. But if she returned to New Symtaria, they would surely lock her away. Her life was ruined.

And now that her stomach was empty, she was starving. As she trudged toward the makeshift bed in the other room, she thought about her mother's cooking and how it had warmed her belly on a cold day. She missed her family. She missed New Symtaria.

She listened as Nivla's craft took off, then lay down on the lumpy cot. She wrinkled her nose. It smelled funny. She'd had to share her bed at home with her older sister. At the time she'd hated it, but at least it had been comfortable.

She closed her eyes as self-pity washed over her. *Fasta, are you there?* She spoke her thoughts to her animal guide.

Yes, I'm here but I'm still angry that you have put us in this position. No good will come of it.

I'll make things right. I swear this to you.

And Excoria would do exactly as she promised, because she hated this life. She only had to come up with a plan.

CHAPTER 15

Jennifer breezed into Darcy's room, plopping down on her bed. "I think Peter might be falling in love with Annette."

Darcy stepped from the bathroom. "That's what I've thought, but I wasn't sure." She sat in an overstuffed maroon chair, curling her feet under her.

"He tried to be subtle, but he mentioned her name more than once. When I asked him if he liked her, he clammed up."

"He's afraid."

"Of Annette?"

Darcy shook her head. "His father."

Jennifer nodded thoughtfully. "You're right. If Peter falls in love with the wrong woman, his father will cut him off quicker than he can say 'trust fund baby.'"

"I feel so sorry for him. He's always been under his father's thumb. I heard his father telling Peter once that he had no head for business, and that he would have to resign himself to living off his inheritance."

"He's an ass." Jennifer curled her lip.

"And Peter is really smart. He's just never been given a chance to be anything more than a playboy."

"Maybe Annette can change all that."

"I hope so."

"Peter's going to the party dressed as a dragon. Annette has to be a princess. Every fairy tale I've read with a dragon in it always had a princess who needed saving. Except Peter is the one who needs saving."

"Then Annette has to be like no princess Peter has ever seen," Darcy said. "She has to be dark and mysterious."

"Did you know the guest list is already over two hundred and that isn't counting people who tag along?"

Great. Surely someone would know Surlock.

Jennifer hugged a pillow. "Anything interesting happen while I was gone?"

"I spoke to my mother."

Her eyebrows rose. "And?"

"And my parents will be here next week."

"And you still think Surlock has amnesia?" Jennifer asked.

Darcy squared her shoulders. "I know he does."

"Then you'd better find out exactly who he is before your mother and father arrive."

Darcy had been thinking the same thing.

Jennifer yawned. "Okay, I'm outta here. If we're going to make this party outstanding, then I need my sleep." She frowned. "I told Peter if he wants me to help him in the future, I need at least two months notice or he's on his own. No more of these last minute, thrown-together affairs." She sauntered from the room.

Darcy was tired, too. Lying to her mother had been pretty stressful. What if she suspected her daughter was lying and showed up early? After all, she'd known who'd broken the glass. No, Darcy had covered her tracks by telling her mother that Jennifer was staying here.

It did bother her that she might not know who Surlock was by the time her parents arrived. As much as they loved her, they wouldn't let Surlock continue to stay in the guest house without knowing more about him. She couldn't bear it if he wasn't nearby.

She snuggled down in the bed, but no matter how many times she changed positions, it was still uncomfortable. She tossed and turned until she was afraid she was going to have sheet burns. Finally, she threw back the cover and rolled out of bed.

She went to the French doors and opened them wide, letting the cool night breeze ruffle her hair as she stepped to the balcony. Her gaze moved to the guest house. It took her a few minutes to realize that the shadow beside it moved. Excitement spread through her when Surlock stepped into the open, completely naked. The man had a serious problem with clothes, she thought as she drank in the sight of him. She liked the idea he was a nudist at heart.

Had she sensed he couldn't sleep, either? When he held out his hand toward her, she didn't hesitate. She went back inside, slipping out of her room, and down the stairs, then out the back door. She ran across the stones and flung her arms around his neck.

"I couldn't sleep," she whispered.

"Nor I when all I could think about is mating with you, feeling your naked body pressed against mine."

He took her hand, a wicked smile curving his lips, and pulled her along with him, past the bushes and trees that surrounded the outer edges of the pool. He stopped, facing her, then slowly and deliberately, he took the hem of her white satin gown and pulled it over her head.

Darcy glanced around, shielding herself. But it was late, and no one would be up. Tilting her chin rebelliously, she moved her hands away from her body. If he could run around naked, so could she.

He laughed lightly, then grabbed her hand as they ran through the lush green grass. She joined in, laughing as well. She had never felt so free in her life. They raised their hands to the moon. Energy flowed through her. Did he feel it, too?

She inhaled the fragrance of the night—the four o'clocks that bloomed after the sun went down. Their sweet aroma filled the night air. Crickets serenaded them as the wind gently caressed their bodies like a lover's touch. She felt like a child discovering something for the very first time.

When they stopped, both of them were out of breath. She dropped to the grass, and he followed. She lay on her back, Surlock on his side.

"It's beautiful out here. It's so quiet and peaceful. As if the night washes everything clean. Do you feel it, too?"

He nodded, tracing his finger around one areola. "I feel as though the moon gives me strength."

She sucked in a deep breath when he dragged his finger across her nipple. A throbbing ache of need weaved its way down her body, settling at the juncture of her legs. She moved to her side, seeing the desire flare in his eyes when she reached down and touched him, lightly stroking her fingernails over his erection. He sucked air when she wrapped her hand around him and slowly slid down his foreskin, then brought it back up.

He closed his eyes and groaned.

"Are you in pain?" she asked with every pretense of innocence that she could muster.

He opened his eyes and growled.

She laughed.

He suddenly grew serious. "I crave your touch, the way you make me feel," he said. Then he was reaching for her, stroking his fingers through her curls, slipping a finger inside her wet heat.

She gasped, arching toward him. The stars above her blurred and became one shining orb. When he stopped, she gasped for air, trying to fill her starved lungs.

Surlock rolled to his back, pulling her on top of him. She moved so that he slipped inside her. Exquisite pleasure rolled off her in waves. When her body had adjusted to his size, she slowly raised herself until she looked into his eyes. His eyes looked golden in the light of the moon and the star-filled sky. She doubted she would ever tire of staring at this man, or feeling him inside her, stroking her.

"You're a temptress," he said, his hands moving from her hips up to cup her breasts. He squeezed and fondled them until every nerve in her body felt raw with the need for more. She didn't want any of this to stop. Darcy wanted to continue feeling like this forever.

"I need you now, Darcy," he whispered. He slid his hands behind her, cupping her bottom, increasing the motion between them, grinding his hips against her.

Her body was on fire. Faster and faster they moved together, each reaching higher and higher. And then the stars exploded all around them. Her body jerked, tightened. He tensed, then growled. She hadn't thought making love with Surlock could get any better, but it could, and it had. Stardust had glittered down on them, filling her world with everything beautiful. She'd never felt so much peace, so much—

"Darcy," he suddenly cried.

"Hmm?" She glanced at him. Her heart skipped a beat when she caught his expression of pain. "Ohmygod, we don't have your eardrops!"

"No," he gasped. "Different this time. Can't stop it." He opened his eyes, holding his head.

Fear swept over her. She slid off him, jumping to her feet. "Surlock, we need to get you back to the house. Take my hand." She held her hand out to help him up.

He shook his head. "Too late. Run! Leave me! I don't want to harm you."

"I'm not going anywhere. Dammit, I won't run away and leave you to suffer alone. Now let me help you back to the house!" If she had to, she would wake the whole house to help her get him home.

He moved his hands away from his face and she was suddenly staring into the eyes of the wolf again, except this time, Surlock's face was hairy. He bared his teeth, then growled from deep in his throat. Shivers of fear wracked her, suffocating her.

She stumbled back, almost falling. Surlock growled again, a demonic sound that sent cold chills down her spine. A fog began to roll in, damp cold making her feel even more chilled. Oh God, this wasn't happening. She was dreaming. She had to be. She'd fallen asleep and this was a really bad nightmare.

"Run, Darcy, run! Don't look back!"

Surlock's voice jerked her back to the present. This wasn't a bad dream. This was real, and happening right now. She turned on her heel and ran for the house. She didn't stop. She didn't look back.

Oh God, Surlock had started changing right before her eyes. What had happened? One second they were having the best sex she'd ever had and then he was turning into a . . . a wolf. She stumbled, caught herself, and kept running.

Her blood suddenly felt as if it were freezing inside her veins. Oh, hell, she knew what he was. It all made sense now. The wolf she'd seen before he appeared. Everything.

Surlock was a werewolf! That's all it could be. She stopped at the place where she'd taken off her nightgown and jerked it over her head, shoving her arms through the arm holes. She glanced around, but a cloud had drifted across the moon—the full moon!—and it was too dark to see anything.

A lone howl echoed over her parents' property. Her whole body began to shake as she hurried around the trees and bushes. She had to get inside where it was safe.

Then it hit her. What if she were a werewolf, too, and just hadn't gone through the change, or whatever it took to become a full-fledged werewolf? Jennifer was in the house. Would her best friend be in danger if Darcy went inside?

Peter would give her sanctuary. He was always there when she needed him. He would take her in. But she didn't want to eat Peter.

She frowned, then shook her head.

She quickly examined her arms. They weren't covered in long hair. She felt her face. It still felt smooth. Maybe there was some ritual that she had to go through before she made the change. Oh, hell, she hoped that was it as she hurried inside. She tiptoed up the steps, then slipped back inside her bedroom. For a moment, she leaned against the door and breathed in deep gulps of air. She was safe.

But what about Surlock? Was he safe?

Darcy went to the French doors and opened them, slipping out onto the balcony. She heard another mournful howl. Surlock was out there somewhere. She hoped he'd retained enough of himself not to eat her neighbors, or anyone for that matter.

"Please let him be okay," she whispered to the night and prayed somehow her words would carry to him.

She went back inside and slowly closed the doors, then locked them just to be on the safe side. If Surlock had turned into a werewolf, she wasn't sure how he would react to her. He might not recognize her.

Tomorrow everything would be back to normal, she was certain. Surlock would be in his bed, and then he would explain what the fuck had happened, because she really needed to know.

She froze.

Oh, no, her parents were probably werewolves. Her biological parents, not her adoptive ones.

She frowned. It was damned inconvenient that her biological parents had left her at an orphanage to fend for herself. What if she had changed? Would the people who ran the orphanage have sent her to the dog pound or something?

Great, her adoptive mother and father would have heart attacks when they found out what she was. How the hell did she even explain something like this to them? Guess what, Mom and Dad, I know where I come from now. Mom, how do you feel about getting a dog? I know you're allergic to them, but you can take allergy pills, right?

Darcy pulled the cover back and crawled beneath it, curling into a tight ball. She really didn't relish the idea of running around the countryside howling at the moon. Or eating people. Even as she yawned, she doubted she would get any sleep tonight.

Darcy opened her eyes, then blinked against the bright light that burst into her room from the curtains as they were flung open. Oh, Lord, someone was torturing her. What had she done to deserve this?

"Wake up, sleepy head," Jennifer called out in a bright cheery voice.

Darcy sat up, rubbing the sleep from her eyes. She felt like death warmed over. Had she partied last night? Maybe drunk a little too much? She had to admit to a fondness for pomegranate martinis.

Then it hit her. "Ohmygod," she said.

"Yes, I know," Jennifer said. "It's after eight. I thought maybe you'd died in your sleep or something. This is like seriously late for you."

"I'm a werewolf," she said.

Jennifer stared at her. "Wow, you have lots better dreams than I do."

"No, it's true. I couldn't sleep last night so I walked out onto the balcony. Surlock was standing beside the guest house."

"He does look kind of dark and dangerous with that black-as-night hair brushing his shoulders." She sauntered over to one of the maroon upholstered chairs and curled up on it. "If you ever get tired of him, I would certainly let him howl at my moon."

Darcy frowned. "I thought you didn't trust him."

"I don't want to marry the guy, only have sex with him. That is, if you ever get tired of him."

Darcy shook her head to try to clear it. It was way too early to have this conversation. "I'm serious." Jennifer didn't believe a word Darcy was telling her. "I went downstairs and slipped outside last night."

Jennifer leaned forward in the chair. "Tell me more. I'll live vicariously through you since I'm not getting any while I'm in the country."

"We went running through the park behind the house. Then we made love."

"It always takes you so long to get to the good stuff."

"And then he grabbed his head," Darcy continued as if Jennifer hadn't interrupted her. "But this time the humming didn't stop. He told me to run away. I think he was afraid he might hurt me."

Jennifer's expression turned serious. "I told you he was strange and couldn't be trusted. It's better if you forget all about him."

Darcy shook her head. "No, there's more. When I looked at him, the eyes of a wolf stared back at me, and his arms and face got all hairy."

"I hate hairy men," Jennifer said. "He could always do laser hair removal."

"I'm telling the truth."

Jennifer untucked her legs and got to her feet. "No, you think I'm as gullible as you and you're trying to pull a fast one."

"It really did happen. Don't you see, if Surlock is a werewolf, then I'm probably one, too."

"Or you could be just losing your mind." Jennifer crossed her arms.

"I'm not crazy." At least Darcy didn't think so. Maybe Surlock could help her sort everything out. Surlock! "I have to make sure he's okay."

She hurried to her closet and flung open the door, then quickly pulled on underclothes, shorts and a T-shirt. She pushed her feet into a pair of sandals and rushed from the room.

"Will Surlock be joining you for breakfast?" Ms. Abernathy asked as Darcy flew down the stairs.

"Yes, why do you ask?"

Ms. Abernathy raised an eyebrow as if she expected Surlock to follow Darcy down the stairs.

"He's not upstairs if you're implying anything." Darcy slowed her steps to a fast walk as she went past the housekeeper.

"One of the maids took fresh towels out to the guest house this morning and said it looked as if his bed hadn't been slept in all night. I thought maybe he'd slept elsewhere."

Darcy skidded to a stop halfway across the room and turned to look at the housekeeper. "He's not in the guest house?"

Ms. Abernathy studied Darcy. "You look a little pale. Maybe you should sit for a bit."

"I'm fine." Surlock hadn't changed back. He was still roaming the countryside as a werewolf. Could he come out in the day-light? She mentally shook her head. She was pretty sure vampires were the ones who couldn't walk in the sunlight. She had to find him before some hunter came along and shot him.

Her parents had problems with hunters sometimes. Some red-neck would see a big buck and want to shoot it for sport. Her father usually made sure the no-trespassing signs were in place, but the hunters didn't always pay attention. She swallowed past the lump in her throat as she pictured Surlock's beautiful head mounted on someone's wall.

"I'm going for a walk," she said as she continued out the door.

"Darcy, wait for me," Jennifer called down to her.

Darcy hesitated. She didn't want to put Jennifer in danger, but right now she really needed her friend, even if Jennifer didn't be-lieve her.

They went to the guest house first. Darcy prayed the whole time that the maid had been wrong, or that maybe Surlock had only been out for an early morning stroll.

The guest house was empty, and worse, his bed looked as though it hadn't been slept in. The maid had been right.

"Where do we look now?" Jennifer asked.

"Are you sure you want to go with me? I don't want to risk your life."

"I don't believe in werewolves," Jennifer reminded her. "I don't know what you saw, but I'm pretty sure it wasn't a wolf."

"You might change your mind. Just remember I tried to warn you."

They made their way past the bushes and trees. Darcy stopped and looked around.

"Why are we stopping here?"

"This is where I took off my nightgown."

Jennifer raised her eyebrows. "You were running around out-side naked? Was he naked, too?"

"Yes. It wasn't a big deal."

"Oh, I'm not judging you. I'm just surprised I never thought of doing it. Of course, it would be a little more difficult to run around naked in the city. Maybe having a country home wouldn't be so bad after all."

Jennifer didn't realize how serious the situation was. They walked down the trail that led through the park. Darcy scanned the area, but didn't see or hear anything unusual.

"No werewolves," Jennifer said. "Darn, and I was hoping Surlock might have a brother. Some big strapping . . . German shepherd." She snickered, then bit her lip when Darcy cast accusing eyes her way.

Darcy should have known Jennifer was just playing along and didn't really believe anything Darcy had told her. Not that she could blame her friend. When she thought about it, the whole story did sound crazy.

"I'm sorry," Jennifer said. "I couldn't help it, but you don't really think Surlock is a werewolf, do you? If you do, then that means your fashion wardrobe this fall might include a straitjacket. This is all a prank you and Peter set up, right?"

Darcy shook her head.

Jennifer drew in a sharp breath. "You're telling the truth."

Darcy nodded.

Her friend threw her arms around Darcy. "Don't worry sweetie, we'll find help for you. I won't let them stick you in any cold institution."

"I'm not crazy."

Jennifer stepped back and looked Darcy square in the eyes. "There are no such things as werewolves."

A low growl came from the woods, followed by rustling in the underbrush. Both girls froze in their tracks.

CHAPTER 16

D arcy took a step toward the dense woods.

"Are you crazy?" Jennifer grabbed her hand and tugged her along as she ran toward the house. "It could be a rabid dog or something."

"No, it was Surlock." But Darcy had to admit that she was a little afraid, too. She wasn't sure if Surlock would recognize her. He might attack first, ask questions later.

Rather than go inside the house, Darcy pulled Jennifer toward the guest house so they would have a little more privacy.

"What are you doing?" Jennifer looked at her as if she'd lost her mind. "We have to tell someone there's a mad dog on the loose."

Darcy could feel the color drain from her face. "No, we can't say anything. That wasn't a mad dog. It was Surlock, and he is a werewolf."

"There are no such thing as werewolves," Jennifer said between gritted teeth.

Darcy had a feeling she would never be able to convince her friend, but she knew what had happened last night. Surlock had changed into something that wasn't human.

"Think what you will, but you can't tell a soul." She couldn't bear it if Surlock was hunted down and killed. "Swear it." She gave Jennifer her steely-eyed look.

"Okay, I won't say anything, but if anyone is hurt by a wild dog that's running loose over the countryside, then it will be on your conscience, not mine."

"I'll take all the blame." Now she only had to hope Surlock didn't kill anyone, and if he did, that he got rid of the body.

She sat down with a thud on the sofa. What if he did hurt someone? Would she be able to live with her guilt for the rest of her life? She didn't think so.

"It will be okay," Jennifer said, sitting beside her.

Darcy shook her head. "No, I don't think it will. I don't think anything will ever be the same."

"Are you sure about what you saw?"

"Yes." She closed her eyes and relived the scene last night. "We'd made love. He grabbed his head." She looked at Jennifer. "He always gets this loud humming noise in his head after we make love. Like someone screaming."

"But it always stops, right?"

"Yes, when I put eardrops in or he goes underwater."

"Underwater?"

She shrugged. "We were in the pool, and we'd just made love. When he went underwater, it seemed to help."

"I'll never go swimming in your pool again." She shook her head. "Never mind. Just go on with your story."

"We didn't have any eardrops or anything. I tried to help Surlock up so I could get him back to the house, but he told me to run. He said he couldn't stop it this time."

"So you ran," Jennifer said. "Don't you see, he didn't change into a werewolf or anything else. He probably had a really bad headache."

"No, he moved his hands away from his face and it was like I was staring at the wolf, and his face was hairy."

"How bright was it outside?"

"Almost like daytime."

"No shadows? The clouds didn't drift in front of the moon and maybe made you think you saw something that wasn't there?"

Darcy closed her eyes and tried to visualize it all again. His eyes had looked strange, and there had been hair on his face. But it *had* gotten darker when the clouds drifted in front of the moon. Could it have been a trick of the light?

There was a dog or a wolf roaming the countryside. Maybe when it howled, she had only connected the dots and thought werewolf. Maybe? But there was still one question left unanswered.

"Then where's Surlock now?"

Jennifer's expression turned thoughtful. "You said he had a horrible humming in his ears."

"Yes."

"It might have scared him. Maybe he thought something was happening to him and the pain was so bad he was afraid he might lash out and hurt you."

Darcy thought about it for a moment. It could have happened like that. "But that still doesn't explain where he is now."

"Maybe by the time the pain stopped, people were up and about. You did say you were both running through the woods naked. He can't very well walk up to the estate without any clothes on."

A few days ago, Surlock might have done exactly that. But would he now since Ms. Abernathy had warned him to keep his clothes on? Darcy rubbed her forehead, wondering if she had only imagined everything.

"It could've happened like I said, Darcy," Jennifer said quietly. "I mean, think about everything you told me. It doesn't make sense. You've been watching too many horror flicks." She raised her hand when Darcy would've protested. "What was the last movie you watched?"

Besides James Bond? Her shoulders slumped. Jennifer was right. "I was bored, and Dad has all the old *Friday the 13th* movies. It's not my fault I'm addicted to them." But Jennifer's answers made more sense than Darcy's werewolf theory.

Jennifer hugged her, then stood. "Come on, we'll have some breakfast, and everything will look better on a full stomach. I'm

meeting with Peter later to go over the final details of the party."
She smiled. "Who would have thought I could be more than a
socialite?" She winked. "I told you my clubbing days would pay
off."

Darcy tried for a smile, but wasn't so sure she pulled it off.
She was glad for Jennifer, but her mind was on other things. Was
Surlock okay?

Once inside, they went to the dining room and fixed their
plates. Darcy did little more than move her food around while
she listened to Jennifer chatter about her ideas for the party.

"Okay, are you ready to go over to Peter's?" Jennifer asked,
interrupting Darcy's thoughts.

Go to Peter's house? When Surlock was stuck in the woods
naked, or in pain? "I think I'll pass this time. I have a bit of a
headache."

Jennifer studied her for a moment. "I think I'll call Peter and
cancel."

That was the last thing Darcy wanted. "I'll be fine. You're
probably right. Too many scary movies, I didn't sleep well last
night, and poor Surlock is probably running around the woods
naked."

Jennifer eyed her. "You're not going to run out to the woods
as soon as I leave, are you?"

"Of course not," she scoffed. "I'm sure Surlock will be back
by the time you return and we'll laugh about all this. He's probably sneaking up the back side of the estate as we speak." Jennifer still didn't look convinced. "Werewolves." Darcy snorted.
"No more spicy food for me at dinner."

"I knew you would come to your senses." Jennifer hugged
her, then said, "I'll see you later. If you get bored, come over to
Peter's." She frowned. "No, call me on my cell. I'm not sure
where we'll be."

"I will."

"I hope you start to feel better."

"I'll take some aspirin."

Jennifer left the room. A few minutes later, Darcy heard the front door close, and Jennifer's car start. She let out a sigh of relief. Now to find Surlock. She pushed away from the table and stood. Before she could make good her escape, Ms. Abernathy came into the room.

"Yes?" Darcy asked.

"Do you think Surlock is okay?" she asked, her forehead wrinkled in worry.

"I don't know."

"I could have Ralph and a couple of the men look for him."

"I'm sure he's fine. He likes to be alone sometimes. I bet Surlock made up his bed, then went for a walk. If he's not back by this afternoon, then we'll worry."

Ms. Abernathy visibly relaxed. "You're right. Men aren't the best about telling women when they're going off somewhere."

Darcy breathed a sigh of relief. "Exactly. In fact, I think I'll take a walk, too. I ate way too much of your wonderful breakfast. It's no wonder I always gain ten pounds every time I'm here."

Ms. Abernathy beamed. "You can stand to gain a little weight."

Darcy smiled and left the room. As soon as she was clear, she hurried to the back door, but at the last minute remembered her father had a dog whistle in his desk drawer. She turned and went back the other way.

She went inside his office, closing the door behind her, and rushed over to the cherry wood desk. She found the whistle at the bottom of the second drawer, and breathed a sigh of relief. Darcy wasn't sure exactly what she would accomplish, but, right now, anything was worth a try. She slipped the chain over her head so the whistle dangled between her breasts, a cold reminder of what she might be up against.

She went outside, stopping at the guest house to grab some clothes just in case she did find Surlock. Maybe he was just hiding in the woods. She smiled. He would probably be mad as hell that he was having to stay hidden because he was naked. Not that she thought he was afraid of Ms. Abernathy, but he had promised not to run around in the buff when there might be staff about.

She started down the path, her gaze scanning the edge of the woods. Her bravery had all but deserted her. She bent and picked up a hefty stick. It might not be much protection, but it wouldn't hurt to have something to defend herself with, just in case.

"Surlock," she called. "It's me, Darcy. If you're out here, make some kind of noise." She didn't add, "But if you're a were-wolf, don't show your face."

Nothing. No rustle of branches or anything. Had it been a ruse? Maybe this was his idea of one big joke. Bed them, make them think you're a werewolf, then move on to the next easy mark.

She shook her head. That was ridiculous, of course. There had been a bond between them. And no matter how much Jennifer wanted her to believe otherwise, Darcy had seen something hap-pening to Surlock that hadn't been normal. But whatever he'd changed into, she would stand beside her man.

Her feet faltered when she realized she might not have much choice. She could be a werewolf, too. What kind of married life could she have with anyone else? She really doubted a normal husband would feel the same way about her if he rolled over in bed and she'd changed into something horrible. Even worse if she ever lost her temper and ate him. What would she tell their children? Sorry kids, your father pissed me off so I gobbled him up.

She stopped and scanned the area. It looked like nothing more than a quiet, peaceful day. She'd been walking about ten minutes and still hadn't seen hide nor hair of Surlock. She grimaced. Not a good choice of words.

Time to bring out the big guns. She brought the whistle to her lips and blew.

Nothing happened.

She frowned and blew again. Still nothing. Damn, why hadn't her father just tossed it if it was broken? She shook it a few times, then blew again.

Not even a little peep.

Her father used it to call stray dogs, the same ones people decided they no longer wanted and would dump on the side of a country road. Then the dogs would go wild. Starving, they'd attack just about anything. Her father tried to call them before that happened. He and Ralph would go out and search for the strays. If they found any, they would take them to the nearby shelter, where they at least had a chance to find a good home.

But the stupid whistle didn't work. She blew and blew until she was sure she was blue in the face. She had just gotten to the point of giving up when she heard a noise, like rustling, then a deep guttural growl.

She held her ground. Not that it mattered. She didn't think her feet would budge. Had this really been a good idea, trying to find Surlock? Right now, she wasn't so sure.

A thick fog began to roll in, just like last night. She hugged Surlock's clothes tighter to her chest with one hand and gripped the stick a little harder with her other one. As much as she loved Surlock, she wasn't about to let him gobble her up. Her mother would be devastated if she stumbled over her only daughter's mutilated body.

"Please don't let him kill me," she prayed just as the fog began to shift and clear. She heard something rustle again and tried to swallow past the lump in her throat.

CHAPTER 17

"I have a weapon," Darcy said, her voice trembling.

"Maybe if you hit me this time, I'll regain my memory," Surlock said as he stepped from behind a tree. He watched as Darcy dropped the stick, and the clothes that were crushed to her chest. She plowed her way through the underbrush and fell into his arms. He pulled her tight against him. He wasn't sure what had happened, but he knew he'd missed being with her.

"I was so scared," she whispered, and he could hear the tears in her voice.

"I know. So was I."

"What happened?"

He shook his head. "I don't remember."

She leaned back and looked up at him. "Nothing?"

"It's as if I lost the time from right after we mated until a few minutes ago. I could feel something trying to take over my body." He grimaced. "I think it might have accomplished it this time."

"But how did you get back?"

"I'm not sure. I heard a shrill, high-pitched sound, different from the humming. It was as though it came from a long distance away. I was able to make out some of the words then." He paused, thoughtful for a moment. " 'Stop that infernal noise.' " He frowned. "Yes, that's what the voice said."

He looked at Darcy, but she didn't meet his eyes. She was holding something back, not telling him what she was thinking. He had a feeling she knew what had happened to him.

"You know what's going on, don't you?" he questioned her.

She did look at him then, and her eyes were full of fear. His own gut clenched.

"You have to tell me," he said.

"Get dressed first. It might be easier to show you." She made her way out into the open, picked the clothes up, then handed them to him. "You're probably starving. You can eat first."

After dressing, he joined her. "That sounds good. I feel as if I've been running most of the night."

"But you are hungry?"

"Starved." He watched her, wondering why she looked relieved.

"Good." She let out a deep breath. "I was afraid you'd be . . . uh . . . full."

They started back toward the house. When they were almost there, Darcy stopped. "If anyone asks, you made your bed this morning and went for a walk. A very long walk."

"Why?"

"Because they think you were out all night. I don't want them to get suspicious if anything happened last night."

"What do you think might have happened?"

"Why worry when we don't know for sure? Everything will be fine," she said, speaking almost to herself.

They went inside. Darcy opened the kitchen door a little and asked Ms. Abernathy if she could fix Surlock something to eat. The next thing Surlock knew, Ms. Abernathy burst past Darcy and hurried to him.

"You're okay, then," she said, stopping only a couple of feet from him. She quickly looked him over. "I was afraid you'd gotten lost or injured."

He tried to look contrite. "I'm sorry I worried everyone. I awoke early this morning and decided to go for a walk. I guess I went farther than I planned. The countryside is magnificent early in the morning."

"Next time leave a note," she scolded. "Now have a seat. We just brought everything back to the kitchen, but it's still warm. I'll fix you a plate. Darcy, would you like anything?"

"Just coffee."

Ms. Abernathy hurried from the room.

"She really was concerned about you." Darcy made her way to the table and pulled out one of the chairs.

Surlock sat in the one beside her. "Ms. Abernathy and I haven't spoken that much."

"But you played a song that moved her to tears, and you listened when she said you couldn't run around naked, and I think she probably sees just how much I care about you."

"Do you care about me?"

"Yes." She folded her hands in front of her. "I was so afraid last night when . . . when—"

"When what?" he prodded when she didn't finish her sentence.

"We'll talk later, after you've finished eating."

Again, she wouldn't meet his gaze and it made him wonder what exactly she had witnessed last night. Before he could question her further, Ms. Abernathy and two of the maids brought the food and drinks.

When everything except Darcy's coffee was sitting in front of him, Ms. Abernathy smiled. "And if you're still hungry after all this, there's plenty more."

He looked at the pancakes piled high, the saucer of bacon. On another plate were scrambled eggs, hash browns and toast. "This will be plenty," he told her, knowing it wouldn't be long until lunch. He might not recognize the food, but he enjoyed it.

Surlock finished off the last bite, then pushed away the plate. "Ms. Abernathy is a good cook."

Darcy smiled and for the first time since they'd found each other, the dark shadows were gone from her eyes.

"She calls it home cooking, stick-to-your-ribs food. Her momma was from the Deep South and she taught her everything she knows. I always gain weight every time I come down here, but it's so worth it."

"My cook is not as good as Ms. Abernathy, but I enjoy her meals. I think I will miss Ms. Abernathy's dishes when I go home to New Symtaria," he said without thinking, then picked up his orange juice and took a drink.

"And where exactly is New Symtaria?" Darcy asked, placing the white napkin beside her cup.

He set his glass down. "Everyone knows where New Symtaria is," he said, then grabbed his head as the humming in his ears increased.

"Surlock, it's okay. Don't try to remember."

He felt her arms go around him; then she cradled his head against her chest. He'd remembered where he was from. Relief rushed through him. "I need to remember it all," he said, straining for something more that would unlock the rest of his memories.

"Shh, it's okay. You remembered a little more and that's good, but now you need to relax. Take a deep breath, then slowly exhale. We at least have the whole name of where you're from. It wasn't just Symtaria. It was *New* Symtaria and that might make a difference when we search for it."

The humming wasn't quite so intense this time and it wasn't followed by the screaming, so he supposed that was an improvement.

"Do you want me to get your eardrops?"

"No, it's easing." It was as if he could hear heavy steel doors slamming shut on the room that contained the rest of his memories. Frustration filled him. He wanted to know everything.

"Don't try to force your memories to return," she told him as she moved away.

He knew she was right, but it didn't mean he had to like it. Something suddenly occurred to him. "If I have a cook, then I probably have money."

"Probably," she said.

That was good because he wanted to take care of Darcy in the style she was accustomed to. Odd, for the life of him, he couldn't remember anything about money or ever having used it.

He needed to know more, and he had a feeling Darcy had the key that would unlock another door. "Tell me what happened last night after I blacked out."

She swallowed hard, and her hands trembled. Surlock had a bad feeling about what she might know, but she had to tell him.

"Okay, but remember that I won't leave you, no matter what." Her mouth turned down. "Actually, since I'm probably part of what happened, then I don't really have a choice."

Now she worried him. What did she know that he didn't?

Darcy bit her bottom lip as she went inside the media room and shut the door behind them.

"Are we going to watch another secret agent movie?" he asked.

She shook her head and went to her father's cabinet. What if she wasn't right? What if it was just a trick of the light when clouds had moved in front of the moon?

No, she knew what she'd seen had been real. Besides, she was pretty sure Surlock had changed back when she'd blown the dog whistle. She'd forgotten that humans couldn't hear the sound. He'd said as much himself. That he'd heard a shrill sound, and then he came to.

They were werewolves and there was no denying it.

She ran her fingers over the titles until she came to the one she wanted. She pulled the case from its slot, then trudged to the DVD player and inserted the disk. After dimming the lights, she took the seat next to Surlock.

The movie began to play. At first nothing seemed to happen. The pace was kind of slow.

"I don't understand," Surlock said.

She sighed. "Just wait. There's a full moon coming up."

In the next scene the sexy hero of the movie was walking with his girlfriend down a quiet street. The moon was bright, but everything around them was shadowed in mystery.

Suddenly, the man grabbed his head. The girl wore a shocked expression and asked what was happening, but the hero only shook his head. She tried to pull his hands away, but couldn't. Her eyes were wild now with terror.

Okay, it was a pretty cheesy movie. Darcy would admit to that, and probably not one of the gorier ones, but she would rather break it to Surlock gently that they were monsters.

The hero moved his hands, but instead of the face of the handsome lover, it was the face of a man/wolf. His hands suddenly changed to hairy claws and his teeth grew long and sharp. The girl raised her hands to her mouth and screamed.

Darcy pushed the remote to pause the movie. Surlock didn't move, only stared at the still frame. Not the best place to stop, but she wanted him to see.

"Are you saying this is what happened to me last night? I became this monster? That's why I lost time?"

She nodded, tears filling her eyes, then slipping down her face. "We're werewolves."

He turned in his seat, grabbing her shoulders. "What happens next in the movie?"

She shook her head. "It doesn't matter."

"It matters to me."

Why had she even told him? What was the saying? Ignorance is bliss? She should've just made something up. Then he wouldn't be looking at her right now with such a dismal expression.

"Darcy, show me the rest of the movie."

She knew if she didn't push play, he would figure out the remote, and watch the rest of it anyway. "Okay, okay," she said when he reached for the remote.

She pushed play and the movie started again. Darcy cringed in her seat. Not because the movie scared her. It was a low-budget film at best. She had no idea why her father had even bought it. No, she was more concerned with the fact that the same plot had played out last night. Surlock had really changed into a were-wolf.

Watching the movie was like watching a train about to wreck, and realizing there were people she knew onboard. The boy-friend in the movie raised his arms, then grabbed the girl and took off running with her. It looked like they had exchanged the girl for a mannequin. The girl he carried was just a little too stiff.

A man suddenly stepped in front of the werewolf and raised a gun. He proclaimed to love the woman. The werewolf growled and dropped the young woman.

Did her leg just fall off? The camera swerved away, almost making Darcy's eyes cross. The new man raised his gun. The werewolf struck a pose that might have passed for fierce, then started toward the new guy. One step at a time. The guy told him to stop or he'd shoot, warning that the bullets were silver.

Of course, the werewolf didn't stop, and the guy shot him. The werewolf clutched his chest, spun around a few times, then crumpled to the sidewalk.

The girl suddenly regained consciousness and ran screaming to her werewolf, who was now changing back into her one true love. The werewolf/boyfriend gasped out his love with his dying breath, then closed his eyes forever.

The new guy dropped his gun and hurried to the girl. He pulled her into his arms and from what Darcy could gather, the girl now had a new, and improved, boyfriend. Poor werewolf lay on the sidewalk as his blood poured from his body. Darcy stopped it there.

Surlock drew in a ragged breath. "You're telling me that I was like this monster?"

"I'm sorry."

Surlock slowly turned his gaze away from the blank screen and looked at Darcy. "You actually saw me turn into this hideous creature?"

She bit her bottom lip. "Sort of," she replied, unable to say more.

He frowned. "What do you mean, 'sort of'?"

"Well, you didn't look quite as fierce and I didn't actually see ferocious looking teeth or claws."

He turned in his seat. "What exactly did you see?"

"You grabbed your head. I knew the humming was even worse than usual. When you finally moved your hands from your face, it was like looking into the eyes of a wolf. And there was hair on your arms." She thought back. "Yes, I'm pretty sure you were hairy."

"But you're not positive."

God, she was so confused. Jennifer had questioned her like the Spanish Inquisition, Surlock was giving her the third degree, and now she wasn't exactly sure what she had seen.

"I thought I saw you turn into a werewolf. At least, a wolf." She closed her eyes and thought back. Surlock had had the same eyes as the wolf. But had she seen hair? The grass had been thick and the clouds had drifted in front of the moon so it might have given the impression of hair. She let out a deep breath. "I don't know, but you screamed at me to run. Then I heard the howl of a wolf."

"And you thought I had changed into this monster."

She nodded.

"Yet today, you came looking for me anyway."

"I had to."

"Why?"

She jumped from her seat. "Because I care about you." She twined her fingers together, unable to look him in the eye. She knew he liked her, and making love was pretty fantastic, but she was afraid her liking him was turning into a lot more.

His arms went around her. She leaned back against his chest, drawing comfort from his nearness.

"Do you think we're monsters?" he asked. "Werewolves that howl at the moon."

"I don't know. Everything just seems so jumbled up in my head."

The door to the media room suddenly opened and Jennifer and Peter walked in.

"Oh, you're back," Jennifer said, when she saw Surlock. She looked at the screen. "What were you watching?"

"A movie about werewolves," Surlock said.

Jennifer snickered. Peter shuffled his feet and looked uncomfortable.

Darcy just wanted to crawl under one of the chairs.

CHAPTER 18

"I forgot to tell you that Darcy thought Surlock was a werewolf," Jennifer said.

"Jennifer!" Darcy glared at her friend.

Surlock watched as Darcy grew more and more uncomfortable. Her gaze darted around the room as though she was looking for the nearest escape route.

"We're all friends. It's no biggie." Jennifer looked at each of them. "Okay, sorry I spilled the beans, but I still think you were joking."

"She was," Surlock said, then squeezed Darcy's shoulder. "We had an argument last night and I'm afraid I stormed off. I think she was embarrassed to tell you the truth." He felt Darcy's sigh of relief.

"I knew it!" Jennifer wore a knowing smile. Then just as suddenly as it appeared, her smile changed to a grimace. "You could've told me the truth."

"You're right. I'm sorry," Darcy said, then cleared her throat. "Uh, what are you two doing here?"

"We needed more input. You know, for the party," Peter explained, eyeing Surlock warily. "Jennifer said she thought Surlock had left for good, and we figured you might be lonely."

Surlock had a feeling Peter had hoped to pick up where he'd left off the other night at the restaurant. Well, that wouldn't be happening. After Surlock had *talked* to Peter in the limousine, Peter had sworn he was only Darcy's friend.

Surlock wanted to hate him, but he knew Darcy could never be romantically interested in a guy like Peter. He had no courage. His wealth had made him soft, and he acted superior to everyone else. Surlock would keep a watchful eye on him.

"Why don't we go downstairs and put our heads together? See what we can come up with." Darcy didn't wait for them to follow. Instead, she grabbed Surlock's hand and pulled him along with her, whispering her thanks that he had saved her from the werewolf story as they hurried down the stairs.

He was glad he could help. It should make him feel better, but he couldn't stop thinking about the movie they'd watched. He'd convinced Darcy that he wasn't like the monster on the screen— the werewolf—but he wasn't so sure. Something had taken over his mind and body. But what?

Once they were downstairs, Darcy took them to a room with places to sit. He stopped at the entryway and looked around. It was familiar, reminding him of another room, except with stone walls, and a fireplace so large he could walk inside and stand. On cold days there would be a roaring fire, the flames crackling and spitting, embers shooting up the chimney.

The vision was so clear he could see a man sitting on one of the chairs, laughing at something another man had said. He had a feeling they were his brothers. He clamped his lips together to keep from calling out to people he knew weren't really there. He could only stand in silence as he drank in the sight of them, searching for something familiar. He closed his eyes tight, then opened them.

A jaguar sauntered into the room. Surlock held his breath, but the cat didn't attack. She went to one of the men, rubbing her head against his leg. The man only laughed and leaned down to scratch the cat behind the ear.

"Come, sit beside me, Surlock," Darcy said, patting the seat beside her.

Surlock looked around. Gone were the stone walls, his brothers, and the jaguar. He drew in a deep breath. The humming in his head was faint.

"You okay?" Darcy asked.

Jennifer and Peter looked at him as they took their seats.

"I'm fine. It's a nice room."

"We like it." Darcy continued to study him.

He smiled and went to sit beside her. What had just happened? The jaguar must be a pet. But somehow, he didn't think so. He thought it was more than that. Nothing clicked.

He would rather be alone with Darcy so he could talk to her about this new vision. He wished Peter and Jennifer hadn't come over. Not that he disliked Jennifer, although he didn't think she trusted him. He couldn't blame her. She didn't know anything about him, and every time Jennifer asked him a question, Darcy would interrupt so Surlock never had to really explain anything.

"Of course, I've already sent out invitations to everyone I know. So far it will be a small crowd. Around two hundred," Peter said. "And I have the catering service. I actually have them on retainer. I'm just at a loss as to what sort of theme I should do, and I'm running out of time."

Surlock watched each one of them closely. It would seem the lack of a party theme was extremely important, although he couldn't understand why. Jennifer kept shaking her head whenever Peter suggested something, which made Peter quite agitated.

"The party is this Saturday, Jennifer, and you've shot down every idea I've had. I have to have some kind of decorations. It's a masquerade party, but I need something cohesive that will pull it altogether," Peter said. He was frowning when he turned toward Darcy. "And you've been absolutely no help, Darcy."

"I'm sorry," she told him.

One of the maids came into the room. "There's an Annette Barrymore to see you, Miss Darcy."

"Show her in," Darcy told her.

Peter sat a little straighter. "What's she doing here? I didn't invite her." He smoothed his hand over his hair and straightened his jacket.

"I called her before we left your house. I thought she might be able to help. Fresh ideas, and all," Jennifer told him. "Besides, I like her."

"Hi, everyone," Annette said as she came into the room, then stumbled to a stop when she saw Peter. Her face turned a bright red. "Oh, I didn't know you would be here, Peter."

"Have a seat. We're having a terrible time trying to figure out the decorations for Peter's party," Jennifer said. She cast a look at Peter that had him shutting his mouth without saying a word. "I'm bringing her to the party as my friend. I knew you wouldn't object, Peter."

"Whatever." He waved his arm in the air. But his gaze kept straying to Annette.

Annette slunk over to the nearest chair and sat down. "I'm not sure how much help I'll be." She hugged the small chair pillow as if it were a shield that might protect her from Peter's sharp words.

"Exactly," Peter said, then looked at Jennifer as if she'd lost her mind inviting Annette.

"We're glad you're here," Darcy stated firmly. "I'm sure you'll come up with something. What do you think of when I say masquerade ball?"

"I'm not sure—"

"Of course not," Peter said. "I mean, how many masked balls have you attended?"

Annette threw the pillow at Peter. He didn't move fast enough and it hit him square in the face with a *thunk*. "I haven't been to any masked balls, Peter, but that doesn't mean I don't have a brain." She glared at him.

"I didn't say you had no brain," he huffed.

"You might as well have. Just because you have lots of money, you think you're better than me, but you're not, so cut the crap."

Surlock didn't try to stop his laughter. He wanted to applaud because Annette had stood up for herself.

"Bravo," Jennifer said.

The exchange was interesting. Rather than look affronted by Annette's outburst, Peter seemed quite pleased.

"Touché," Peter said. "I apologize for my rudeness."

"Apology accepted," she said, raising her chin.

Ahh, so Darcy had been correct when she'd said Peter was interested in Annette. He'd forgotten what else she'd told him. Something about Peter never being given the chance to think for himself, and that his parents expected him to join with the right woman. Surlock was starting to like Annette, and couldn't understand why she would not make Peter a suitable mate.

"Do you have an idea for the theme of the party?" Peter asked Annette.

"Well," she began, her confidence slipping just a fraction. "When I think of masked balls, I think of Mardi Gras. You know, like they have in New Orleans with parades."

"Well done," Darcy said. "That's a brilliant idea. You could even have a king and queen."

"Ohhh—" Jennifer sat forward. "You could give out beads at the door. What fun."

Everyone looked at Peter, who hadn't said a word. He looked at each of them, but his gaze stopped and stayed on Annette. Then he smiled. "I think it's a brilliant idea, but can we pull it off by this Saturday?"

"Of course, I can," Jennifer said. "I can do anything."

Peter clapped his hands, and came to his feet. "We have a ton of work to do before Saturday, so back to my house to make all the arrangements." When Annette didn't move, Peter held out his hand. "You'll come as well, won't you?"

"You don't need me," she said, blushing.

Peter studied her. "I think I do. I think I need you more than I ever could have imagined."

She shyly took his hand and rose to her feet.

"Every king needs a queen, and of course, since it was your idea, you'll be my queen."

"I couldn't." She looked at everyone.

"Yes, you can." Jennifer laughed. "You might even make Peter look good."

"That was not funny." Peter frowned.

"Actually, it was," Darcy said as she stood.

"You're ganging up on me, too, are you? Not fair."

Darcy chuckled. "You'll have one less female causing problems. I think Surlock and I will hang out here. I have some work to do for him."

Peter's face fell. "Are you sure?"

She nodded. "But we'll visit later."

"I'll hold you to that."

Surlock stepped closer to Darcy. "We'll both see you later." So what if Peter was interested in Annette. Surlock wanted to make sure Peter understood Darcy was not available.

After they left, Darcy turned to him. "And what exactly was that last remark supposed to mean?"

He looked at her with all the innocence he could muster. "What remark?"

"You know exactly what I mean—'we'll *both* see you later.'"

"Just that I don't trust him alone with you," he said casually enough, holding back what he really felt.

"Peter is only a friend."

"You think so, but I'm still not convinced he believes that."

She rolled her eyes. "Sheesh, men can be so hardheaded."

He raised an eyebrow.

"You didn't see how taken Peter was with Annette?"

He snorted. "I'll withhold my judgment for now. I know what we saw, but he held back his feelings."

She shook her head. "He's been brought up to believe he's better than everyone else. His parents wouldn't approve of Annette, so Peter is fighting his attraction to her."

"So you told me. I like Annette. Why wouldn't his parents?"

"She doesn't come from money. Peter's family can be traced back for hundreds of years. They originally came from England. His father has a duke in his ancestral lineage."

"A duke is important?"

She grinned. "It is to Peter's parents. They think they're royalty sometimes. No, they wouldn't approve of Peter dating someone they thought was a lower-class citizen."

"And your parents, would they disapprove of you dating someone like me? I have no background. What if I'm just a common man?"

Her eyelids lowered as she pressed close to him, her arms going around his neck. "You may be the poorest man on earth, but you'll never be common."

He wrapped his arms around her and pulled her closer, nuzzling the side of her neck, then moving his lips to hers. He kissed her, reveling in her taste, absorbing her essence.

She rested her head against his chest when the kiss ended. Her breathing was ragged. The kiss had affected her as much as it had him. He wanted her. He wanted to remove each article of her clothing and mate with her.

Only one thing stopped him. He knew when he lost control, whatever was inside him took over. He couldn't afford to lose control again. What if he was a monster? Would he harm Darcy? He couldn't take that chance. He moved out of her arms.

"I'm not afraid," she whispered.

He looked at her, glad he'd put some distance between them because it was difficult to resist her when she looked at him like that. He sucked in a deep breath and braced himself to fight the attraction.

"Until I know what happens to me when we mate, I think we should step away from an intimate relationship." He could see the struggle going on inside her.

"Okay, fine," she finally said. "I don't like it, though."

"But I'm right."

She raised her arms, then let them fall back to her sides. "Yes, you're right. I know that, but it doesn't mean I have to like it."

"I don't like it, either."

"Then we need to find out exactly who you are. We at least have a last name—Prince."

"Maybe."

"It's better than nothing. And we know the place you come from is called New Symtaria and not just Symtaria. Let's check on the computer and see what we can find."

He only hoped this time they would be successful. No matter what his good intentions were, he wasn't sure how long he could keep his promise not to mate with her. Darcy was too tempting. He should have led the way to the computer. It wasn't helping that he couldn't take his eyes off the gentle sway of her hips.

Darcy sat down at the computer and he breathed a sigh of relief as she typed "Surlock Prince" into the search engine, then scrolled down page after page. He pulled up a chair and sat beside her.

"There's nothing listed," he said.

"Which doesn't mean a lot. It only means you haven't done anything that would get you on the Internet. Obviously, you don't have a webpage."

He had no idea what she spoke about. Webpage? Again, everything seemed so unfamiliar.

"There's nothing here," she muttered, clicking on one site.

"Wait," he said. "What's that?" He pointed toward a stone structure.

She looked at it. "The castle?" She touched her finger to the screen to make sure that's what he was talking about.

"Yes, the castle. It looks familiar."

She slowly turned in her seat and stared at him as if she were seeing him for the first time.

"What?" he asked.

She swallowed hard. "I think we need to change the order of your name. It's not Surlock Prince. I have a feeling it's Prince Surlock."

CHAPTER 19

Excoria yawned as she leaned against a tree and stared at the house. It was a beautiful home, very majestic. She bet it was cool inside. She hated this land, especially this place called Texas, where it was cool one day, then burning hot the next.

Her stomach growled, reminding her she hadn't eaten today. Damn Nivla for not giving her money. He'd only been more cruel because she'd almost gotten sick on him, which was his fault, too. If she didn't eat something soon, she wouldn't be able to keep an eye on Prince Surlock.

That was another thing she had a problem with. Nivla had told his son, Ekon, to oversee Excoria and make sure Prince Surlock didn't escape before they had a chance to capture him.

And where was Ekon?

Excoria knew. He was back at the warehouse sleeping. His father had made sure his son had a nice comfortable bed in which to lay his head while she still had the lumpy cot. He also had money and food. It wasn't fair.

Besides, she loathed Ekon. He wasn't hard to look upon, not like his fat father, but in a few years time she had no doubt he would be just as slovenly. A shudder of distaste ran through her.

She straightened when a man came around the corner. He carried a brown sack in one hand and a tool in the other. The breeze carried the aroma of what was in the sack over to her. Her mouth watered. It didn't smell at all like the burrito, which had been pretty awful.

The man set the brown paper bag on a metal table and leaned the long wooden handle of the instrument against the chair opposite the one he sat in. Then he opened the bag.

Excoria gritted her teeth as she tried to hold back a moan.

"Hey, Ralph, Ms. Abernathy wants you to look at her sink. It's leaking."

The man frowned, then closed the bag as he stood up. "She'll owe me another one of her peach-fried pies for this." He walked off, leaving the bag on the table.

As soon as he rounded the corner, Excoria raced over and grabbed it, then ran past her hiding place as if her feet were on fire. She didn't stop in case the man came back. By the gods, Nivla could not expect her to keep an eye on the prince under these circumstances.

When she was deep inside the cover of the woods, she sat on the ground, and leaned against a tree. She didn't hurry. No, she slowly opened the bag, savoring the smell. The unknown aroma wafted up to her.

Her stomach rumbled as she brought out a biscuit of some kind with meat in the middle. She knew the earth food because she'd been here for quite some time searching for impures. This particular food she'd seen before, but never eaten.

When she bit into the bread, she knew she'd never tasted anything like this, either. It practically melted in her mouth. She forced herself to eat slowly since she wasn't sure when her next meal would be.

Even after she finished the bread with meat, her stomach felt as though it was hollow. There was a flaky crust pastry of some kind inside the sack. When she bit into it, fruit oozed out. Peach. They had peaches on New Symtaria and her mother had made sweets with them, but nothing that compared to this.

She finished the last bite, then licked her fingers. Her stomach was comfortably full. As she sat there, she realized exactly what her life had come to—stealing food just to survive. Now, she didn't have a choice. If she left the rogues, they would hunt and kill her just like they did the impures. To them, she would be an impure. Her eyes narrowed. Nivla was evil and mean. She should have demanded he give her money.

The world suddenly came crashing down on her. Even her animal guide wasn't talking to her except to complain about the mistake Excoria had made when she joined the ranks of the rogues. She had retreated into stony silence.

"I'm sorry," Excoria whispered, wiping away the tear that slid down her cheek. "I'll make it up to you."

Silence.

Somehow, some way, she would, too. She missed her guide. Her guide had always been her best friend. Now she was alone, deserted by everyone. She wasn't important to anyone.

A thought suddenly occurred. If she could capture the prince, then she would be very important. They would probably shower her with jewels. She only needed to be the one who captured him.

She got up, brushing away crumbs. She looked deplorable. If she was going to get close to him, she would need to clean up. Nivla or Ekon would have to give her money. She squared her shoulders, anger filling her. It was time she made a few demands of her own. What was the worst they could do?

She frowned. They could kill her. It was against the law to kill a pure Symtarian, but since they were breaking the law anyway, it wouldn't matter to them.

Demanding money might not be the best way to earn their favor. Her stomach clenched. She might have to sleep with one of them. Death was more welcome than Nivla's slimy arms, but she might be able to stomach Ekon.

She glanced toward the big house, a smile forming. She hadn't yet told Nivla or Ekon where the prince was staying. She might have more leverage than she thought.

CHAPTER 20

"You're a prince," Darcy whispered. "Do you know what that means?"

Surlock shook his head.

Her face suddenly turned pale. "Oh, good Lord, I clobbered a prince over the head and caused him to have amnesia. Is that treason? I don't think so, but I'm pretty sure there's a law against it."

Her pout was too tempting. Surlock leaned over and captured her bottom lip with his teeth, tugging gently, then he began to kiss her. She sighed, leaning in closer, her arms going around his neck.

When he ended the kiss, he saw her eyes were glazed with passion. She blinked several times until they cleared, then quickly moved away from him.

"You make me forget everything," she complained.

He grinned. "Good."

"No, it's not good. If you really are a prince, then we need to find your . . . your . . ."

"My kingdom?" he supplied.

Her eyes narrowed. "This is not funny."

"Was I laughing?"

"I think you were. If you want to keep your vow of celibacy, then you're going to have to keep your distance."

"I apologize." He didn't think she believed him. But she was right. It would be difficult to keep his hands to himself.

"I'm surprised it hasn't been on the news or in the papers." She drew in a sharp breath. "Maybe you were kidnapped and they're waiting for a ransom." Her eyes suddenly filled with tears. "You had probably gotten away, stripped of everything, including your clothes, and then I battered you over the head."

He had a feeling she was about to apologize again so he quickly took her hands in his. "We don't know I'm a prince. I recognized a building. That was all."

"Castle." She sniffed. "It's a castle."

He looked at the picture. Castle? It sounded familiar. Again, he saw the room with the two men.

"What do you see?" Darcy whispered.

"Two men. I think they're my brothers. A jaguar with a glittery necklace around its neck."

"A jaguar? Like the cat?"

He heard the confusion in her voice. That was okay, he was confused, too.

"One of the men is rubbing the cat behind the ear. There's a fog." He shook his head. "I can't see anything. Wait, it's starting to clear." He blinked several times.

"What?" Darcy asked.

"A naked woman. The jaguar is gone." He watched as another woman brought a robe and held it out to the naked woman. She slipped her arms inside the sleeves and belted it at her waist. The vision slipped back into the shrouds of his mind. He blinked. "I think the woman was my sister."

"What happened to the jaguar?"

He drew in a deep, ragged breath. "I think they were one and the same."

Her forehead wrinkled. "Huh?"

"They both wore the same necklace. I think my sister was the jaguar, then she changed into the woman."

She shook her head. "That doesn't make sense."

"I know, but it might explain who I am." The humming in his ears was back. He closed his eyes tight against the noise.

"Are you okay?" Worry laced her words.

"The humming. It's back."

"I'll get your eardrops."

He opened his eyes and blinked several times until the noise eased. "No, it's not as bad as it was the last time. I think it's beginning to go away."

She sighed with relief. "We're still back at square one, though."

"But maybe the visions are showing me who I am."

She pushed out of the chair and began to pace. "It doesn't explain anything. It only makes things more confusing. That would mean you're some kind of shape-shifter. They don't exist. No more than a werewolf exists." She stopped walking back and forth across the room. "I put these thoughts in your head. I should never have made you watch that stupid werewolf movie. I'm sorry. I watch too many horror movies."

"But it looked real, and it seemed familiar." He felt as though he was losing his mind.

She knelt in front of him and took his hands. "It'll be okay. You probably do have brothers and sisters, but your memories are a little confused right now. That's all. Maybe there was a little statue of a jaguar that you liked and it got mixed up in your memory banks."

"You might be right."

"I know I am." She smiled. "There are no such things as vampires, or werewolves." She laughed. "Or aliens or things that go bump in the night. But there is one thing we know."

"What's that?"

"You're starting to remember things. Maybe you're not a prince. You could be a pauper, but none of that really matters. I like who you are right now."

The phone rang. Rather than waiting for someone else to answer it, Darcy reached over and picked it up. "Spencer residence."

"This is Dr. Wilson calling for Darcy."

"This is Darcy." Her heart pounded inside her chest.

"We have the blood work back, but I'm afraid there's a problem."

Darcy looked at Surlock. He watched her intently. She tried to keep her voice calm, even though that was the last thing she was feeling. She was almost afraid to ask what was wrong. What if she'd caused Surlock to have a slow bleed or something? Dammit, she had to know—good or bad.

"What . . . uh . . . exactly is the problem?" She smiled at Surlock reassuringly while she felt her insides tighten into knots.

"Oh, nothing to do with Surlock. The lab made an error and I will be filing a complaint with them, *and* the x-ray company."

"Exactly what was the error?"

"They screwed up the results with a vet or something. The blood work came back abnormal. There apparently weren't any of the antibodies that humans have."

"I don't understand."

"Ah, yes, let me see if I can explain in layman terms. We, as humans, have natural antibodies. These antibodies recognize and attack foreign invaders, which is why you have to type and cross match blood. If you give a human the wrong type blood, it could kill the patient."

"And the lab results didn't have these natural antibodies. Isn't that a good thing?"

"It might be if he ever needs a blood transfusion, except the tests are wrong. Unless he's a canine." Dr. Wilson chuckled.

"Huh?"

"Simply put, dogs don't have these natural antibodies."

She swallowed past the lump in her throat. "Dogs, you say."

"Which is why I'm irritated at the results. Shoddy work. It's nothing like the old days when people took pride in their jobs. We'll have to repeat the tests, of course. I'm leaving on vacation tomorrow, but you can bring Surlock in any time."

Everything was slowly sinking into her brain. The X-rays were wrong because there were two types of bone structure, the blood work was incorrect because the results were those of a canine. She closed her eyes for a moment. Or wolf. The howling in the woods. Thinking she was looking into the eyes of a wolf.

"You still there, girl?"

"Yes," she squeaked, then cleared her throat. "That will be fine. I'll get him down to the office."

"Good. I apologize for the inconvenience."

"No, that's okay. These things happen."

"How's the boy feeling? Any more humming in his ears?"

"He's better. Remembering more every day, and the humming is getting better, too."

"Good. I told him that his memories would come back."

Darcy didn't mention that Surlock's memories were a little crazy. She didn't want to take the chance Dr. Wilson would commit him, because they might commit her as well. "Have a good vacation," she said instead, and replaced the phone in the cradle.

"That was the doctor," Surlock said rather than asked.

She faced him with a bright smile on her face. "Yes. There was a mix-up with your blood work and he only wants to repeat it."

"What kind of mix-up?"

She shrugged. "Stuff like this happens all the time. Nothing at all to worry about."

He watched her, but rather than pressing the issue, he nodded. She let out a deep breath. He was not a monster. This was all a coincidence. The idea that he could be a werewolf was so crazy, she didn't want to think about it.

She sat in her chair in front of the computer again and continued her search on the Internet. Surlock didn't say anything, but she could feel him close to her. She was not going to mention what kind of error the doctor had found. That was all it was, just an error. People made them all the time. It was ludicrous to think he could change into—what? A wolf? Or worse—a werewolf. And if he could, what did that make her?

An hour later, she pushed away from the computer. Nothing. Not a blasted thing. There was no Prince Surlock, no New Symtaria. Nothing whatsoever. She'd hit another dead end.

"I guess I'm not much of an investigator," she said, turning in her seat until they faced each other.

He pulled her onto his lap before she could think to protest. Once she was there, she didn't want to leave. It felt too good having him hold her close. It wasn't as if they were going to mate. She frowned. Make love.

"I think you're a very good investigator."

"I haven't found out anything."

"I wouldn't say that. I could be a secret agent, or a werewolf, or I could be a prince."

Oh, great, now she felt a whole lot better. Everything she had come up with sounded totally ridiculous. No wonder her mom didn't want Darcy to get a job—she knew she couldn't cut it in the real world.

"What are you thinking?" Surlock brushed his lips across the top of her head.

A shiver of need spread through her. "That I suck at the only job I've ever had." She felt the rumble of his chest. Oh, yeah, now she felt a whole lot better.

"I'm not laughing at you," he finally said.

"Of course not. You're laughing *with* me. Uh, I hate to tell you this, but in case you haven't noticed, I'm not laughing at all."

"Why does it have to be so complicated?" he asked. "Going to the party was a great idea. Someone is bound to know me. You did say Peter always has a large number of people there, right?"

She'd forgotten about the party for a moment. So maybe everything wasn't a hopeless cause.

"We'll need to get you a costume," she said. "What do you want to go as?"

"How about a wolf?"

Was he laughing again?

CHAPTER 21

Nerves of steel, that was Darcy.

Jennifer and Annette had already left for the party. Darcy was taking her time. She wanted to arrive when there were more people so Peter could announce them. She was hoping someone might recognize Surlock.

And if no one knew him, then what? Her nerves of steel melted around her feet like warmed butter. Deep breath. She was meant to be an investigator. Peter's party was the perfect place to be seen, and hopefully recognized.

She slipped her foot inside the stiletto and stood, but her movements were slow and jerky. If no one knew him, then once again, she would have slammed into a brick wall. What would she tell Surlock? What *could* she tell him? Nothing. She squared her shoulders.

Think like Dick Tracy, she told herself. Be Dick Tracy. She closed her eyes and breathed in deeply, then exhaled. What would Dick do?

She grimaced. She wasn't sure what Dick would do, but she knew what her father would do. He'd taught his daughter the ins and outs of the financial world. One of the first things he told her was to know when to back out of a negotiation, even if it cost you money. Losing a little was better than losing a lot. Maybe it was time to get Surlock an experienced investigator. She didn't like the idea of throwing in the towel, but she was there to help him, and she wouldn't let her ego stand in the way.

With her decision made, she looked one last time in the mirror. She hadn't worn her cat costume in a few years. The black glittery material clung to her curves. The ankle-length dress was cut in a low vee neckline, and it had a very high slit on the side.

Annette had painted Darcy's face so that her eyes were catlike, dark and mysterious. She'd passed on the black nose and just went with the whiskers. She'd covered her blond hair with a long black wig. Not bad. She had a feeling she would definitely have all of Surlock's attention tonight. Her blood heated, flowing hot through her veins as she imagined his reaction.

Just as quickly, she tamped down her lustful thoughts. They couldn't make love until they figured out just who he was. But then again, if they found out tonight, then they could make love when they got home.

There was a light knock on her door. Darcy smoothed the material over her hips and called out, "Come in."

The door opened and Surlock entered, stopping when he saw her. His gaze slowly moved over her, touching her in all the right places. Then she noticed how he was dressed and her mouth went dry. Good Lord, did he realize that he could send women into cardiac arrest?

She swallowed. "I'm not sure it will be safe to let you out of the house looking like that."

He looked down. "Is this not the right costume?"

"I doubt we could have found one more perfect," she said. He wore a short apron of wolf fur. It was fake, of course, but no one would be able to tell. Not that they would be looking at the apron of fur. No, they would be drooling over his muscled thighs. His rock-hard abs and chest were also bare, displaying a very sexy expanse of skin. On his head, he wore a wolf head with fur that came down on both sides. He reminded her of an Indian warrior—strong, powerful and damned sexy.

His forehead wrinkled. "I don't understand."

"The women will be drooling."

He grinned. "Do you think so?"

She frowned. "Don't get any ideas. You're . . ." What had she been about to say? You're mine? But he wasn't.

"I'm what?"

"Never mind," she said as she turned back to the mirror and fastened a diamond pendant earring in her lobe.

"I like what you're wearing," he said as he came to stand behind her.

Her hands trembled. It was all she could do to fasten the earring. When she brought her hands down to her sides, his trailed over them, lightly caressing, leaving tingles of pleasure in their wake.

"You make me want you very much." He kissed her shoulder, then moved to her neck.

She sucked in a breath, caught his scent, and knew she wanted him as much as he wanted her. Before she turned in his arms and pressed her body close to his, she came to her senses and stepped away from him. This was the night they could possibly discover exactly who he was. As much as she wanted to drag him to her bed, she had to look out for his interests.

"Are you ready?" she asked.

He hesitated. "What if we do find out who I am? Then what?"

"What do you mean?"

"What if I have none of the money that it seems everyone holds in high esteem? What if I have nothing that will compare to"—he waved his arm around her room—"this? Does it matter to you?" His gaze captured hers.

Her heart swelled. "None of this matters. I wouldn't care if you were raised by wolves and had nothing to your name. What I care about is what's on the inside of a person. If you were a jerk, no amount of money would make me like you.'

He seemed more than satisfied with her answer.

But would everything change after tonight? Would the bond between them be broken? No, she wouldn't think like that.

She squared her shoulders. "Everyone should be at the party by now. Are you ready?"

He nodded, and they left her bedroom. A good thing they didn't linger. She wasn't so sure she could keep her hands off him. The guy was definitely too sexy for his shirt.

"What's a 'jerk'?" he asked as they went out the front door.

She smiled. "A person no one likes."

"But you like me a lot."

Darcy hadn't seen that one coming. She opened her car door and slid into the driver's seat. After she started the car, she turned to look at him. "Yes, I like you a lot."

He grinned, and again she thought about not going to the party. What if she found out something she didn't want to know? Just because a man didn't wear a wedding ring didn't mean he wasn't married.

Then there was the little problem that he might be a prince. Sure, she came from money, but she was also adopted. Her pedigree might not be good enough to marry a prince. And if they did come from the same race of people, she might be so low on the food chain there was no way he would be allowed to get serious.

So many problems. She sighed. And since when had she started thinking about marriage? Sheesh!

The drive over was pretty quick since Peter's estate was the next one over. She pulled into the circular drive. As usual, Peter had valet parking. She had a feeling he kept staff on retainer for just such an occasion. His parties were usually planned at the very last minute, but everyone would cancel just about anything to go. Peter was the ultimate party-giver.

"It looks festive," Surlock said.

She looked around as she pulled up. "Peter always outdoes himself when it comes to parties." And it looked like he had this time, too. Well, with Jennifer and Annette's added input.

There were lights strung in the trees; the fountain had been replaced with a dolphin ice sculpture. Up-lights cast a soft glow of changing pastel colors in a fog mist. The front of the house was decorated with loops of beads. Darcy could only imagine how many people Peter had hired to pull everything together in such a short amount of time.

A valet opened her car door and she climbed out. She hoped Peter wouldn't mind that Surlock didn't have a mask. Darcy wanted people to see his face.

Surlock took her arm as they went up the steps to the veranda. Peter's family estate reminded her of Tara from *Gone With the Wind*. It definitely had plenty of Southern charm.

The butler opened the front door. "Welcome, Miss Darcy."

She grinned. "Charles, you're not supposed to know who I am." No mask, but her face was painted.

"Of course, Miss Darcy." He smiled.

She laughed lightly as they went inside. Peter had changed his costume to King Neptune, and Annette was his mermaid queen. She was wearing a glittery gown of aqua. Darcy had to admit it was the perfect choice. She looked absolutely stunning wearing a tiara, and diamonds at her throat. If she knew Peter, the jewels were real. He would want her to look as classy as possible.

"You look perfect," Darcy told Annette, taking her hands.

"I feel like a princess," she said.

"No, darling," Peter interrupted. "Tonight you're my queen."

Annette blushed. Darcy smiled, happy Annette was so excited.

"There you two are. I wondered when you would get here," Jennifer said as she came up. Her gaze slowly wandered over Surlock, then moved back to Darcy. "Not that I can blame you. In fact, I wonder why you bothered to show up at all."

"Because I throw the best parties and she knows it," Peter said.

Jennifer's snakeskin costume molded to her body. A gold snake band hugged her upper arm and gold snake earrings dangled from her lobes. Annette had painted Jennifer's skin so that it looked like the scales of a snake. Only Jennifer could pull the look off and come across as the sexiest woman in the room.

"Did I tell you that you look positively lethal?" Darcy asked.

"I do, don't I?" Jennifer gave her a slow smile. "Okay, I'm off to see if I can get lucky." Her gaze swept the room. "Yum. I think I've found my first victim of the night." Hips swaying seductively, she headed toward a vampire.

After she left, Surlock turned to Darcy. "Lucky? Victim?"

Darcy really didn't want to get into this conversation with him so she pulled him by the arm toward the main ballroom. "Let's make sure we're announced."

Other people were being announced according to their costume to keep their real identities secret. She could already see that Peter had spent lavishly and had continued the Mardi Gras theme in here as well.

The walls had been draped with purple and gold material. There were beads everywhere and colorful decorations, along with waiters and waitresses carrying heavy trays of drinks and food. She could hear a band playing outside and someone singing something bluesy.

When they reached the announcer, Darcy gave their names as Prince Surlock, prince of wolves, and his mate, the Black Cat. Not very imaginative on her part, but who she was didn't really matter as long as someone recognized the name Surlock. Darcy scanned the crowd when the announcer called out their names. It was impossible to tell if anyone recognized him or not. How could she have forgotten that most of the people here tonight would be wearing masks?

There were plenty of people looking at Surlock, but she had a feeling it wasn't because they knew him. His costume, or lack thereof, was a definite distraction.

He was getting noticed, though, and that was a good thing. As long as none of the women hit on him. She might be tempted to do a little more clobbering if that happened.

"There are a lot of people here tonight," Surlock said.

"At least two hundred just in here. There are probably more outside. Just smile and look at everyone and we'll work our way toward the back doors."

"It doesn't look safe," he said.

Safe? Probably not, the way the women were starting to look at him as if he was one of the appetizers. But mingling with the crowd was their only chance of running across someone who might know him.

"Why, Darcy, you've been holding out on us," a female drawled in the fakest Southern accent Darcy had ever heard.

Darcy looked at the woman dressed as a leopard. Her yellow and black-spotted costume had to have been painted on. Not a good choice. The woman would have done better to wear something with a support bra.

She moved her mask on a stick away from her face. "It's me. Nita Hayfield."

Darcy smiled. "Nita, I didn't recognize you. Uh, great costume."

She leaned in closer. "Jack painted it on," she whispered loudly, then let her gaze fall on Surlock. "It was quite erotic. He has that wonderful little shop at Eighth and Monroe. You should check him out sometime."

Heat flooded Darcy's face and she took a quick half-step away from the woman. Eww. She grabbed Surlock's arm and pulled him closer to her. "Do you know my friend, Surlock?"

Nita's gaze roamed over him as if she could eat him alive, and Darcy had no doubt she would if they'd been the only two in the room.

"No, I don't believe I do. Would you like me to get to know him?" She met Darcy's eyes. "We could make a night of it together. All three of us."

"Sorry, Surlock isn't into that sort of thing." She smiled and pulled him quickly away from the other woman.

"Was her costume really painted on?" Surlock asked.

"Afraid so." She barely knew Nita. "She's recently divorced. A very messy one. I think she's trying to prove she's still sexy." She glanced his way. "She didn't go about it in the right way."

"You would look good in a painted-on costume."

She stumbled. He caught her elbow to steady her. "That is so not going to happen in my lifetime."

"Oh, I would only let you wear it for me." His thumb traced circles on her arm. "And I would be the one who painted you."

Flames shot down to her lower regions, then curled into a tight little ball of passion. If he kept this up, it was going to be a long night.

They chatted their way to the French doors that were open to the outside, spilling people out onto the large patio. More lights twinkled in the trees, and again, beads draped everything. The bandstand was a makeshift float in bright colors.

Any other time, Darcy would have loved to be outside with Surlock. Since there were no walls, it seemed less like she was crammed into a can of sardines.

But she was working, and getting more and more frustrated. No one seemed to recognize Surlock, but Darcy told herself the evening was still young. More people would probably show up.

Outside, they continued their meet and greet.

She noticed one woman seemed to be staring at her intently. The woman had followed them outside. Darcy knew it could just be a coincidence, but what if she knew Surlock? Darcy was pretty sure she'd never met her. She was just taking a step toward her when Annette and Jennifer hurried up to them.

"Come on, Peter wants you both inside for the first parade," Annette said, grabbing her arm while Jennifer latched on to Surlock's.

Before Darcy could protest, they were herded back inside. A parade? No, she wanted to talk to the woman. But the group grew in size and she was forced to move along with them or be trampled. She looked back for Surlock, met his gaze, then lost him.

"Let the parade begin," Peter said. Bowls of beads were passed around.

"Grab some," Annette yelled over the noise of the band, which had gotten louder.

Her smile was infectious. Darcy knew she would find Surlock again as soon as the parade was over. She grabbed a handful of beads, laughing. Someone shoved a champagne cocktail in her hand. She realized how thirsty she was and downed the drink, then placed the empty glass on a waiter's tray as he passed.

Bleh, the drink had a bad aftertaste.

"Let the good times roll," Peter called out.

The music changed to a sexy beat as they pranced through the ballroom. One of the bead throwers yelled out that he wanted to see some skin. A female voice laughed and told him to keep dreaming.

Darcy joined in on the fun. She caught sight of Surlock briefly before she began to throw beads into the crowd of clapping, yelling people. She smiled and waved at him. He smiled and waved back.

When she turned back around, the room blurred. Wow, the cocktail she'd drunk had gone straight to her head. It was a good thing she was in the middle of the crowd because she was afraid the tight press was the only thing keeping her upright. Next time she would remember to eat before she went to one of Peter's parties.

"Over here," a man yelled, then raised his hands for beads.

Darcy tossed some his way, laughing when he caught them. She glanced around. No Annette. People were disappearing. No, just her friends. No problem, she would find them later.

The room blurred again and she had to blink several times until it cleared, but even then everything still looked slightly out of kilter. Not that it mattered that much. She was having too much fun!

"Isn't this great?" a female voice asked beside her.

Darcy laughed and turned toward the other woman. "I love Peter's parties," Darcy yelled above the noise, but when she got a good look at the woman, anything else she was going to say died in her throat. It was the same person who had been watching her and Surlock earlier.

This was her chance. Maybe this woman knew Surlock. Darcy's heart pounded. Damn it, her vision was freakin' blurry. The woman weaved beside her.

"You okay?" the stranger asked with concern.

"I'm Darcy Spencer. Do you happen to know the man I'm with?"

The woman smiled. "Of course, I know Surlock."

CHAPTER 22

Relief flooded Darcy. She'd known they'd meet someone who would recognize Surlock. She looked around, but didn't see him anywhere. Not that she could see very well at all. Jeez, why was everything so fuzzy?

"You really do know Surlock, right?" Darcy asked.

"Of course. My name is Excoria. Has he not mentioned me?"

"No." She didn't tell her he had amnesia.

"I saw him go out that side door," Excoria said, pointing to an exit that would lead them to the opposite side of the yard.

Now why would he go out that way? Everyone was gathered on the other side of the house. Maybe he just needed some quiet time. She had to admit it was pretty noisy.

"We need to catch up to him," Darcy told her. As big as the estate was, Surlock might get lost. He needed to talk to this woman.

Darcy glanced her way. She wore a really bad costume. What was she supposed to be, an alien? She should've watched *Star Trek* or something because this was the worst alien costume she had ever seen.

The humming started in Darcy's ears again. She closed her eyes, willing it to go away. Talk about bad timing. Maybe she could just ignore it.

"Let's hang on to each other so we don't get separated."

"Good idea." Darcy could barely walk a straight line. How embarrassing. Actually, she wasn't real sure she was even accomplishing that small feat. Hanging on to someone helped.

"I'm afraid Peter's drinks are a little strong."

"I agree," Excoria said, then laughed lightly.

Darcy would definitely talk to Peter about this tomorrow. They stepped into the night. The crisp air lightly teased her. It was nice outside. "Wow, look how beautiful the stars are. They're so bright. 'Twinkle, twinkle little star,' " she sang off key.

"Over this way," Excoria urged.

Darcy blinked several times. What the hell was she doing? Oh, yeah, looking for Surlock. She needed to find him.

Darcy glanced around. "But there aren't any people over here. I don't see Surlock, either. I think we went through the wrong door."

"No, I'm positive that was the door." Excoria dragged Darcy down the path and around a corner.

"Wait a minute." Darcy came to a sudden stop, tumbling into a bush. A thorn stabbed her arm. Damn, that hurt.

Excoria helped her out of the bush. "Watch where you're going!"

Why the hell was Excoria pissed? Darcy was the one who'd been hurt. It wasn't her fault Peter made his drinks so strong. "How do you know Surlock?" she asked.

"He's a prince from New Symtaria."

"He's really a prince," Darcy said in wonder. "We have the same birthmark, you know."

"Oh, yes, I know. You're an impure."

"I beg your pardon," she said, then stumbled again as they made their way farther from the house, away from the noisy revelers. "I am not impure." She frowned. "Oh, wait a minute. I'm not pure, either." She shook her head, falling against Excoria again. They nearly lost their balance. "It wasn't my fault I lost my virginity. I got horny." She stumbled again.

"Could we just walk without talking?" Excoria ground out.

Darcy looked around. "Where are we going?"

"To my car."

"But we're supposed to be looking for Surlock. Oh, wait, I suppose I should call him Prince Surlock. Protocol and all, you know."

"Whatever," Excoria mumbled.

Darcy blinked, looking around. "I don't think Surlock would have come out this far. We should go back." She started to turn around, but Excoria grabbed her by the waist.

"Not so fast. Surlock told me to bring you to him."

"Why would he do that?"

"There are bad people after him. He is in danger."

Darcy couldn't breathe. Oh, no, what if she had put him in greater danger? First, she'd whacked him over the head and given him amnesia. And now she'd waved him like a white flag in front of the bad guys. Come and get him! Sheesh.

"Let's hurry." Darcy stumbled faster.

"That's what I've been trying to do."

They walked for what seemed like miles. The farther they went, the clearer Darcy's thoughts became, and the more suspicious she started to get. When they arrived at a beat-up green Ford, her worries increased.

"Where's Surlock?"

"He'll be here in a minute." Excoria opened the back door. "Hurry and get in."

Darcy crossed her arms in front of her. "No, not until I see Surlock."

Excoria pursed her lips. "Get in. You're wasting time."

Darcy shook her head. "Nope. Not gonna happen."

Excoria plowed into her, taking Darcy completely unaware and knocking her against car. She fell inside the open door, hitting her head against the seat with a thud. She was still woozy from the drink, which she guessed must have been drugged, so her reaction time was slowed. Before she could sit up, Excoria had shoved Darcy's feet inside and slammed the door.

"Let me out!" She reached for the handle, except it wasn't

where it should be. She kicked on the door, but only managed to hurt her foot.

"Temper, temper." Excoria laughed as she slid into the front seat. She started the car and began driving away.

Oh, hell, what had she gotten herself into this time? The woman up front, Excoria, if that was even her real name, headed away from town. A partition separated the backseat from the front or she'd jerk the bitch's head off.

Darcy looked around the backseat for a weapon of some kind. Nothing. She glared at Excoria. "Surlock will kill you." If the car hadn't swerved just a fraction, she would've wondered if Excoria had even heard her. "He won't stop looking for me. This is fair warning—let me go. If you release me, I won't say a word."

"Not a chance. You're my ticket to more wealth than I could ever spend in one lifetime. I'm finally going to have everything I want."

"All you're going to get is a jail cell and a long prison term."

The woman only laughed.

Darcy leaned against the backseat. "He will find me, you know," she said calmly and with enough confidence that she knew the woman was at least a little worried.

"I'll let you in on a few things," Excoria told her. "Before this night is over, Prince Surlock will be captured, and there's nothing anyone can do about it."

Darcy was suddenly very cold, even though the inside of the car was warm and stuffy. Surlock captured? She didn't even want to think about it. The woman turned onto the main road, but she didn't head toward town as Darcy had hoped.

"Why are you doing this?"

"I want wealth. I don't care about causes. It's nothing to me."

Darcy thought she might faint. She quickly took a deep breath, then exhaled. "Causes?"

"Your lover is going to be exchanged for my leader. At least, that's the plan. We could've gotten a king's ransom for him, but

no, they want to free Zerod. Why, I don't know. The guy is totally crazy. He scares the hell out of me."

Terrorists. Oh, God, terrorists didn't care who they killed.
That must have been the reason Surlock was wandering the
woods without clothes or any kind of identity. He must have escaped them.

Then she'd clobbered him. Lord, he'd been through a lot. She
frowned. Then why take her? "But why did you kidnap me?"

"Bait. You'll lure him into our trap."

She couldn't let that happen. Not when she had leverage of
her own. "My parents are rich," she said. "They would pay you
a lot of money if you returned me safely to them." Darcy met
Excoria's eyes in the rearview mirror and saw the calculating
gleam. This might just work. "By tomorrow, you could be long
gone. No one would ever find you. A new identity. You could
have the life you've dreamed about."

The woman's thoughtful expression turned angry. "Quit
messing with my head. You probably think I don't know what
you're trying to do, but I'm not that dumb. You might have
money, but you're just an impure. The lowest of the low have
more status than you."

There she went with that "impure" stuff again. "Who cares if
I'm a virgin or not? It's not like I'm going to be a nun or anything."

Excoria laughed. "You think that's what it means?"

Now she was confused. If Excoria wasn't talking about virginity, then what was she talking about?

But she didn't have a chance to ask as Excoria pulled down a
bumpy dirt road. Darcy figured the woman was crazy. After all,
Excoria planned to kidnap Surlock. Darcy would not want to be
in her shoes when she did because she was pretty sure he wouldn't
go down without a fight.

The humming in her ears intensified. She reached up, massag-
ing them. Excoria chuckled. Bitch.

"Problems?"

"Whatever you put in my drink, and I know you put something in it, has made the humming in my ears worse."

Her laughter only grew louder. It didn't mix well with the humming and Darcy could feel a headache coming on. At least the bumping down the road had stopped. They were in front of a large abandoned warehouse. Darcy was pretty sure no one had used it in a long time. Most of the windows were broken out.

"Don't try anything," Excoria said as she cut off the engine, and climbed out.

"It's not likely I could overpower you, so why try? I'm still tipsy from the drink and this horrible humming is making my head pound."

"You still haven't figured it out, have you?" She opened the back door and motioned Darcy to get out.

No, and she didn't care if she ever did. Her first priority was escaping, and she knew she could take this scrawny bitch. Her self-defense classes were about to come in very handy.

As she scooted out, she moaned, holding her head. When she was standing, she slammed her elbow into Excoria's face, connecting with her nose. The other girl screamed. Darcy didn't waste any time, but took off running back down the road. She would cut across the pasture as soon as she rounded the corner.

The main road wasn't that far. She could jog to it. Except her jog was more of a stumble and weave, but she had one thing going for her—determination! Surely whomever she flagged down would have a cell phone so that she could call the police. Everyone had a cell phone nowadays.

She had almost reached the corner when she heard a high-pitched sound, and then something slammed into the middle of her back. She gasped for her next breath, stumbled and fell to her knees. It was all she could do to take a breath.

No, this couldn't be happening. She had to get to Surlock. She had to warn him before they took him. She began to crawl, but every time she moved, excruciating pain stabbed her. Now she couldn't even feel her legs. Had Excoria shot her? Was Darcy dying?

She heard Excoria's laughter as if it was coming from a long way off. Then a foot shoved Darcy onto her back. She cried out as pain set her body on fire.

Excoria squatted beside Darcy, shaking her head. In her hand was a gun. So this was it. She would take her last breath lying in the middle of a dusty dirt road and Surlock would never know she had fallen in love with him.

Love?

A tear slipped out of the corner of her eye and slid down her cheek. Yeah, she loved him.

Her gaze moved to Excoria. "Bitch."

Excoria laughed. "You're a fighter. I don't see many impures who are. Good thing you're so weak from the drink or you might have broken my nose. Then I would've been really mad."

"If you kill me, Surlock will make sure your death is slow and painful."

Excoria's humor died a quick death. "You aren't dead yet. Only temporarily paralyzed. If you're lucky, it will knock you out."

She wasn't dying? Relief washed over her. There was still a chance.

"Dying will come later, but not until we don't need you anymore. Now I have to get you to your cage."

She grabbed Darcy's ankles and began dragging her toward the warehouse. If being dragged down the road didn't hurt so much, Darcy might have laughed that Excoria had to exert herself.

Once they were in the warehouse, Excoria dragged her inside a cage. There were two of them. One for her, and one for Surlock. The humming in her ears grew louder. As if she didn't have enough to deal with.

She hurt all over and her hair was matted with dirt and twigs. She sniffed. She wanted to kill this bitch, but she couldn't move. Whatever Excoria had shot her with had almost completely paralyzed her. She could only glare at the other woman as she fought the drug weaving its way through her body.

Excoria slammed the door, then locked it, her chest heaving from the exertion. She glared at Darcy. "That should keep you nice and safe while I go back to the party." She ran a hand over her hair, then smoothed her stupid alien costume. "How do I look? Presentable, I hope." She smirked.

"You look like a moron," Darcy said, glad she could at least form words.

Anger flared in the other woman's eyes, but just as quickly dissolved. "But I'm free and you're locked in a dirty old cage. Oh, and don't bother screaming. No one will hear you."

"If Surlock doesn't kill you, I will."

Excoria stretched her arms out. "Come on, kill me then. What? Can't move? That's a shame. I'll tell Surlock you said hello." She waltzed out of the warehouse. The car started a few minutes later. Darcy listened as she drove away.

Now would be a good time to come up with a plan to escape. She tried to move her arm, but only managed to wiggle her fingers. That was a start. Maybe the drug was wearing off.

"Help!" So what if no one could hear her, and she sounded more like a dying goat than a human. Screaming made her feel better. "Help!" Her voice echoed in the hollowness of the room.

Silence.

This wasn't fair.

But at least something good had come from it all. She knew who Surlock was now. Correction, Prince Surlock. Unless Excoria was totally crazy and didn't even know who she was.

The humming in Darcy's ears worsened. She was totally screwed.

CHAPTER 23

Surlock had been searching for Darcy almost two hours and still hadn't located her. Panic seared through him.

Peter had laughed and said they were probably both searching for each other and not crossing paths. Surlock could see his point. There were twice as many people at the party now. There was barely room to breathe.

Surlock headed for the French doors, planning to use the band's microphone to call out to Darcy. Just as he stepped outside, a man wearing a red cape and horns approached. He grabbed Surlock's arm.

Surlock frowned, and the man released him.

"Are you Surlock?"

"Yes." Surlock looked at him. Could this man know him? Surlock didn't recognize him. He was of average height with dark hair. Something about him seemed familiar, though.

"Darcy sent me to find you. Said you were dressed like a wolf." His voice shook as if he were nervous or scared.

"What's the matter? Where is she?"

"She fell. I told her I would get you. I think her ankle is broken."

"Take me to her." What had she been doing that she would fall? Probably trying to find him. He should never have let her out of his sight, but there had been so many people jostling him, he'd let go of her arm and the next thing he knew, she'd been swallowed by the crowd.

He followed the man down the steps toward the side of the house. No wonder she had fallen. There was no light here, and as they continued, no people. Surlock began to get suspicious. He grabbed the man's arm.

"Where did you say she was?"

"Just on the other side of those bushes."

Someone moaned.

"Darcy!"

"Surlock," came a muffled response.

Relief flooded through him that Darcy could respond. He hurried around the bush and saw her lying on the ground, her back to him, softly crying.

"Where are you hurt?"

She turned over. Surlock saw it wasn't Darcy at all. "What is this?" he growled.

"Your worst nightmare." The man behind him laughed. Surlock whirled around, and saw the gun. It didn't matter. He roared, and charged the man. The man fired, hitting Surlock in the chest.

The roaring in his ears was back, but he couldn't stop it this time as his legs buckled and he went to the ground. "Darcy," he managed to say.

"She'll be dead before you come to. Sorry, but you know as well as I that impures are an abomination."

Surlock's head pounded as the world around him went dark. No, Darcy wasn't going to die. He wouldn't let that happen. But right now, he knew there wasn't anything he could do. The humming slowed, then stopped, and he didn't hear anything else.

"Is he breathing?" Excoria asked. By the gods, Nivla would have her head if Surlock died, even though she wasn't the one who'd shot him. Nivla couldn't very well kill his own son.

"He's breathing," Ekon said. "I knew it would take a lot to keep the prince knocked out. He's a big man."

She looked down at Prince Surlock. Not bad looking, either.

There was a lot of naked flesh showing. What would it feel like to run her hands over his muscles and pretend for a moment that he lusted after her as she had lusted after him through the years?

"Let's get him on the cart. It's going to take us a while just to get him to the car."

And Excoria was pretty sure she would be doing most of the work. Ekon wasn't going to exert himself too much.

They rolled Prince Surlock onto a cart with wheels. The prince was definitely big, but she did enjoy touching him. His body was hard and muscled.

He was also very heavy as Ekon pulled one end of the cart and she pushed the other. They were both breathing hard by the time they got to the car. Surlock was still out. She was thankful for that. She hadn't liked the look in his eyes when he'd realized she wasn't Darcy. How she wished to be Darcy for a brief moment and have him look at her with desire.

But no, she hadn't been good enough for the prince on New Symtaria. He'd sneered at her advances. But who was sneering now?

They got him inside the car. She climbed into the driver's side again. Ekon didn't like to drive, so that chore was also left to her. Not that she really minded. She just let him think she did.

It wasn't far to the warehouse. Once they were there, they used another cart to haul Surlock inside, putting him in the cage next to the woman's. The drug had almost worn off the impure. She was sitting up, leaning against the bars of the cage. When she saw Surlock, she tried to move. It apparently took too much effort, and she gave up.

"Surlock," she said.

Ekon curled his lip. "Quiet, impure! You will not say the prince's name. You are unworthy."

"Screw you!" Darcy spat.

Excoria hid her smile. She would have enjoyed telling Ekon that, but didn't have the courage. When Ekon took a menacing step toward the impure, she grabbed his arm.

"Leave her. She's not worth your time."

He took a deep breath. "You're right. Nivla will be here soon."

Her eyebrows rose. "Nivla? Will the exchange take place so soon?" Her stomach curled. He was the last person she wanted to see right now. She knew he would come sooner or later, but she preferred later. Much later.

"There's been a change of plans." He looked at her with all the innocence of a rattlesnake. "Didn't I tell you?"

"No, I guess you forgot."

There was a whirring outside. Dread filled Excoria. Nivla was here. She had a feeling she wasn't going to like what was about to happen.

Ekon went to meet his father after the craft landed. Excoria hurried in his wake. The craft's door was opening. Three high warriors came out first. Then Nivla appeared, standing at the threshold. She was pretty sure he did it for effect. She rolled her eyes, then quickly bowed her head.

"Ekon, you have been successful?"

"Yes, Father."

"I didn't doubt you would be. After all, you're my son." His forehead wrinkled. "Why are you dressed like this?"

"I'm in costume, Father. So I could blend in at the party."

"Very wise." His lip curled in disdain when his gaze moved to Excoria.

She raised her chin. Could she help it if this was all she had to wear? She'd asked for funds and had only been laughed at.

They breezed past her without a word. She fumed silently as she followed.

"This is the impure?" Nivla asked as he glanced in Darcy's direction.

"Yes."

He stared at her for a long time. Excoria knew exactly what was on his mind. The slit up Darcy's dress had ripped and most of her legs were exposed. Nivla licked his lips as if he would like to join the impure inside her cage, but then he must have decided he didn't have time. He turned to the other cage.

"Ah, Prince Surlock." He clapped his son on the back. "You have done well, my son."

Excoria cleared her throat. Really, did he actually think his imbecile son had done everything by himself? Not hardly, and she wasn't about to let Ekon steal all the glory.

"Excoria, did you want something?" Nivla asked.

"I helped," she whined. That hadn't come out like she had planned. "I mean to say that I was the one who kept an eye on Prince Surlock, and I lured the girl here."

"You mean the impure?" He scoffed. "I wouldn't think she would be a problem."

"Well, she wasn't."

"Then it's settled. We're taking the prince to Rovertia to make the exchange for our Great Leader. You will stay here and dispose of the impure."

"And then what?"

He waved his hand as though she was a bothersome gnat buzzing around his face. "Then you will continue as before, hunting other impures."

"But—"

Nivla squared his shoulders while his son smirked. "You have a problem with my orders?"

She bowed her head, placing the back of her hand against her forehead. "No, Great Leader."

"Good." He turned to his men. "Load the prince on the craft. It's time we leave."

They were none too gentle with the prince as they carried him to the craft. Excoria stepped outside and watched them take off. There went her dreams of riches. They wouldn't even bother to mention her part in the prince's capture. All of the credit for this mission would go to Nivla and his son. She was nothing to them, so nothing in the way of wealth or honors would come her way.

She picked up a rock and threw it as hard as she could at the departing craft. Not that it would even come close to its mark, but it made her feel a little better. If there was any way she could get revenge, she would!

Now she had to dispose of the impure. And worse, she still hadn't eaten, and she was starving.

She stomped back inside the warehouse. The woman eyed her warily.

"I have to kill you," Excoria told her. "If I don't, someone else will. Then they would come after me." She shrugged. "You know how it is."

Excoria opened the door and stepped inside. The girl tried to move away, but the drug hadn't worn off completely. Excoria knew from experience it would leave her incapacitated for several more hours. Excoria wasn't sure if that made her job more difficult or not. She hated watching the impures struggle as they attempted to escape. They were like worms on the floor, wiggling and squirming.

She really, really hated this part.

"I can't die," Darcy said, her voice bleak with denial.

"Everyone has to die," Excoria said. "It's a fact of life. You'll just be leaving a little sooner than you'd planned."

"But I haven't lived my dream," she murmured.

Excoria knew she shouldn't engage in conversation with the impure, but she was curious. She knew about dreams and what it felt like to have them crumble at your feet.

"What was your dream?" she asked.

"I wanted to work as a private investigator."

Excoria snorted. "That's it? You wanted a job? Why didn't you just do it?"

"Because I lacked the courage."

"Think about it this way: You won't have to worry about it anymore."

CHAPTER 24

Surlock opened his eyes and blinked, trying to clear the fog that shrouded his thoughts. Where was he? His gaze moved about the enclosure. He was in a cage. It was small. Barely enough room for him to lie on his side and even then, he had to curl his legs.

But why? He tried to stand, but his legs wouldn't cooperate. He finally grabbed the bars and pulled himself up. It took all his strength. His mind was foggy, and it was difficult to concentrate.

Then it hit him. The party. Darcy. Looking for her. Some woman pretending to be her. He'd been shot with something that had knocked him out.

The breath went out of him, and if he hadn't been holding on to the bars, he would have gone to the floor. Where was Darcy? He looked around, but didn't see her.

"Darcy!"

A few moments later a door whooshed open and a man stepped inside. He was short and fat, with a large nose. "I see our captive is awake," the man said.

"Where's Darcy?"

"Dead, by now. I had her killed," he said as if she had been nothing.

Everything around Surlock stopped moving. His knuckles

turned white as he gripped the bars. The weakness he'd felt threatened to topple him. Darcy was dead? He closed his eyes tight against the pain that ripped through him. By the gods, not Darcy.

Surlock glared at the man and saw pleasure flit across his face. "You lie!" Surlock said.

"Lie? No, I haven't lied." He shook his head. "Why do you look so shocked? She was an impure. I'm a rogue. Second in command," he puffed out his chest. "I'm Nivla, and rogues kill impures." He brushed at his coat sleeve.

"No, she can't be dead."

"Please tell me that you didn't care for her," he sneered. "But of course you did. Your brothers have mated with impures. They might as well have wallowed in sewage. Symtarian blood should never mix with other races."

Surlock reached through the bars of the cage, growling. Nivla stepped back, fear on his face. Then he relaxed and smiled.

If Surlock could've gotten a few inches closer, he would have strangled the life out of this man. He was a lunatic with his talk of impures. What was that supposed to mean?

"Ah, yes, I see it in your eyes. You really don't remember who you are." He laughed. "This is quite amusing. I wish I could keep you around longer. What fun I would have."

Surlock stretched his arm farther, but it was still not far enough to reach Nivla. He looked at the bars as if he would rip them out.

"The cage is quite strong. You can't escape," Nivla told him with a cocky smirk.

"Know this." Surlock glared at the man. "I will kill you." Some of the color left the man's face. "If it takes the rest of my life, I will hunt you down and squeeze the very breath from your body. I'll do it slowly so the pain lasts for a very long time."

Nivla visibly swallowed. "You can't kill me. I'm a pure Symtarian. It's against the law to kill me. You would be put to death." As he talked, Nivla began to gather his confidence, his words becoming stronger.

Surlock wanted to smash the smirk off his face. "I don't care," he said. "My life *was* Darcy, but you've taken her from me. I would welcome death rather than live without her."

The man opened and closed his mouth like a fish out of water, then abruptly turned. The wall opened when he waved his hand. He stepped over the threshold without another word. The door closed silently behind Nivla, leaving Surlock alone with his thoughts, his pain and building fear that the man hadn't lied.

No! He shook his head. Darcy couldn't be dead. He would feel it, and he didn't.

When he closed his eyes, she was as alive as she had been at the party. He saw her smile, smelled the sweet scent of the perfume she liked to wear. He could feel the heat of her body as it pressed against his, the softness of her lips.

"By the gods, you can't be dead."

There was a roar throughout the craft that had others looking warily around as if the demons of the night had been let loose.

Surlock dropped to his knees, all his strength drained. How could he live without her? She was his heart, and now it had stopped beating. He loved her, and he hadn't realized it until he no longer had her in his life.

His strength ebbed. It was as though his soul had left his body. He let the drug that still lingered consume him once again. At least in dreams, he could still be with his love. He closed his eyes. Darcy smiled, opening her arms. He walked toward her, and found peace.

"Wake up!"

Surlock forced his eyes open, blinking as the bright lights shone in his eyes. When memory came back, it brought deep searing pain that made him gasp.

He looked up and saw the face of the man who had so callously told Surlock that he'd had Darcy put to death. Surlock slowly came to his feet, his eyes never leaving Nivla's face. The man shifted his weight from one foot to the other.

"Are you ready to die?" Surlock casually asked, as though he'd only made a simple comment about the weather.

"You're in a cage." Nivla squared his shoulders. "You cannot hurt me."

"But I won't always be in a cage. Do you want to wait? It would be easier for you if I killed you now. You wouldn't have to worry about it for the rest of your life. Not that I'll let you live very long."

Rather than answer, Nivla raised a gun. Surlock hadn't seen it tucked close to the man's side.

"Are *you* ready to die?" he countered, then fired.

The pellet hit Surlock square in the chest with a hard thud. He looked down, saw a drop of blood trickle down his chest. He staggered back, falling to his knees.

"It's only a tranquilizer, and not as strong as the last one. Just something to keep you a little more docile during the exchange. You asked if I was ready to die. I'm not, and I plan to take every precaution to stay alive." He laughed. "Don't look so angry. Someday you'll thank me for killing the impure."

The room swirled, then darkness closed around Surlock again. He welcomed it. At least drugged, he couldn't think, he couldn't feel the pain. Nivla was actually doing him a favor. When he was free, there would be plenty of time to hunt Nivla down and kill him . . . very slowly.

But sleep didn't come. Nor did Darcy's image. Nivla was right, the drug only made everything around Surlock move in slow motion.

The craft he was on touched ground. The door swished open and men entered his room. Surlock watched through blurry eyes as the back of the craft opened. His cage was moved to a platform with rollers. He growled and reached for the bars, but his movements were slow and awkward. He heard laughter, and knew Nivla was amused. Let him find humor in the situation. Surlock would have his revenge some day.

They wheeled him outside. It was dark, but different from the dark he knew. It was more of a deep gray-black and the air was heavy, muggy and smelled much like rotting flesh. Where was this place? He could feel death hovering around him. Maybe Nivla planned to kill him after all.

The humming in his ears grew louder.

"I don't care," he mumbled. There was no fight left inside him.

He heard another craft. It didn't look like the ones he'd seen on the Internet, but it looked familiar. After it landed, another cage was rolled out, with a man inside, but this one stood tall. Surlock watched him, and saw the evil oozing from his pores.

"Nivla, it's good to see you again." The man in the cage spoke in a silky smooth voice.

"Zerod." Nivla touched the back of his hand to his forehead and bowed slightly.

Zerod? The name sounded familiar.

"What have you done to our brother?" a strong male voice asked.

Familiar again. Surlock tried to push himself up, but his arms refused to cooperate. He finally gave up. He recognized the voice, though, and he knew this man would help him.

"Open my cage," Zerod ordered.

"Enjoy your freedom while you can," the other man said harshly. "We'll have you back behind bars before you can harm anyone else."

Zerod laughed. "You would have made a great rogue warrior, Rogar. Are you sure you won't join my ranks?"

"No, but I will destroy you."

"Give my best to your mate."

Surlock had Nivla in his line of vision. The man was starting to sweat and the longer the other two men talked, the more nervous he looked.

"Great Leader, we should leave," Nivla finally said.

"I agree. This planet stinks," Zerod said. "Release me so I can be gone from it."

Planet?

Visions flashed across Surlock's mind. A castle high in the wilderness. Surrounded by forest. Quick flashes. His head pounded. The humming was deafening. He grabbed his head, moaning. He knew these men, but yet, he didn't. He saw pictures, but nothing made sense, nothing connected.

"Unlock the cage!" Rogar said.

The door opened. Surlock struggled to his knees, grabbing the bars. Nivla was getting into his craft, but he turned at the last minute and smiled, his eyes full of all the cruelty that lived inside him. Surlock bared his teeth as the craft's door closed.

"Surlock, are you all right?"

Hands lifted him. He turned, seeing the face from his earlier vision. Confusion filled him.

"Kristor, help me with him," Rogar said.

"By the gods, I'll kill them all," the other man said, grabbing Surlock's other arm as they half carried him toward their craft.

Surlock looked at him. The other man from his vision. These were his brothers. Yet he didn't really know them.

"I don't know who I am," he said.

The two men exchanged looks.

"It's okay, little brother. Our mother will help you remember."

"Can she help me forget?" he asked.

Surlock didn't think so. As they took him to their craft, his mind was a tumble of questions. But right now, he couldn't summon the energy to ask any of them.

Once inside the craft, they put him on a bed. Another man began to examine him. He was elderly, and reminded Surlock of Dr. Wilson. A healer, he supposed. There were some things he remembered automatically.

"We were told he has no memory," the one called Rogar said.

"I still think you should have let me go after them, especially now that Zerod is loose again."

This was his brother Kristor speaking. He was bigger than Rogar and looked as if he could tackle a whole army of men without blinking twice.

"Do you know who you are?" the healer asked.

"I think I'm Prince Surlock. But I don't know this person," Surlock said.

Kristor fisted his hands. "Did Nivla do this to you? Did he cause your loss of memory?"

Surlock's smile was slow. "No, Darcy did."

The healer cleared his throat. "It may be a few days before he starts to make sense. It could be the drugs they gave him."

Surlock shook his head. "No, Darcy hit me over the head because I scared her. I lost my memory. She was helping me find it, but they took us captive." He swallowed hard, but his pain rose to the surface despite his best efforts to keep it at bay. "Then they killed her."

He closed his eyes, letting the dregs of the tranquilizer, and his depression, lull him back to sleep. He didn't know when the craft landed, didn't see the worry on his mother's face, the pain in his father's eyes or the concern of his sisters. Nor did he know when they carried him inside the castle.

He didn't care. He was content to stay lost in his dream world.

"I'm here, Surlock," Darcy said.

He looked around, and then his gaze landed on her. By the gods, she was the most beautiful thing he'd ever seen. "I've missed you," he told her.

She laughed, the sound swirling around him like a tumble of beautiful colors. He took her in his arms and lifted her high, then let her body slide slowly, sensuously down his.

"I think you're very bad, Surlock."

"That would be Prince Surlock."

"Oh, Prince Surlock, is it?"

"Yes, and I'm going to carry you off to my castle and keep you safe. I'll not let any harm come to you."

Her eyes were sad as she looked into his. "But how can you keep me safe. I'm dead, remember?"

He sat up with a start, his cry of pain echoing through the halls of the castle. "Darcy! Come back!" He reached out, but was surrounded by darkness.

And silence.

CHAPTER 25

"He won't awaken, Mother," Karinthia said. "He's suffered a great loss." Her mother's soft blue eyes filled with tears.

Karinthia had never seen Jadar cry and it broke her heart that her mother would suffer so, almost as much as seeing Surlock in this condition. "What can we do?"

"We have to cast the circle of power and healing," Jadar said.

"He's so weak it could kill him."

"If we don't, he will die for sure."

"And if he returns to us, what will he be like then? He's lost his lifemate. I've seen Symtarians go crazy or die because they've lost the one they were meant to be with. Surlock won't like being brought back."

Jadar fisted her hands. "I'm his mother. I refuse to lose one of my children. We will prepare the circle and may the goddess of all things living grant me his life."

"But—"

"No, we will cast the circle. It's the only way to save him."

Karinthia bowed before her Queen Mother, touching the back of her hand to her forehead. "Yes, Mother." Her mother left the room to prepare.

Karinthia straightened and stared down at her brother's sleeping form. Tears filled her eyes. She had always been closest to

Surlock. It broke her heart that he would have found his life-mate, only to lose her to a rogue. She clamped her lips to keep her anger inside.

Nivla was almost as evil as Zerod. If her father hadn't created the law that no Symtarian could kill another Symtarian, Karinthia would have killed him long ago. He'd hurt too many of her people.

Fear weaved through her as she thought about the ramifications of what Nivla's actions had produced this time. He might have already caused Surlock's death. Losing your lifemate could be a slow, painful way to die. She gripped the footboard on his bed. Maybe she would risk the consequences of killing Nivla if Surlock crossed over.

No, she wouldn't let Surlock die! The end of his life wouldn't happen as long as she had breath left in her body! The goddess would save him. Karinthia had to believe that.

She walked around the bed. "As much as you would like to step to the other side, brother, I refuse to let you go. We will cast the circle and bring you back to us." She leaned over and kissed his forehead. Unnatural heat radiated from him, almost burning her lips.

This wasn't good. They needed to cast the circle soon or he would be lost to them forever. She hurried from the room to ready herself.

Karinthia knew where her mother would be. She quickly changed into her blue robes and joined Jadar outside. Deep in the woods, six stones standing like sentinels surrounded a large stone slab. The sun dipped low on the horizon, casting eerie shadows around them.

The scent of sweet night flowers perfumed the air. Karinthia began to relax. Magic was all around her. Her pulse quickened in response. This was where she was most comfortable, surrounded by the elements. Where she felt closest to the gods and goddesses that once walked among the people.

There was a rustle through the leaves. Karinthia turned, then smiled. Her sister Ciara wore her red robes. She moved to her place. Her sister Mischa, wearing black robes, came with her. Their mother took her place at the head of the circle wearing her white robes.

Jadar began to chant the prayer of strength and guidance. Then, one by one, she removed five small stones from the pocket of her robe, invoking the spirit of the goddess to join them this night as she placed them on the slab.

When all was made ready, her brothers and father carried Surlock into the circle, placing the jewel-encrusted litter on the stone slab. They didn't look at the women as they moved to the outside of the circle, then to the edge of the woods, offering protection if needed.

Symtarian men were fierce warriors and had courage beyond compare. Some even had powers of their own, but it was the women who were gifted with magic. The men knew when they were not needed. Instead, they would stand guard on the fringes, one man at each point, so the women would not be interrupted.

Jadar raised a golden chalice. "To the goddess of light, I ask that you bring my son, your prince, out of the darkness and back to us." She lowered the chalice, then set it on the slab. Next she took a knife of silver and made a cut above her wrist. She didn't flinch. This was her son. Her blood ran into the chalice; then she bound her wound tight before taking her place in the north.

Karinthia stepped forward. For a moment, she could only stare at her brother. Was he alive? Were they too late to save him?

"He still breathes, daughter," her mother's voice whispered as if she'd read her eldest daughter's pain.

Karinthia drew in a ragged breath and raised the chalice. "To the goddess of rain, I pray you will wash his soul clean of his pain and let him live again." She took the knife and made a cut above her wrist, letting her blood flow into the vessel. She set the chalice and the knife down, bound her wound tight, then took her place in the south.

Ciara moved next to the slab. Karinthia saw tears shimmering in her sister's eyes, the only visible sign that she was shaken to see her brother like this. She raised the chalice.

"To the gods of fire, I pray you will warm his blood with life." She then made a cut above her wrist and let her blood flow into the chalice. She also bound her wound tight, then took her place in the west.

Mischa, the youngest of the daughters, moved to take her place. She raised the chalice with hands that trembled, but her voice was strong and sure. "To the gods of wind, I ask that you breathe life back into my brother." She, too, made a cut above her wrist and let her blood flow into the chalice. After she bound her wound tight, she carried the chalice to her mother, then took her place in the east.

Their mother raised the chalice high. "I give the goddess the blood of her children and call on the powers of light, wind, rain and fire to descend from the four corners of the universe and save Surlock, Prince of New Symtaria."

Glittery light swirled around the stones like a snake, then lit the slab as though the sun had come out from behind the clouds. Next came fire. Flames licked at the stones. Fire engulfed the slab, but before it could burn, gentle rain quieted the heat and it became a warm glow. As wind joined them, it brought the fragrance of life and all things living.

"Thank you, goddess, for your power so that my son can be healed if it be your will." She took the chalice, raised it high once more, then poured the blood down the center of Surlock's chest. "With this blood we, the children of the goddess, the keepers of the magic, ask that you return Surlock to the realm of the living."

Lightning streaked across the night sky, followed by thunder so loud it made the ground shake.

A voice filled the air. "You have always served me well, Jadar, and you have taught your daughters to do the same. I give your son back to you."

"Surlock," Darcy cried. *"Don't leave me."*

Something was drawing Surlock out of the cold gray darkness that swirled around him. He fought against the pull. He wanted to stay deep in the shadows that protected him from pain, but the force bringing him back was too strong.

He sat up, crying out with a roar that echoed through the woods. His head whipped to the side. Where was she? Where was Darcy? Who dared to rip her from his arms!

Torches lit the area. He lay on a stone slab. He saw his mother and three sisters, and he knew them. Memories returned in rapid succession. His life, and who he was, playing out as though watching one of Darcy's movies. Anger and pain ripped through him as he realized how much he'd lost.

"Chinktah, I am back!" he told his animal guide. "And vengeance will be mine!"

His mother blew across her open palm. Silvery dust sprinkled over him.

"No!" Surlock knew what she had done as his body grew weak.

"You must sleep now. Let your mind and body heal. It is for the best."

But it wasn't for the best. He wanted to destroy those who had harmed Darcy.

Ah, no, not Darcy. Not his love, his life.

Darkness closed over him, but this time it was different because Darcy wasn't there, and the pain was unbearable.

CHAPTER 26

Surlock slowly came awake. He was in his old room at his parents' castle. For a moment, he lay there, looking at the canopy above him. He didn't want to think, he didn't want to feel.

His stomach growled, reminding him it had been a while since he'd taken nourishment. Hunger pangs gnawed at his insides—along with guilt. How could he think about eating when Darcy was gone?

He sat up, swinging his legs over the side of the bed. He sat there for a moment. Pain gripped him. By the gods, he couldn't bear the pain. He finally stood, going to the closet. He grabbed the first thing he came to and dressed. A bathroom connected to his old room. He used the facility, then stared at his reflection above the sink, noting how haggard he looked. Then, for a brief moment, he saw the eyes of the wolf.

It is good that you have returned, Chinktah, his animal guide, told him. *I had thought you would be lost forever.*

You tried to reach me through the humming in my ears and my dreams. I see that now, Surlock said.

But as usual, you were too stubborn to listen.

Forgive me, Chinktah.

We are a part of each other. I can do no less.

Surlock left his room, going down the stairs, and with each step he took, anger forced his depression aside. He would make Nivla pay for what he'd done to Darcy.

Muted voices grew louder as he approached the main area. He walked inside the room, saw his family gathered, saw the worry etched on their faces. His brother Kristor's lifemate, Rianna, looked at him, eyes filled with pity before her gaze skittered away. Callie ran her hand over her stomach, which was swollen with his brother Rogar's child. Conversation stopped when the others saw him.

"You have connected with your animal guide?" his mother asked.

"Yes, and I have my memories back." He saw the bandages on his mother and sisters' arms and knew they had cast a healing circle. "Thank you for what you have given me."

"I'm glad that you are back, brother," Karinthia said.

His gaze fell on his older sister. "It's good to know who I am and where I come from."

"You are well, son?" Surlock's father looked toward his wife, who nodded her head. He strode to Surlock and hugged him tight. "I worried about my youngest son. It would have grieved me greatly if you had not returned to us."

An ache grew deep inside him. Surlock knew his pain would never heal. But he could understand why his family had not wanted to suffer the same. His father stepped back, clearing his throat.

"Thank you for saving my life," Surlock told Kristor and Rogar.

"You would have done the same," Rogar said.

Kristor nodded in agreement.

Surlock knew they were right. No risk would have been too great. "But now we have another problem. Zerod is free again. We must capture him or more impures will be killed. I won't let that happen to another one."

"Are you strong enough to travel?" Rogar asked.

"I am."

Karinthia stepped forward. "I'm going this time." She looked at her brothers. "I can use my magic if need be."

Their mother nodded. "Yes, it's your time. I have seen it coming. We must do more to protect our people, and the impures are our people, too."

"Then are we ready?" Surlock asked.

"Yes," his siblings answered as one.

Leaving took longer than Surlock expected. He wanted to wrap his hands around Nivla's throat. Surlock knew he couldn't kill him, but Nivla didn't know Surlock wouldn't break his father's law. He would make Nivla suffer for the rest of his life, though.

By early morning, they were on their way back to Earth. His brothers and Karinthia talked and planned. Surlock listened. He knew what he had to do first.

"We'll be landing near where your craft is," Kristor said.

Surlock nodded. "Excoria pretended to be Darcy. That's how they captured me. She may still be in the area. I will pick up her scent and see what I can find, but I have to take care of something first."

"You will find Darcy's essence there." Kristor spoke solemnly.

Surlock was surprised to see the bleakness in his brother's eyes.

"I could not live without my mate. I can only imagine the pain you're going through, and it hurts me. It hurts us all. You must find peace within yourself." He handed Surlock a small device. "When you need us, push the button, and we will find you."

Surlock nodded, unable to speak. Kristor was a strong warrior, but since he'd found his lifemate, a softer side had come through.

They landed. When Surlock stepped from the craft, what he had lost hit him with full force, almost taking him to his knees. Karinthia grabbed his arm to steady him.

"I'll be all right," he told his sister. "I have to face this alone."

She nodded and stepped away.

Surlock walked through the woods, making his way back to the trail where Darcy had hit him over the head. He stopped for a moment, closing his eyes. He could almost smell her scent.

A hawk cried overhead.

Surlock looked up and saw that Kristor had shifted into his animal guide. He would find the warehouse Nivla had told him about. He doubted the female rogue would be there, but they would check it out just the same.

Surlock walked up the trail that led to the house. The last time he'd walked it, he and Darcy had mated in the meadow. He hadn't lost the time afterward; Chinktah had been able to emerge for a short period.

As he approached the house, he wondered what Ms. Abernathy had thought when they hadn't returned from the party. He didn't want to tell everyone Darcy was dead. But how could he not tell them?

He took a deep breath and stepped to the back door, lightly knocking.

There was a clicking noise behind him.

Surlock turned and stared at the weapon Ralph held.

"Make one wrong move and I blow your brains out," Ralph said, and from his expression, Surlock thought he might do just that.

"I offer you no harm," Surlock told Ralph. "I came to speak about Darcy."

"Yeah, and you'd better tell us where she is, too."

The door behind him opened, but he dared not take his eyes off Ralph.

"Is this the man who kidnapped Darcy?" a man behind Surlock asked.

"That's him all right," Ralph said.

"I didn't kidnap Darcy," Surlock told them. Now he wasn't so sure he wanted to tell them she was dead, either. He only hoped Ralph didn't suddenly develop a nervous twitch.

The man stepped from behind Surlock. He had dark hair threaded with streaks of gray. His face was aged and lined with worry.

"Just tell me where my daughter is and we'll pay the ransom."

"Ransom?"

"The note that came yesterday said you wanted two million dollars. We're gathering it now. All we care about is our daughter, and if you've harmed her, I'll kill you with my bare hands."

The world stopped moving as the blood rushed to Surlock's head. "Darcy is alive?" Hope sprang inside him. Hope and joy and a burst of love. The emotions hit him full force, almost toppling him. "She's alive?" he asked again.

Ah, no, if this was a lie, then he would surely be doomed. He couldn't bear the pain of losing her twice.

Chapter 27

Darcy glared at Excoria's back. First chance she got, she was knocking this chick's lights out. Not that she would get that chance any time soon. The bitch had tied the ropes pretty damned tight.

And if Excoria shot her with that tranquilizer gun one more time, she'd do more than knock her lights out. She'd cram the gun down her throat—then knock her lights out.

Even in her dazed state, Darcy recognized the estate next door to her parents' place. The Bishops were still in France. She was so close to her parents, to her home and everything she loved, yet so far away.

No, that wasn't quite true. She wasn't close to Surlock. She had no idea where he was. From what she could gather from El Stupido, he was being used to trade for some high-up official who was imprisoned in Surlock's country.

When Excoria suddenly turned around, Darcy quickly lowered her gaze and became the docile captive again.

"I'm going to call them." Excoria reached for her cell phone.

"It's too soon," Darcy told her. "It will take time for my parents to gather that much money without raising suspicion." She only hoped she could stall Excoria long enough for her parents to contact the FBI and get them involved. Excoria had been a little smarter than Darcy had given her credit for and warned her parents she would kill Darcy if law enforcement of any kind was brought in.

"No, I think I should call them." Excoria paced back and forth, plucking at her clothes as if they scratched her. She stopped to glance nervously out the window. "This was a bad idea," she mumbled. "Nivla will be really mad if he discovers I didn't kill you."

Darcy had to distract the other woman so she would stop worrying about what would happen if the others found out she hadn't carried out their orders. Excoria was clearly off her rocker. Darcy would never understand why a bunch of terrorists would even enlist this woman's help. She kept talking about im-pures.

Apparently, everyone thought Darcy was an impure. They were all lunatics. Maybe they were against people who weren't virgins and still unmarried. A weird religious cult. Wow, they were going to have their work cut out for them if they planned to destroy all the unmarried non-virgins.

Right now, fear and indecision were written all over the woman's face. Darcy certainly didn't want Excoria to regret not killing her.

"You know, there are a bunch of places to hide," Darcy said. "You could go anywhere you want with the money my parents are going to give you for returning me *safe* and *unharmed*."

Excoria was thoughtful. "Yes, I can, can't I?"

"You won't have to take orders from anyone."

Excoria sighed, then plopped down on the sofa. She'd removed most of the sheets that covered the furniture. Ms. Bishop was going to be really pissed that Excoria was staining her expensive white sofa with her dirty boots. Not that Darcy would mention that to her.

"You could easily afford a house like this," Darcy said.

Of course, by the time Excoria paid all the taxes, and bought furniture, and paid any HOA fees, there wouldn't be much left. Besides the fact the IRS would want to know how she'd acquired so much money in the first place. No, she'd let all that be a surprise. That is, if Excoria even had a chance to spend any of the money.

Excoria looked around with a dreamy expression. "I could have all the jewels I wanted, too."

Obviously, she'd been living in a cave and hadn't heard the economy was in the crapper.

"Oh, well, yeah." Darcy nodded her head. "You could drape your body in jewels. Diamonds and rubies. Emeralds as big as your thumb." Mostly paste, of course. Two mil just didn't go as far as it used to.

Excoria sighed. "I've heard that on Nerak they have jewels just lying around. Can you imagine that?"

Nerak? Darcy had never heard of the place. "Is that somewhere in Australia?"

Excoria snorted. "You still don't have a clue, do you?"

No, and Darcy doubted she ever would. But, just to play along, she shook her head. "I don't guess I do."

"Nerak isn't another country," Excoria smugly stated. "It's another planet."

Great, the woman was crazier than she'd thought. What? Had they all escaped from a loony bin? Had they taken Surlock because they wanted to break out this Zerod guy? He was probably crazier than all of them put together. Maybe Surlock was a doctor who worked there or something.

A cold chill swept over her. What if Surlock was one of the crazies?

Surlock was not crazy! Just because he had humming in his ears didn't make him crazy. She had humming in her ears that was steadily getting worse, but that didn't mean she was crazy. . . .

Lord, she hoped it didn't mean she was crazy.

She had to think, and keep Excoria talking. The woman was clearly off her rocker. But if Excoria was busy talking, maybe she wouldn't be thinking about killing Darcy.

"So, does that mean you're an alien?" Darcy asked as nonchalantly as she could.

Excoria chuckled, leaning forward. "I'm an alien. You're an alien."

"I'm an alien," Darcy repeated. The situation was worse than she'd thought.

"Part alien, which makes you an impure." Excoria crossed her legs at the ankles. A clump of dirt fell off one boot and landed on the sofa.

"Oh, I thought it meant I wasn't a virgin," Darcy mumbled.

Well, at least now they wouldn't be going around killing off the non-virgins who weren't married. That would save a lot of lives.

"And my parents were aliens?" Darcy asked. Uh-huh, sure.

"Only one of them. I know that much about your ancestry. They were disposed of by rogues."

Disposed of. Hmm, she supposed that meant they were dead. "How sad. Did you kill them?" It was best to play along with the lunatic.

Excoria frowned. "No, of course not. I didn't become a rogue until a couple of years ago."

"Up until then you were just your run-of-the-mill alien."

Excoria cocked an eyebrow. "A Symtarian isn't an average alien, and New Symtaria is far more advanced than Earth. And we're not aliens where I come from. You would be the alien."

"And New Symtaria is a planet." Wow, now this was getting strange. How could this chick know that she and Surlock had been searching for New Symtaria?

"Of course it's another planet."

"And Surlock is a prince."

"Exactly." Excoria smiled as if she was a teacher and her dumbest student had just figured out how to add one plus one.

Time to make her worry just a little. "Then since Surlock and I care deeply for each other, if you harm me in any way, he will probably hunt you down and squash you like a bug."

Excoria's mouth opened and closed, then her brow wrinkled in thought. Suddenly, she brightened. "I'll have a lot of money, and I'll make sure he never finds me." She stood up. "I'm going to get some air and check the perimeter. You'd better not try to escape or I'll squash *you* like a little bug." She sashayed into the other room.

A few minutes later, Darcy heard a door open, then close. She might have ten minutes or so to make her escape. Thank goodness, Excoria had left her hands and feet tied in front.

As she tried to wiggle loose, Darcy realized Excoria was pretty good at tying knots. All she had accomplished so far was rubbing her wrists raw.

She began to gnaw at the ropes with her teeth, cringing at what her mother would think if she could see her, especially since she'd forced Darcy to wear ugly braces until she was fifteen. It had not been fun when the kids tagged her with the nickname "Metal Mouth."

Her teeth were not strong enough to even gnaw a strand of the rope. Frustration filled her. She was only two miles from home, and the thought was killing her.

Was Surlock looking for her? Was he even alive? Her stomach clenched. His captors were as crazy as Excoria. Were they both doomed?

No, she wouldn't think about the lunatics who'd taken him prisoner. Or the fact that terrorists usually killed their hostages. But if he was really a prince, would that make a difference?

She didn't know what to think anymore and this infernal humming in her ears was driving her up a freakin' wall! She couldn't stand it. She struggled to her feet and began to hop toward the front door.

"Where are you going?" Excoria said behind her.

"Out of here."

"I don't think so."

Darcy knew she was screwed when she heard the click of the tranquilizer gun. Ah, hell. It popped her right on the butt. Tears filled her eyes as she sank to the floor, thankful the carpet was plush. The Bishops had spared no expense. Still, it wasn't the most comfortable landing.

Excoria strolled over, then rolled Darcy onto her back.

"Think of it this way—you can take a nice long nap. You don't have to worry about getting free. I loaded this one with a little something extra, so enjoy all the colors and pretty lights." She laughed as she moved out of Darcy's line of vision.

Excoria was right about one thing, Darcy didn't feel the urge to run. No, she was just going to lie here and trip out. Her mom would be so pissed when Darcy told her Excoria had given her drugs. Darcy had never even experimented in college.

Wow, what an intense shade of blue. This was really cool. Her mouth was so dry, though, and she was getting the munchies. Maybe some chips and French onion dip and chocolate cake.

Yep, she was screwed. But the lights were pretty.

CHAPTER 28

"Don't move or I'll blow your brains out," Ralph repeated, the gun aimed at Surlock's head.

Surlock vaguely heard Ralph's voice. The words kept repeating over and over in his head that Darcy might still be alive. If there were any kind of chance she might be . . .

Surlock squared his shoulders and looked Darcy's father straight in the eye. "I may be the only one who can save her," he told him.

The man studied him for a moment, then sighed warily. "Put the gun down, Ralph. Even if this is a trick, we have no choice but to go along with him. I want my daughter back alive. Let's go inside."

Ralph didn't look happy about taking the gun off Surlock, but he did. Mr. Spencer and Surlock went inside. Ms. Abernathy was in the hall, arms crossed in front of her.

"Do you know where our girl is?" Her words were cold and hard, but Surlock noticed her bottom lip tremble.

"No, but I'll find her, and I'll make sure she comes home safely."

She nodded. "I'll put a pot of coffee on." She looked at Surlock. "And I'll make some fresh juice."

"I know you've been staying here, but I'm not sure why," Mr. Spencer said. "I think I need more of an explanation than what

I've been told." He looked at Ms. Abernathy. "We'll be in my study. Make sure Mary isn't disturbed. She was up most of the night and this is the first decent sleep she's had." His hard gaze landed on Surlock. "The doctor had to give her a shot early this morning."

Ms. Abernathy dabbed at her eyes with the hem of her apron, then quickly left the room.

Surlock followed Darcy's father into his office. Once he was seated behind his desk, he began firing questions so fast they all ran together.

Surlock held up his hand. "I think I need to start from the beginning and tell you everything."

Mr. Spencer frowned, but motioned for him to take a seat. "It will be nice to hear the truth. Just make sure it is the truth."

"I was sent here to protect Darcy," Surlock said.

"My daughter doesn't need protection. At least, she didn't until you arrived." When Surlock didn't speak, Mr. Spencer waved his hand. "Go on, go on."

"She was walking in the park behind your home when she saw a wolf. The wolf left, and when I stepped from behind a tree, I startled her. She held a heavy branch and acted on instinct, hitting me over the head."

"Good for her! I made sure she took self-defense classes before she went to college. It served you right for scaring her!"

Surlock wasn't so sure in this instance.

"Go on," Mr. Spencer urged.

"I lost my memory and only recently did it return, but too late to protect Darcy."

"You know who has her?"

"I do."

"Then we should call the authorities." He reached for the phone.

Surlock shook his head. "That's the last thing we need."

His hand stilled. "You can't get her back by yourself unless you're some kind of James Bond. Are you?"

"No."

"One thing I don't understand—why does my daughter need your protection?"

He hesitated. "Because of who she is."

"You mean because she's rich?"

"No, because of her mother and father."

Mr. Spencer sat forward, resting his hands on his desk. "She's adopted. If we couldn't find out any information on her biological family, then why would I believe you could?" His eyes narrowed. "Maybe you're in on the kidnapping and you want to make sure I deliver the money. Who are you exactly?"

Surlock rose to his full height, bowing slightly. "I am Prince Surlock Valkyir from the planet New Symtaria. We're a race of shape-shifters. Darcy was born to a Symtarian mother and a man from Earth. Because she's an impure, rogue Symtarians want her dead. That is why I was sent here to protect her." He downed his head in shame. "Except I failed."

Mr. Spencer came to his feet, his chair slamming against the wall behind him. "Now you listen to me, you fruitcake. If my daughter isn't in this house within the next hour, I'll have so many FBI agents crawling all over you that you'll wish you had never heard the name Spencer."

He wasn't taking the news as well as Surlock had hoped.

"I can prove it," Surlock told him.

Mr. Spencer clamped his lips together.

Surlock figured he only had a short time to actually prove his words. This might be too much information, too soon, but he didn't have time to break it to Mr. Spencer gently. "The wolf Darcy saw was my animal guide. It lives within me."

Chinktah, I need you.

Of course you do. I don't know how you survived so long without me.

Chinktah, I really don't think we have time to argue the point.

Okay, okay.

Surlock felt the familiar pain grip him, but held steady. The pain wasn't so bad he couldn't stand it. Over the years, shifting had become more of a discomfort.

"What's going on? Where did this fog come from?" Mr. Spencer jerked his gaze from side to side.

"This is what happens when a Symtarian shifts," Surlock managed to tell him before everything went dark. He closed his eyes. The change was taking place. Hands became paws, a thick coat of fur covered his skin.

It is good to be out again, Chinktah said.

Surlock opened his eyes and blinked. As always, it was as if he saw through Chinktah's eyes.

Mr. Spencer eased behind his chair, using it as a shield. "How did a wolf get in here? If this is some kind of trick—" He rubbed his hands over his eyes. "This isn't happening. Lack of sleep, that's all it is."

Chinktah jumped to the desk, and papers scattered to the floor.

Don't scare him to death, Surlock warned.

Well, I don't see what's so hard to believe. You told him the truth, and now here it is, staring him in the face.

I think that's the problem. Can you look a little less menacing, and stop staring him in the face?

Whatever.

Chinktah lay down on the desk, then lowered his head to his paws.

"There's a wolf on my desk. A really big wolf. This isn't a trick. It is real." He took a deep breath. "Okay, I believe you, I think."

Chinktah stood and jumped to the floor. *Good enough?*

Very well done, Surlock told his guide.

Then find your soul mate so we can leave this planet. I tire of people who refuse to accept anything they cannot see or touch. Besides, you were quite depressing when you thought she was lost forever.

The fog began to roll in again. Surlock felt the change taking place.

The fog began to dissipate. He blinked. He was always a little confused when he returned.

"You're naked," Mr. Spencer said.

Surlock rose to his feet, casually reaching for his clothes. "On my planet, we don't perceive the naked body as something embarrassing or shameful."

"You are what you say you are," he mumbled as if he were still digesting everything.

"I am, and now I need to find Darcy. She is with one of the rogues."

Mr. Spencer's face drained of color. "The ones who kill people like my daughter."

Surlock grimaced. "Yes."

He reached for the phone. "I have to call the FBI."

Surlock grabbed Mr. Spencer's hand. "No, it will only give the rogue more reason to kill her."

"But how can you find her by yourself?"

Surlock's smile was grim. "I'm not alone." He took the small device Kristor had given him and pushed the button. It would lead his siblings to him. "Help will soon arrive. Then we will find her."

Mr. Spencer wearily rubbed his forehead. "Darcy, my baby girl, is part alien."

"That's one way to look at it," Surlock said. "If you came to New Symtaria, you would be the alien."

The door to the office opened and Ms. Abernathy poked her head inside. "You'd better come quick. We have company."

"I think my brothers and sister have arrived," Surlock said as he hurried out of the room.

"I should've known," Ms. Abernathy said. "They look as handsome as you."

He followed Ms. Abernathy out back.

His sister was holding Ralph's gun, examining it actually.

"Careful, sister."

"It's very antiquated," she said, looking up.

"But it will still kill."

She handed it back to Ralph, who took it with a grateful sigh.

"You summoned us?" Rogar said.

"Darcy may still be alive. The rogue who has her asked for ransom money." He nodded toward Mr. Spencer. "This is her father."

"I found a warehouse not far from here," Kristor said, nodding toward the east. "There were signs of rogues, and a female."

"That warehouse has been vacant for years," Mr. Spencer said. "You didn't find Darcy, though?"

Kristor shook his head. "No, I'm sorry, she's been moved. The rogue who has Darcy probably guessed we would eventually find out Darcy was alive and come looking for her. They must have left in a car because I lost the trail quickly."

Mr. Spencer's shoulders drooped. "Then she could be anywhere."

"We'll find her," Surlock said.

"Our animal guides can find her easier," Rogar spoke quietly so only Surlock and his other siblings heard.

Surlock turned back to Mr. Spencer. "Do you have something of Darcy's?"

He stuck his hand down in his pocket and brought out a necklace with a silver heart. "She wears this a lot. I thought if I kept it close she would be okay."

Kristor took the necklace, then looked between Mr. Spencer and Ralph. Ms. Abernathy had also joined them outside. "We'll find her and bring her home, but we need a private place to . . . change. You can understand our need for privacy."

Mr. Spencer nodded. "The guest house. You can leave through the back," he said quietly. Then he said louder, "Ralph, give me that gun and go inside. Ms. Abernathy, do you think we could have some of that coffee now?"

"Yes, of course." She hurried inside.

Surlock quickly led his brothers and sister inside the guest house, then looked at each one of them. "We have to find her. Do you think you could give us a little magic, sister?"

He handed Karinthia the necklace. She closed her eyes, holding it close, then passed it to Rogar. He did the same, then Kristor, before he gave it back to Surlock. Surlock placed it in the center of their circle.

"I'll do my best." Karinthia took Surlock's hand, then Rogar's. Kristor clasped his brothers' hands and the circle was joined. "Spirit of the goddess, go with us as we search for Darcy." The sound of thunder roared around them even though the sun shone brightly outside.

They each called their animal guide. The fog rolled in, thick and heavy as the four shifted. When it cleared, a hawk, a jaguar, a wolf and a unicorn stood in a circle. They each left in different directions as they began their quest to find Darcy.

And heaven help the rogue if Darcy was harmed, Surlock thought. Maybe he would break his father's law after all.

Surlock had to believe she still lived, though. She was his life, his love, and soon they would be together.

CHAPTER 29

D arcy was definitely going to kill Excoria. After the pretty swirling lights had gone away, she was left with a headache the size of Texas, and a damned humming in her ears that could have vibrated the walls.

Where the hell was Surlock? He should have saved her by now. She sniffed. If he was still alive, that is. Oh, Lord, he had to be alive. She loved him.

What if he didn't love her?

She didn't care. Well, she did, but it would be enough to know he was alive.

"I hate tears," Excoria snarled. "You're not going to start crying, are you?"

"No, I'm not going to cry." Darcy sniffed. She'd be damned if she'd let the bitch see one tear slip from her eyes.

"Good." She flipped open her cell phone and punched in a number. Then waited. "Have you got the money?" she asked the person on the other end. Excoria gripped the phone tighter, her mouth turning down. "Your daughter might not have a few more hours."

Darcy's heart skipped a beat. Excoria was talking to her dad. At least, she hoped Excoria was talking to her father and not her mother. She groaned. Her mother would probably know what was going on, though. She would be hysterical. No, she would be beyond that by now. Her mom would have taken to her bed, trying to escape her worst nightmare. Maybe the doctor had given her a shot to knock her out.

Great, her mother would never let Darcy become a P.I. now. That is, if Darcy lived through all this, because she wasn't quite so sure Excoria would keep her end of the bargain. She might take the ransom money and still kill Darcy. That way, her crazy cohorts wouldn't come after her. Excoria could truthfully tell the terrorists she had done away with the impure. Sheesh, it sounded like something out of one of her dad's James Bond movies.

Excoria suddenly turned to Darcy. She'd had the decency to help her back into the chair. Only after Darcy had whined a lot, though.

"He wants to speak to you." Excoria held the phone up to Darcy's ear.

"Dad?"

"Oh, God, you're alive. I was so afraid."

Her heart began to break. "I'm fine, Dad. I—"

Excoria moved the phone. "There, are you satisfied?" She paused. "She'll only be fine for one more hour. If I don't have the money by then, she won't be fine." She snapped the phone closed.

"I hate you," Darcy said.

"So what else is new?"

"You're going to regret ever taking me captive when Surlock finds me."

Excoria's hands trembled. That was the only sign she was paying attention. "But he won't find you," she finally said.

"Are you so sure about that?"

Excoria straightened. "By the time he discovers your body, it will be too late for him to do anything. I'll be long gone and I'll make sure he never finds me."

The room began to spin around Darcy and she could barely breathe. "You never planned to let me go."

Excoria shrugged. "Sorry. I can't take that chance."

Oh, God, her parents would be devastated when Excoria didn't deliver their daughter. They would never stop looking for her. Not until they discovered her lifeless body.

Surlock would be furious. She knew him well enough to know that he would find Excoria, and God help her when he did. No, Darcy didn't want God or anyone else helping the bitch. She wanted her to rot in hell.

Excoria seemed quite unconcerned she was about to end someone's life. What kind of a monster was she? Darcy was glad when the other woman left the room. If she had to be around her much longer, Darcy was afraid she might say something to anger her even more. There was no guarantee that Excoria might not go ahead and kill her at any time.

Damn it, Darcy wasn't ready to die. She hadn't lived her dream. Hell, she hadn't lived. She'd always been too afraid to take a chance. Her mother had only been an excuse. She could have talked her mom into letting her get a job if she'd tried hard enough. No, Darcy had been too afraid of failing to push the issue.

She finally saw how really dumb that was. She might have succeeded as a P.I., too. Not that she had done such a great job discovering Surlock's identity. He might be a prince or he might not be. Although right now she was pretty much leaning toward believing he was a prince. Why else would terrorists take him prisoner so they could trade him for their leader?

Excoria, of course, had already lost her mind. The terrorists probably dealt in illegal drugs, and she had inhaled more than she should have. Her brain was already fried. She was not an alien. But that still didn't change the fact she was evil and planned to kill Darcy.

She wiggled her wrists—again. The ropes were too damned tight. She'd only managed to rub her wrists bloody.

She looked around the room for a weapon. The lamp was too heavy to lift. There was a candy dish of sorts on the coffee table. Could she hop over to it, and get back without falling down? Maybe her ballet lessons would finally pay off. It was worth a try. But when she tried to stand, nothing happened. She frowned. Her legs were still numb from the tranquilizer.

She tried rocking her body to a standing position, but she had no strength. Now what was she going to do?

Excoria strolled back into the room. "Good news!"

"You're going to let me go?"

She frowned. "No, your father has the money. I told him where to take it. I said that as soon as I had it, I'd call and tell him where you are."

Hope rose inside her. "You're going to let me go after all?"

Excoria shook her head. "No, I just told him that."

"And that's your good news?"

"Well, yeah." Confusion wrinkled her brow.

God, could she be *that* stupid? "You can't just kill me!"

"Yes, I can." She held up the small gun. "I'll just load up the gun with enough of the drug to kill you. It won't hurt. I'm not that cruel. Just think of it like this, you'll be going to sleep . . . forever."

She went to a black box that was sitting beside the sofa and began going through the pellets.

"Please don't kill me," Darcy begged. She hated begging, but it was her last hope.

"You know what I look like. You'd tell everyone. I've watched enough of your television and that's what they do. The victim tells the captor she won't say anything, but the minute the captor lets her go, bam, she runs to anyone who will listen. Then the poor captor is locked away when all the kidnapper was trying to do was make a decent living."

"You've got to be fucking kidding me?" Darcy said, staring at her.

"No, I'm not. I saw it on television." She stood and raised the gun, pointing it at Darcy.

"Yes, but did you see the *CSI* episode where they capture the kidnapper?"

"*CSI*?"

"Oh, yeah, that's the show to watch. You've got to be careful of the evidence you leave behind. Pffft, they could have you in custody within a few minutes after getting the ransom money. You wouldn't want that to happen."

Excoria glared at her.

"You'll tell me everything you know about this evidence," Excoria said.

"Or what? You'll kill me?"

"I can remove the sleep agent and exchange it for something that will make you scream in pain for hours before you finally die."

"You can do that?"

"I can do many things."

"I'll tell you everything I know," Darcy said and wondered how many investigative procedures she could come up with before Excoria felt she knew enough, and then killed her anyway. It didn't matter. Darcy would suck up every last second she could get.

Ten minutes later, Darcy knew she was quickly running out of time. Excoria's eyes were glazing over. Hell, Darcy's brain was glazing over.

"You'll need to get some booties to wear on your feet," Darcy said. Yes, she was inventing stuff now. "That way they won't be able to trace the tread of your shoes. And a surgical mask."

"Why would I need a mask?"

Mask? Why would she need a mask? Think! She drew in a deep breath. "So they won't pick up your scent." Okay, that was really lame.

Excoria nodded. "You're right."

"I am?" She cleared her throat. "I mean, of course, I am. I told you I could get you through this."

"I have plenty of information." Excoria looked sad. "Now I must say good-bye."

She looked sad? Ha, she wasn't the one about to sleep forever. "You don't have to kill me. Just leave me tied up. At least give me that much. We're practically friends now. I swear I won't tell a soul."

Excoria shook her head and Darcy knew this was it. Her mother and father might never know what had happened to her.

"I'm truly sorry."

"At least let my parents know I'm"—she cleared her throat—"dead. Give me that at least."

Excoria nodded, tears filling her eyes. "I will send them a letter."

Darcy sighed with relief, then closed her eyes and braced herself.

Something crashed through the window in the other room.

Darcy's eyes flew open. "I'm saved!"

Excoria jumped and screamed. The gun went off, the pellet thudding into Darcy's chest.

Well, hell!

She glanced down at her chest. "Great, someone crashes through the window to save me and it's too damned late." She blinked, wondering if it was the drug that was making her see a wolf. It was crouched in attack mode, teeth bared, hair standing up on its back.

Darcy's gaze transferred to Excoria. She looked scared shitless, which served Excoria right for killing her. She sniffed. Now no one would ever know what had happened to her. The wolf could dine on them for a solid week. Her bones would be buried all over the neighbors' estate.

Eww.

"No, don't hurt me," Excoria screamed.

A hawk suddenly flew into the room, circled, then landed on the coffee table. Next came a jaguar, then a unicorn.

Wow, she was really tripping. If this was what drugs were all about, she wanted no part of them. Although the unicorn was pretty. Still, she'd much rather live in the real world. Except that would never happen.

A tear slipped from the corner of her eye as a heavy fog rolled across the room. This must be the end. Everything was getting foggy. Good-bye, Mom and Dad. Good-bye, Surlock. Oh, God, they could've been so good together.

The fog began to clear.

Maybe this wasn't the end just yet. She blinked, but her eyes were still filled with tears so it was hard to tell what exactly she was looking at.

Had she died and gone to heaven? There were three naked men and a naked woman in the room and the animals were gone. She blinked again.

One of the men was Surlock. What a nice fantasy to have before she checked out. Damn, she was so sleepy, she couldn't . . . she couldn't . . .

She closed her eyes on a sigh.

CHAPTER 30

Surlock rushed over to Darcy and began untying the ropes that bound her wrists. He glanced at the woman who was cringing on the sofa, immediately recognizing her. She'd thrown herself at him more than once on New Symtaria, but he'd rejected her advances, knowing that she only wanted his wealth.

"Darcy, I'm here. Can you hear me?"

Nothing. Darcy didn't move.

"I should kill you for this, Excoria," he said.

"You can't. It's against Symtarian law." Her voice trembled.

"Maybe I'll get my father to change the law. He is, after all, the king."

Excoria whimpered

"What did you shoot her with?" Rogar asked.

"Perepsicol mostly," she whispered. "But I added the sleeper so she wouldn't have pain. I'm not so cruel that I would want her to suffer," she whined.

Karinthia had grabbed one of the sheets that covered a piece of furniture and was tucking the end between her breasts, but when she heard Excoria's words, she drew in a sharp breath. "The drug of death. Do you have the antidote?" She didn't wait for Excoria to answer, but rushed to the box on the floor and began searching inside.

"The green capsule, but it may be too late," Excoria whispered.

Surlock hurled himself toward Excoria and wrapped his fingers around her throat. "By the gods, I'll kill you for this," he growled. He wanted her dead, no matter the outcome, no matter the consequences.

Rogar grabbed his hands, but couldn't break his hold. Surlock watched Excoria's eyes begin to bug out and felt intense satisfaction.

"Kristor, I can't break his hold," Rogar said.

"Leave me!" Surlock told his brothers, but they didn't listen and pulled him off Excoria.

Excoria grabbed her throat, coughing, then curled into a ball and began to cry hysterically.

"Our laws will take care of her," Rogar told him. "Would you end Excoria's suffering now? Or let it carry out through the rest of her life?"

At his words, Excoria began to cry louder.

"You're right," Surlock agreed.

"I have the antidote." Karinthia loaded the capsule, aimed, and shot Darcy.

Darcy's body barely flinched when the pellet entered. Surlock knew they might be too late. He couldn't lose her, not after just finding her again.

"I have to cast a circle," Karinthia told him, placing her hand on his arm.

"Can you do it alone?" Surlock asked.

Her expression was grave. "I don't know, but I will try."

"What can we do?" Kristor asked.

Karinthia scanned the room. "Take her to the long table." She pointed to the other room. "Lay her on it." She turned to the eldest of the siblings. "Rogar, you help Surlock. Kristor, bind the rogue."

"With pleasure." He walked toward Excoria.

Excoria tried to shrink into the sofa.

Kristor might not be the oldest, but he was the largest. He

controlled the security on New Symtaria. No one dared invade their planet. He did not take kindly to someone in his family being threatened.

Surlock lifted Darcy's limp body and carried her to the table while Rogar cleared the surface with one sweep of his hand. Darcy reminded Surlock of a broken doll. Only traces of the makeup she'd worn to the party streaked her face, and her dress was torn and tattered so that it barely covered her.

After he laid her gently down, he took her hand and raised it to his lips. Her skin was cold, lifeless. "Darcy, you can't leave me," he said. He knelt beside the table and began to pray.

Karinthia hurried from the room. When he heard her return a few minutes later, he looked up and saw his brothers had also knelt beside the table to pray with him.

They stood up as their sister placed on the table a wineglass, a knife and five small stones she must have found outside.

Rogar and Kristor had both donned sheets, knotting them at the waist. Rogar caught Surlock's frown and smiled.

"We remember how our soul mates reacted to our nakedness. We don't want to frighten your soul mate when she comes back to you."

"Will she come back to me?" Surlock asked and all the pain he felt came through his words.

Rogar gripped his shoulder. "Our sister is powerful. If anyone can bring Darcy back, it will be she."

"It is time," Karinthia said.

Surlock brushed his lips across Darcy's, then the three brothers stepped away from the table, moving out of the circle his sister would cast. For as long as he could remember, men were not allowed in the women's circles. The most powerful of all Symtarians were high-born women. Magic had been passed down from the goddesses for centuries, though sometimes a little would spill over to the men.

Surlock only prayed this would work. Was his sister strong enough without their mother and other two sisters? Could she bring Darcy back? He drew in a deep ragged breath. Karinthia had to succeed. If she didn't, he would surely go crazy without Darcy in his life.

The three brothers quickly lowered their gazes so that their sister could create her magic.

Karinthia began to chant the prayer of strength and guidance. Then one by one she raised the stones, invoking the spirit of the goddess to join her.

Next she took a knife of silver and made a cut above her wrist and let her blood run into the glass, then bound her wound tight before she raised the crystal glass once again.

"To the goddess of light, I ask that you bring this woman out of the darkness and back to us. To the goddess of rain, I pray you wash her soul clean of pain and let her live again. To the goddess of fire, I pray you will warm her blood. To the goddess of wind, I ask that you breathe life back into her. I give the goddess my blood and call on the powers of light, wind, rain and fire to save this woman, soul of my brother."

Glittery light swirled around the stones like a snake, then illuminated the table as though a bright light had been turned on. Next came fire. Flames licked at the stones, then engulfed the table. But before it could burn, gentle rain quieted the heat and the fire became a warm glow. As wind blew softly in, it brought the fragrance of life and all things living.

Surlock clenched his fists as he offered up his own prayer to the goddesses, begging them to give Darcy back her life, to give him back his life. Without her, he knew he couldn't live.

Karinthia poured the blood over Darcy's still form. For a moment, it looked as if nothing would happen, then a shining light began to appear in one corner of the room. Karinthia dropped to one knee and bowed her head. The brothers did the same.

Surlock raised his head just enough to watch this miracle. His chest began to ache just looking at the beautiful sight before him. The light had begun to take the shape of a woman.

"Goddess," Karinthia breathed.

"You have used your gift well, my child." Her voice was as light as air.

The warmth of her voice flowed over Surlock. Tears filled his eyes. She was too beautiful to look upon for any length of time. Silver hair trailed over bare breasts and her body glowed with an ethereal light. Though her top half was that of a goddess, her bottom half was that of a prancing white horse.

"It is good that you wish to protect the ones who were born part Earthling and part Symtarian. They are not impures as some have called them. They are new life that will save our people from extinction."

"Thank you, goddess." Karinthia's whispered words floated over to Surlock.

"You must protect them from the rogues. I give this charge to you, Karinthia."

"Thank you, goddess, for placing your trust in me," she replied reverently.

The goddess reached out, waving her hand slowly over Darcy. The goddess faded and as she did, Darcy sat up straight, gasping for air as though new breath had just been breathed into her body.

"Darcy!" Surlock ran to her, wrapping her in his arms. "I was so afraid I had lost you forever." Tears filled his eyes as he clasped her tightly to him.

"Surlock, what happened?" She looked around. "Ohmygod, I thought I was dying. I saw the wolf again, and some other animals. But then there was a fog and the animals were gone, but there were two other men and a woman and they were naked," her words spilled out, then just as suddenly stopped as she looked at his siblings. "Actually, they looked a lot like these people. What's going on?"

"These are my brothers, and my sister."

Darcy suddenly smiled. "You remember."

"Yes."

"Are you really a prince?"

"From New Symtaria. It's another planet. We're a race of shape-shifting people. The wolf, Chinktah, is my animal guide and he lives within me."

She sniffed as tears filled her eyes. "I know a good psychiatrist. We'll get you all the help you need."

His siblings began to laugh. He frowned at them and their laughter changed to coughs.

"You're part Symtarian as well. The humming in your ears is your animal guide trying to communicate with you."

"Darcy, I'm Rogar, Surlock's older brother and it was nice meeting you."

"You're leaving?" Surlock asked.

"I'm going to take Excoria back to the craft. I think you need time to explain everything to Darcy."

"I'm Karinthia." His sister stepped forward. "Surlock and I have always been close. I'm glad he found you." She smiled.

Kristor was next. "Little Darcy, it is good you came back. I don't think Surlock would have been worth being around if you hadn't."

All three stood together as the fog began to roll in. Surlock took Darcy's hand. When she opened her mouth to ask about the fog, he placed a finger against her lips. "Just watch. This is who we are. Who *you* are."

The fog cleared. Three animals were in front of them. Sheets on the floor. Darcy gripped his hand.

The jaguar jumped to the table, then regally bowed her head before jumping down. The hawk landed on the table, spread his wings, then flew away. The unicorn stopped beside the table and lowered his head briefly before joining the other animals.

Darcy turned to him. "I . . . I don't understand."

"I'll explain everything. First, you'll call your parents and tell them you'll be home tomorrow. Then I'll tell you everything."

"Yes, I think you're right," she said. What else could she do?

He helped her off the table. As they went into the other room, Excoria was stumbling out the door, surrounded by animals.

Darcy stopped in her tracks. "Are you sure I'm not hallucinating? Maybe I'm dead and just don't know it." She looked at him. "If I am, then I must be in heaven because you're here with me."

He shook his head. "You're not dead. My sister used her magic to heal you."

"I'm not going to die? I mean, like within the next few hours?"

He shook his head.

She breathed a sigh of relief. "Good, I'd hate to tell my parents I was alive only to keel over dead." She looked around, saw the phone Excoria had been using, and punched in the number of the house.

"Hello?" Her father answered in the middle of the first ring.

"Dad. I'm fine. Everything is okay."

"Darcy, is this really you?"

"Yes, Dad. Surlock and his brothers and sister saved my life. The rogue—uh, I mean my kidnapper—will be transported someplace where she won't be able to hurt anyone else." She took a deep breath.

"When will you be home?"

"Tomorrow. Surlock needs to explain some things to me. It's complicated, Dad."

"You mean about you being part alien and all?"

She moved the phone away from her ear and stared at it, then looked at Surlock. "You told him I'm part alien?"

"He needed to know."

She nodded. Of course, he was right. She moved the phone back to her ear. "And you believed him?"

"Not at first. I thought he'd escaped from the state hospital, but when a man changes into a wolf right in front of your eyes, it's hard not to believe aliens exist."

And yet, Darcy still had trouble grasping it. She supposed it was better than being werewolves. She mentally shook her head. "How's Mom?"

"She'll be much better when I tell her you're okay."

"Are you going to tell her I'm part alien?"

He paused. "I might wait to tell her that. Sometimes seeing is believing. Besides, she's had enough shocks."

"True." She cleared her throat. "Dad, I love you."

"I love you, too."

"I'll see you tomorrow." She slowly closed the phone. "That's done." She set the phone down, then turned and went into Surlock's arms. "Have I mentioned how much I love you?" There, she'd said the words out loud.

He pulled her closer. "I love you, too." His lips lowered to hers in a searing kiss that curled her toes. His tongue caressed hers, causing an explosion of desire to flood her body. When they finally broke apart, they were breathing hard.

Her heart soared. She'd never once imagined she could feel so much love for this man or that he would return her feelings. Darcy felt as if her world was completely in sync.

Well, except for the fact she was part alien. "Maybe you'd better tell me exactly who I am."

"Then you should sit on the sofa and I'll take the chair because if I'm too close, I'll never be able to tell you everything."

She knew what he was saying. It was all she could do to keep her hands to herself, but she needed to know where she came from. "Maybe you could give me the short version."

CHAPTER 31

"New Symtaria does exist," Surlock began, "but it's another planet. When the old planet was dying, the elders went in search of a new one. There weren't enough spacecraft so some of our people chose other planets. When a new home was found, there was much to be done. Many years passed. The old ruler died; the lost people were forgotten. They integrated with people from Earth, adopting their ways."

"How sad that your own people would forget about you," she said. "But why are these rogues trying to kill us?"

"Your blood isn't pure. Your father was an Earthling and your mother a Symtarian. They think it's an abomination, but it isn't. Our blood has become too pure. In some of our people, the animal guide has become more aggressive. That isn't what our goddesses and gods had hoped to accomplish when they chose to join with our people centuries ago. They wanted us to coexist."

"And I have an animal guide living in me?" Okay, she wasn't so sure about all this now.

"The humming in your ears, that's your guide trying to speak to you, but you've pushed her away for so long she can't communicate with you unless you let her out."

"I'm not sure I want her to come out."

He stood and moved next to her, taking her hands in his.

"Your animal guide is just as much a part of you as your Earth side. If you'll let her, she'll protect you from harm."

"I'm scared."

"Don't be. I'll stay with you."

"Promise?"

"Yes, I love you and I'll never leave your side."

"And all I have to do is let my animal guide through?"

He nodded.

"Will I shift into an animal?"

"If she thinks you're ready." He brushed his hand down her cheek. "Just close your eyes and think about her." His hand rested over her heart. She could feel the warmth of it against her skin and knew he wouldn't lead her down the wrong path.

She closed her eyes.

Silence.

"Nothing is happening," she whispered.

"Just concentrate. Communicate through your thoughts."

"You won't leave me?"

He took her hand in his. "I promise to stay right here with you."

"Good." She held fast to his hand and took a deep breath. Okay, he'd said she had to communicate through her thoughts. That would be like thinking to herself. She could do it.

Hi, I'm Darcy.

Sheesh, how lame could she be?

Surlock said I have an animal guide and that you've been trying to reach me. Her hands began to tremble. This wasn't quite as easy as it had sounded. Okay, she had to concentrate.

Did you know I was adopted? Learning I'm part alien is all kind of new to me. I'm sorry that you tried to communicate with me. I didn't know. That scared me, too, I guess. But I want to meet you. That is, if you still want to meet me.

The humming in her ears grew louder. Rather than block the sound or cover her ears, she accepted it, even though it became so loud, she could barely stand the noise.

There was a loud *pop*, as though her ears had cleared, then silence.

Are you there? Darcy asked.

I'm here.

The voice was soft, almost like musical notes. *You do exist,* Darcy said with awe. She hadn't really believed until this moment. Oh, she'd seen Surlock and his siblings shift, but she hadn't actually thought it could happen to her.

I've always been inside you, but I couldn't communicate. You always shut me out, her guide told her.

I'm sorry.

I understand you were frightened. We're together now.

What's your name?

I am called Amara.

Amara, it's a beautiful name. Darcy didn't quite know how to ask what she needed to ask so she just decided to blurt it out. *Am I going to shift into your animal form?*

Maybe we should get to know each other first.

Darcy tried to hide her relief, but she had a feeling Amara sensed her reluctance. *I think I'd like to get to know you better, too.*

They communicated their thoughts for what seemed like hours, and maybe it had been hours because when she finally opened her eyes, it was getting dark outside. Surlock was still beside her, still holding her hand. She smiled at him, then threw her arms around his neck.

"Thank you for giving my animal guide to me."

"She's been with you the whole time. I just aimed you in the right direction."

She pulled away and looked into his face. "The humming in your ears, that was your animal guide trying to communicate?"

Surlock laughed. "Yes, and he was getting quite irritated that he couldn't get through to me." His forehead wrinkled. "There's something I should tell you. When a male Symtarian mates, if he has extreme pleasure, he'll shift into his animal guide."

Her eyes widened as it dawned on her what he was saying. "You shifted in the park. I thought I saw the eyes of the wolf. Your animal guide is the wolf?"

"Yes. His name is Chinktah."

"I guess I'll meet him the next time we make love. Will he attack me?"

He snorted, then quickly covered the sound with a cough, but she knew he thought her question was funny. Well, what did he expect? She was new to this shifting stuff.

"It was an honest question," she said, scooting to the end of the sofa and crossing her arms in front of her.

He quickly joined her, wrapping his arms around her. "I swear I will never laugh at anything you might wish to ask."

"You're forgiven. Now, if you don't mind, I'd like to meet your animal guide." Her words were husky with need. She turned until she could wrap her arms around his neck.

He was only too happy to oblige as his lips met hers in a heated kiss. Surlock tore away what there was left of her clothes with little effort. Not that she cared. The dress was ruined anyway.

No, she was more concerned with the way his hands came around the front to cup her breasts, to squeeze the nipples. He ended the kiss and lowered his mouth to one breast. She cried out as his tongue scraped across the nipple, then sucked it inside his mouth.

She leaned back as the pleasure he created exploded inside her body. It was all she could do to pull away, but she did. She wanted this to be special. She came to her feet, then tugged on his arm. She already knew the utilities were still on.

"You've changed your mind?" he croaked out.

She laughed. "No, but I've been dragged through dirt, and locked in a cage. I feel grimy and dirty. There's something I've always wanted to do. Now's a good time. I'll race you upstairs."

Not waiting to see if he followed, because she was certain he would, she took off toward the stairs. He caught up to her before she had made it up the first step and scooped her into his arms. Not really fair since she was still so weak, but she didn't offer any protest.

"Which way?"

"To the first door we come to." She clung to him while he took the rest of the steps as if she weighed nothing at all. He made her feel sexy and oh, so alive.

At the top of the stairs, he turned right, then balancing her with one hand, he opened the first door. Good, it was the master bedroom.

"Ah, a bed. You want to mate in bed."

She laughed, wiggling out of his arms, and waltzed over to the bathroom door and opened it. "In the shower." Her voice was seductively husky and by the look in his eyes, she had pulled off being a temptress.

He didn't move.

Or maybe not. She wondered if there was a reason he didn't like the idea of making love in the shower. "Is something wrong?"

He slowly raised his gaze. "No, I just don't think I will ever tire of looking at you. You're beautiful."

Heat rose up her face, but her embarrassment was soon forgotten when he sauntered toward her, and the heat that flooded her body turned to that of passion.

He stopped when only inches separated them, and brushed the hair away from her face. "I thought I'd lost you forever. Nivla told me you were dead. I wanted to die. My life would have been nothing without you."

"I know because I feel the same." She took his hand and led him to the shower. She turned the water on, tested the temperature, then pulled him inside with her.

She kissed his lips, then his chest. She met his gaze, saw the fire flare in his eyes. She moved lower, her lips lightly kissing him. He drew in a sharp breath, moaned when she took him into her mouth and began to gently suck. She wanted to do this, wanted to know everything there was to know about him, wanted to make him feel like he'd made her feel.

She tasted, she caressed, then she moved back up, stroking, touching. He slipped inside her, filling her. She gasped, wrapping her hands around his neck. He pulled her legs up so they were around his waist, and he sank deeper inside her heat.

"Yes," she cried out.

He drove inside her. Flames of passion licked her body. He increased the tempo. In and out. In and out. She threw her head back, moaning, body quivering.

He cried out, and his body stiffened.

They gasped for each breath, clinging to each other.

"I don't think I will ever tire of making love with you," she finally managed to say.

He suddenly groaned. "I can't stop the shift," he said as he doubled up, sliding to the floor.

"Then don't. This is who you are, who we are." She turned off the shower and stepped out, grabbing a robe, glad that her neighbors had left so much behind.

She belted the robe as the fog rolled in. She heard Surlock moan. The fog slowly dissipated and she was left staring into the eyes of the wolf.

"Chinktah," she said. She braced herself as the wolf stepped from the shower and walked toward her. She tentatively held out her hand, praying Surlock had told the truth and the wolf wouldn't harm her.

The animal sauntered closer and licked her hand.

She smiled. This was her past, this was her future. A burst of adrenaline rushed through her. She was part alien. *Amara, I welcome you into my life!*

Sudden pain gripped her and she wasn't so sure she welcomed her after all. A moan escaped from between her lips as she crumpled to the floor. Chinktah lay down beside her as if he offered his support.

Was she dying? Her gut clenched. She blinked as her world went dark. The burning inside her intensified. She clutched her stomach. She could feel her body shifting, voices swirling inside her head.

Do not be afraid.

Not as long as you're with me, Darcy said. She closed her eyes tight and prayed for strength.

Then nothing.

Darcy didn't move. Something was definitely different.

Amara, are you here?

I am. Open your eyes and see your world through mine.

Darcy blinked several times. It was as though she were seeing through someone else's eyes. She saw Chinktah, but everything looked different.

What happened?

I'm Amara, your animal guide.

She could feel herself moving, and yet, she wasn't moving her feet. Then she was looking into the mirror and seeing her animal guide. Darcy relaxed as she looked into the eyes of a wolf.

Hello, Amara.

I have much to show you. Much more to tell you.

I'm ready.

With Chinktah at her side, they left the house, running through the woods. Darcy felt a freedom such as she had never known before. Her thoughts melded with Amara's. They were separate, yet one. Darcy realized her life had never really been complete until now. The missing piece of who she was had been found. Happiness soared inside her.

The circle of her life had finally joined.

CHAPTER 32

Darcy had called her father to let him know they were on their way home. He still hadn't told her mother that their daughter was part alien. That should prove interesting.

Or not.

"I'll be here beside you," Surlock told her as they walked up to the front door.

She nodded and took a deep breath, then straightened her clothes. Karinthia had returned to the Bishop estate with a database. It was a handy little device much like an IPod, only a little bigger. She had only to punch in what she wanted and it appeared.

Darcy liked Surlock's sister, and after talking to Karinthia, she discovered that the goddess had told Karinthia that she was to protect the impures and bring them safely home. Darcy had had a brilliant idea; now she only needed to convince her mother.

She opened the door and stepped inside her home, making sure Surlock stayed right beside her. Ms. Abernathy was walking down the hall, but stopped when she saw Darcy.

"It's about time you were getting yourself home," Ms. Abernathy scolded, but in a soft voice filled with unshed tears.

Darcy rushed to her and wrapped her arms around her. The housekeeper hugged her tight, sniffed loudly, then let go and stepped back.

"Your mother has been fit to be tied. You'd best make an appearance soon or we'll be calling the doctor to give the poor woman another shot."

Darcy smiled. "Then I'll do just that. Where is she?"

"In the living room with your father."

Ms. Abernathy looked at Surlock and gave him a rare smile. "Thank you for bringing her home."

"I could do no less," he said.

Ms. Abernathy looked between the two. "Yes, I suspect that's the God's honest truth."

Darcy and Surlock went to the living room. Her mother was half sitting, half lying on the sofa, a tissue wadded in her hand. Her father was sitting in one of the armchairs, looking more haggard than she'd ever seen him.

"Mom, Dad."

Her mother looked up, then jumped from the sofa and ran to Darcy. "My poor baby." She squeezed her tight, then held her at arm's length, then pulled her back for another bear hug. "I was so afraid. Dad told me you were okay, but I refused to believe it until I saw you with my own eyes." She suddenly let go of Darcy and turned a frown on Surlock. "Who are you?"

Darcy took Surlock's hand in hers and pulled him close. "Surlock saved my life." She glanced at her dad, who had moved to stand close to her mother. "Did you tell her anything?"

He suddenly grabbed Darcy and hugged her close. "I love you, baby girl." Then he whispered, "No, I didn't tell her. I'm a coward."

This was going to be a long day.

The phone rang. A few minutes later, Ms. Abernathy came into the living room. "Jennifer's on the phone." She glanced at Darcy. "She hasn't been back since the night of the party, so she doesn't know a thing. I thought you might say something to her just to let her know you're okay."

Darcy nodded, then took the phone. "Hi, Jennifer."

"And just what are you up to, girlfriend? I've been trying to call your cell since yesterday. It was as if you'd dropped off the face of the earth. I was starting to worry so I thought I'd call the house. What? Did that handsome hunk kidnap you?"

Jennifer didn't know just how close to the truth she was. "Something like that," Darcy told her.

"I crashed at Peter's, then we took a plane to Paris. We've decided to go into the party business together." She laughed. "Do not even ask what got into us. Annette came along for the ride, and I have to admit, they make a great couple. And I've met this wonderful man who has the most seductive Parisian accent you'll ever hear. I'm so sorry to leave you out of the loop, but I figured you and Surlock were having your own party." She chuckled.

"Uh, my parents are here. Let's talk when you get back."

"Sounds good, darling. I have a feeling my news will top yours. This guy is very delicious."

Darcy really doubted Jennifer's news could even come close to hers, but decided now was not the best time to mention it. "Talk to you later."

After she turned the phone off, Darcy looked at her mother. This was so not going to be easy.

"Mom, you'd better sit down."

EPILOGUE

D arcy stood outside her San Antonio office with Karinthia, admiring the new sign. Surlock came up behind her and wrapped his arms around her.

"It looks good, doesn't it?" he asked.

She smiled and nodded. "I finally have everything I want. My own business since my mother finally cut the apron strings, and best of all, I have you. I think she took the news that I'm part alien rather well."

He nuzzled her neck. "Because she loves you—as do I."

She chuckled and the three of them walked inside.

Okay, so it was sort of what Darcy had envisioned. She'd just never thought her business would be Alien Investigations, Inc. She and Karinthia had come up with a great advertising slogan:

> *Does your neighbor act a little odd? Does the cat you've been feeding look at you strangely? Did you hear a bump in the night? If so, for a nominal fee, we'll make sure you don't get probed.*

When Karinthia had told Darcy the goddess had given her the task of finding impures and bringing them home, Darcy realized what her mission in life was supposed to be. With the help of Surlock's family, they would make sure no more impures were killed. At least, they would to the best of their ability, and maybe they would be able to capture Zerod and Nivla in the process. No one would be safe until those two were locked away in a cage.

And who else to investigate reports of alien activity than aliens? Not that anyone would know they were really aliens. But if clients reported something odd, they could investigate, and maybe save an impure.

"I have something that needs your attention in my office," Darcy said in a loud voice as she pulled Surlock along with her. His sister snickered. Once they were behind closed doors, she turned and pressed her body intimately against his. "I don't think she believed me," she said, smiling.

"I don't think so, either. Do you care?"

She shook her head. "Not really."

When he lowered his lips to hers, she knew she had spoken the truth. She wanted to shout to the world just how much she loved him. Life was good.

Be a little IMPULSIVE with HelenKay Dimon's latest novel,
in stores now . . .

"Hello?"

Katie froze at the sound of the familiar male voice. Then her head whipped around. The main door was open, but the metal security screen was closed and locked. It would be hard for people to see inside and impossible for anyone to break it down, but, oh boy, could she see out.

It couldn't be. It couldn't be. It couldn't be.

She repeated the refrain as she stared at the outline on the other side of the steel screen. Dark hair, broad shoulders, and relaxed stance. She'd know that body anywhere.

That would teach her to want fresh air. If the stifling heat hadn't bothered her, she'd be hiding in the storage closet and ignoring him right about now.

"Can you hear me?" He looked right at her as he said it. Clearly he knew she was there. Could see her, despite the promises in the sales brochure about the door providing protection and privacy. It didn't seem to be doing either at the moment.

With wet hands dripping on the floor beside her sneakers, she stood there. "Uh . . ."

"Not sure if you can see me." He waved his hand. "We met at the Armstrong-Windsor wedding."

Met? Now there was an interesting word for what they did. "Oh, I know who you are."

"Yeah, I guess so." Eric chuckled in a rich open tone that vibrated down to her feet.

She could hear the amusement in his voice. Figuring out how to take it was the bigger issue. She rubbed her hands on the towel hanging out of the waistband of her khaki shorts and adjusted her white tee to make sure everything that should be covered was. "What are you doing here?"

"I can explain if you'll let me come inside."

Talk about a stupid option. "No."

After a beat of silence, he spoke up. "Really?"

He sounded stunned at the idea of being turned down. Apparently the big, important man didn't like it when people disagreed with him.

That realization was enough to make her brain reboot. While running held some appeal, it wasn't very practical. They lived on an island, after all. And she needed to know how he'd tracked her down. "I mean, why do you want to come in?"

She could see his broad shoulders through the thick safety mesh and the way he balanced his hands on his lean hips. He was a man in control of his surroundings, even though this part of town didn't fit him at all. He wore tailored suits and walked into a fancy high-rise office every day.

Many of the folks in the Kalihi neighborhood never ventured near the expensive restaurants and exclusive communities around the island. This was a working-class area with an increasing crime rate, older and lined with warehouses, a little rough. A place where words like "redevelopment" were thrown around but never brought to fruition. In other words, not the place where one would expect to find Eric Kimura.

"I wanted to talk with you," he explained.

She'd been afraid he would say that. "Okay."

He pressed his face close to the screen. "And people are starting to wonder why I'm screaming into a door, so could we take this inside?"

Last thing she needed was for him to be mugged. She tried to imagine explaining that bit of news to the cops . . . and to Cara.

"I'm coming." Katie rushed over, jangling the keys in her hand as she tried to find the one for the top deadbolt. "Here we go."

Eric didn't hesitate. The second she opened the screen, he pushed his way in and closed the solid door behind him. The controlling move should have made her nervous. Instead, she was strangely intrigued. Hunting her down took some work. Stepping into this neighborhood at five o'clock, which probably qualified as the middle of his workday, created a bit of mystery. Clearly he wanted to find her. Now he had.

He held out his hand. "Eric Kimura."

She stared at his long fingers before sliding her palm inside his. "Oh."

The corner of his mouth kicked up. "But you knew that, right?"

"Pretty much." The feel of that smooth skin against hers brought a rush of heat to her cheeks. She looked down at their joined hands, wondering at what point long turned to *too long* and she had to let go. "I watch the news now and then."

"Ah, yes. Not always the most flattering place to pick up information about me, but not a surprise." He frowned as if the notoriety didn't sit all that well with him. "So, do you have a name?"

"I figured you knew it since you tracked me here and all."

"I have my sources but the exact name was tougher."

Yeah, he had something all right. "Katie Long."

"The caterer."

Looked like he didn't quite know everything. She dropped his hand and backed up a step. No need for them to be this close, sucking up all the air in the room, when there was a big No-Eric zone right behind her. "Her assistant and sister. I'm surprised you went to the trouble to find me."

His head tilted to the side. The wide-eyed look made him look younger, less imposing, if only for a few seconds. "Why?"

This qualified as the strangest morning-after type conversation she'd ever had. "I guess this is the part where I say I've never done that at a wedding before."

He nodded. "For the record, me either."

"And where I insist I'm not the kind of woman who engages in thirty-minute sex romps with strangers." She actually wasn't but there was no way to sell that as a convincing story after the way they'd met.

"I'm not judging."

Of course he was. Hell, she was. When she'd vowed to turn her life around, she'd promised the days of putting herself at risk were over. She wouldn't do dumb things or get involved with the wrong guys. Eric didn't appear to be a loser, but he was most definitely wrong. He was her assignment. She was supposed to keep a safe distance and being under him didn't cut it.

"Maybe just a little judging?" She held up two fingers and squeezed them together.

"Any name I call you would apply to me."

"Very logical."

"You weren't alone in that room."

She tried very hard not to conjure up a visual image of his hands up her skirt. "Oh, I know."

"I admit, that sort of thing isn't a weekly occurrence for me."

She laughed. The contrast between the serious way his brows came together and the humor in his tone did her in. He might be good at sex, but he wasn't all that comfortable with the way they'd met.

That made two of them.

Be sure to look for
A DARKER SHADE OF DEAD
by Bianca D'Arc out now!

"This blows."

Dr. Sandra McCormick's voice echoed around the morgue. Well, it wasn't really a morgue. At least it hadn't been. The large room had been a perfectly good laboratory until the senior team members had decided to perform tests on cadavers. Now it was a morgue.

The temperature had been lowered to near freezing, and Sandra shivered in her lab coat. She'd donned her heaviest jacket under the lab coat she had borrowed from one of the men on the team who wore a much larger size, but it still wasn't enough. She was cold, dammit.

Cold, miserable, and all alone on night shift because she was low man on the totem pole. The science team had been together for a few months, working for the military on ways to improve combat performance. Specifically, they'd been trying to come up with substances that, when injected into people, would improve healing and endurance in living tissue. They were at the point now where they'd graduated from *in vitro* testing in Petri dishes to something a bit more exotic.

They weren't ready to try *in vivo* testing on living animals or people. Instead, the senior scientists had decided to take this grotesque step, administering the experimental regenerative serum to dead tissue contained in a whole, deceased organism.

Personally, she would've preferred to start with a dead animal of some kind, but only human cadavers would work for this experiment since the genetic manipulation they were attempting was coded specifically for human tissue. They didn't want any cross-contamination with animals if they found a substance that actually worked.

As a result, she was stuck in a freezing cold lab in the middle of the night, watching a bunch of dead Marines. It was kind of sad, actually. Every one of these men had been cut down in their prime by either illness or injury. They had all been highly trained and honed specimens of manhood while they were alive. Some of them had been quite handsome, but their beauty had been lost to the pale coldness of death. They were here because they had no next of kin—only their beloved Corps—and their bodies had been donated to science.

The room was dimly lit. Sandra only needed the individual lights over each metal table on which the bodies rested to do her work. She'd holed up at a desk in the far corner of the giant lab space, entering the data she collected hourly for each body into a computer. Her fingers were already numb from the cold, and it had only been three hours. Five more to go before the day shift would release her from this icy prison.

She heard a rustling sound in the distance as she blew on her fingers to try to warm them. Her chair swiveled as she lifted her feet, placing them on the runners of the rolling office chair.

"That better not have been the sound of mice scampering around in here."

Contrary to most medical researchers, Sandra had never really been comfortable with mice. Little furry rodents still made her jump, and she shied away from any lab work that required her to deal with the critters.

The room was dimly lit. The only illumination came from the computer screen and desk light behind her and the single light over each table. The whole setup gave her the creeps.

Deciding to brave the walk to the bank of light switches on the far side of the room near the door, Sandra stood. If she had to sit here with a bunch of dead bodies all night, the least she could do was put on every light in the damned room. Why she'd ever thought the desk light would be enough, she didn't know.

She'd gone on shift at midnight and was slated to take readings every hour until 8 a.m. when her day shift counterpart would relieve her. Scientific work sometimes required a person to work odd hours. Experiments didn't know how to tell time. When the researchers were running something in the lab, she usually got tapped for the late night hours. Normally she didn't mind. The lab was usually a peaceful, comforting place.

But not now. Not when it had been turned into a morgue. Or maybe it was more like Dr. Frankenstein's dungeon, only without the bug-eyed servant named Igor. She'd definitely seen that old Mel Brooks movie one too many times in college. Thinking about some of the funnier lines from the comedy classic made her smile as she walked down the aisle of tables toward the door and the light switches.

"*It's alive . . .*" She did a quiet imitation of Gene Wilder from the scene where he'd given life to his monster as she walked, chuckling to herself.

On either side of her were slabs on which the cadavers rested. A breeze ruffled one of the sheets that had been pulled over the body on her right.

It must've been a breeze. The sheet couldn't move on its own, right? She quickened her step, a creepy feeling shivering down her spine as the smile left her face.

A hand shot out of the dark and grabbed her wrist. She screamed. The fingers were cold. The flesh was gray. But the grip was strong. Too strong.

It pulled her in. Closer and closer to the body she'd checked only forty-five minutes before. He'd been dead at the time. Immobile. Now he was moving and—oh, God—his eyes were open and he was looking at her. His stare was lifeless as he drew her closer.

She did her best to break free, but the dead man was just too strong. She beat against his fingers with her other hand. When that didn't work, she tried pushing against his cold shoulder. Nothing seemed to help. She hit his face, his chest, anyplace she could reach, but he wouldn't let go.

He drew her closer until she was leaning across him, her arm over his head. Then he opened his mouth . . . and bit her. She gasped as his teeth broke through her skin. Blood welled as the icy teeth sank deep. Dull eyes looked through her as the dead man chewed on her forearm.

She went crazy, struggling to break free. She must've twisted in the right way because after a moment, she felt herself moving more easily. The next second, she was free.

He sat up, following her progress. She heard noises all around the lab now, echoing off the shadowed walls. She looked around in a panic. Other bodies were rising all around the makeshift morgue.

"How in God's name . . . ?" She gasped, clutching her bleeding arm to her chest as six tall bodies slid off the laboratory tables to stand in the dim, chilled room. She was so scared, she nearly wet her pants. The fear gave her a spike of clarity. She had to get out of there.

She ran for the door. Hands grabbed at her lab coat. She stumbled but caught herself before she could fall to the cold floor. She let her arms slip backward so the oversized lab coat came off, held in those strong hands that had come at her out of the darkness. She had no idea what had gone wrong with the experiment, but she wasn't about to stick around to ask questions. These guys were huge. Big Marines who were easily twice her size. And they didn't seem friendly. In fact, they kept grabbing at her.

If she could just get to the door. She ran, dodging and weaving around the tables and the reaching arms. They tried to grab the jacket she'd worn under the oversized lab coat, but they had a hard time getting hold of the slippery nylon fabric, thank goodness.

She crashed through the door, running for her life. She had to get help. She had to rouse the entire team. She had to get the

MPs, the Marines, and, hell, the National Guard if she could, to stop these guys.

She turned to look over her shoulder just once as she ran into the fringe of trees on the heavily wooded outskirts of the base. What she saw chilled her to the bone. In the dark of the night, she could see the dim, yellow, rectangular glow of the open doorway. Outlined there were the hulking shapes of dead men. The dead Marines were following her path outdoors at a slow, steady, lurching pace.

Don't miss Elizabeth Essex's Brava debut,
THE PURSUIT OF PLEASURE,
coming next month!

"I couldn't help overhearing your conversation." He wanted to steer their chat to his purpose, but the back of her neck was white and long. He'd never noticed that long slide of skin before, so pale against the vivid color of her locks. He'd gone away before she'd been old enough to put up her hair. And nowadays the fashion seemed to be for masses of loose ringlets covering the neck. Trust Lizzie to still sail against the tide.

"Yes, you could." Her breezy voice broke into his thoughts.

"I beg your pardon?"

"Help it. You *could* have helped it, as any polite gentleman *should*, but you obviously chose not to." She didn't even bother to look back at him as she spoke and walked on but he heard the teasing smile in her voice. Such intriguing confidence. He could use it to his purpose. She had always been up for a lark.

He caught her elbow and steered her into an unused parlor. She came easily, without resisting the intimacy or the presumption of the brief contact of his hand against the soft, vulnerable skin of her inner arm, but once through the door she just seemed to disolve away, out of his grasp. His empty fingers prickled from his sudden loss. He let her move away and closed the door.

No lamp or candle branch illuminated the room, only the moonlight streaming through the tall casement windows. Lizzie looked like a pale ghost, weightless and hovering in the strange light. He took a step nearer. He needed her to be real, not an illusion. Over the years she'd become a distant but recurring dream, a combination of memory and boyish lust, haunting his sleep.

He had thought of her, or at least the *idea* of her, almost constantly over the years. She had always been there, in his brain, swimming just below the surface. And he had come tonight in search of her. To banish his ghosts.

She took a sliding step back to lean nonchalantly against the arm of a chair, all sinuous, bored indifference.

"So what are you doing in Dartmouth? Aren't you meant to be messing about with your boats?"

"Ships," he corrected automatically and then smiled at his foolishness for trying to tell Lizzie anything. "The big ones are ships."

"And they let *you* have one of the *big* ones? Aren't you a bit young for that?" She tucked her chin down to subdue her smile and looked up at him from under her gingery brows. Very mischievous. And very challenging.

If it was worldliness she wanted, he could readily supply it. He mirrored her smile.

"Hard to imagine isn't it, Lizzie." He opened his arms wide, presenting himself for her inspection.

Only she didn't inspect him. Her eyes slid away to inventory the scant furniture in the darkened room. "No one else calls me that anymore."

"Lizzie? Well, I do. I can't imagine you as anything else. And I like it. I like saying it. Lizzie." The name hummed through his mouth like a honeybee dusted with nectar. Like a kiss. He moved closer so he could see the emerald color of her eyes, dimmed by the half light, but still brilliant against the white of her skin. He leaned a fraction too close and whispered, "Lizzie. It always sounds somehow . . . naughty."

She turned quickly. Wariness flickered across her mobile face, as if she were suddenly unsure of both herself and him, before it was just as quickly masked.

And yet, she continued to study him surreptitiously, so he held himself still for her perusal. To see if she would finally notice him as a *man*. He met her eyes and he felt a kick low in his gut. In that moment plans and strategies became unimportant. The only thing important was for Lizzie to *see* him. It was *essential*.

But she kept all expression from her face. He was jolted to realize she didn't want him to read her thoughts or mood, that she was trying hard to keep *him* from seeing *her*.

It was an unexpected change. The Lizzie he had known as a child had been so wholly passionate about life, she had thrown herself body and soul into each and every moment, each action and adventure. She had not been covered with this veneer of poised nonchalance.

And yet it was only a veneer. He was sure of it. And he was equally sure he could make his way past it. He drew in a measured breath and sent her a slow, melting smile to show, in the course of the past few minutes, he'd most definitely noticed she was a woman.

She gave no outward reaction, so it took Marlowe a long moment to recognize her response: she looked *careful*. It was a quality he'd never seen in her before.

Finally, after what felt like an infinity, she broke the moment. "You didn't answer. Why are you here? After all these years?"

Her quiet surprised the truth out of him. "A funeral. Two weeks ago." A bleak, rain-soaked funeral that couldn't be forgotten.

"Oh. I am sorry." Her voice lost its languid bite.

He looked back and met her eyes. Such sincerity had never been one of Lizzie's strong suits. No, that was wrong. She'd always been sincere, or at least truthful—painfully so as he recalled—but she rarely let her true feelings show.

"Thank you, Lizzie. But I didn't lure you into a temptingly darkened room to bore you with dreary news."

"No, you came to proposition me." The mischievous little smile crept back. Lizzie was never the sort to be intimidated for long. She had always loved to be doing things she ought not.

A heated image of her white body temptingly entwined in another man's arms rose unbidden in his brain. Good God, what other things had Lizzie been doing over the past few years that she ought not? And with whom?

Marlowe quickly jettisoned the irrational spurt of jealousy. Her more recent past hardly mattered. In fact, some experience on her part might better suit his plans.

"Yes, my proposition. I can give you what you want. A marriage without the man."

For the longest moment she went unaturally still, then she slid off the chair arm and glided closer. So close, he almost backed up. So close, her rose petal of a mouth came but a hairsbreadth from his own. Then she lifted her inquisitive nose and took a bold, suspicious whiff of his breath.

"You've been drinking."

"I have," he admitted without a qualm.

"How much?"

"More than enough for the purpose. And you?"

"Clearly not enough. Not that they'd let me." She turned and walked away. Sauntered really. She was very definitely a saunterer, all loose joints and limbs, as if she'd never paid the least attention to deportment and carriage. Very provocative, although he doubted she meant to be. An image of a bright, agile otter, frolicking unconcerned in the calm green of the river Dart, twisting and rolling in the sunlit water, came to mind.

"Drink or no, I meant what I said."

"Are you proposing? Marriage? To me?" She laughed as if it were a joke. She didn't believe him.

"I am."

She eyed him more closely, her gaze narrowing even as one marmalade eyebrow rose in assessment. "Do you have a fatal disease?"

"No."

"Are you engaged to fight a duel?"

"Again, no."

"Condemned to death?" She straightened with a fluid undulation, her spine lifting her head up in surprise as the thought entered her head, all worldliness temporarily obliterated. "Planning a suicide?"

"No and no." It was so hard not to smile. Such an arch, charming combination of concern and cheek. The cheek won out: she gave him that feral, slightly suspicious smile.

"Then how do you plan to arrange it, the 'without the man' portion of the proceedings? I'll want some sort of guarantee. You can't imagine I'm gullible enough to leave your fate, or my own for that matter, to chance."

A low heat flared within him. By God, she really was considering it.

"And yet, Lizzie, I think you may. I am an officer of His Majesty's Royal Navy and am engaged to captain a convoy of prison ships to the Antipodes. I leave only days from now. The last time I was home, in England, was four and a half years ago and then only for a few months to recoup from a near fatal wound. This trip is slated to take at least eight. Years."

Her face cleared of all traces of impudence. Oh yes, even Lizzie could could be led.

"Storms, accidents and disease provide most of the risk. Don't forget we're still at war with France and Spain. And the Americans don't think too highly of us either. One stray cannon ball could do the job quite nicely."

"Is that what did it last time?"

"Last time? I've never been dead before."

The ends of her ripe mouth nipped up. The heat in his gut sailed higher.

"You said you had recovered from a near fatal wound."

"Ah, yes. Grapeshot, actually. In my chest. Didn't go deep enough to kill me, though afterwards, the fever nearly did."

Her gaze skimmed over his coat, curious and maybe a little hungry. The heat spread lower, kindling into a flame.

"Do you want to see?" He was being rash, he knew, but he'd done this for her once before, taken off his shirt on a dare. And he wanted to remind her.